ROOTS OF THE BAY

Esther Schultz

Backyard Studio Publishing
Harris, MN

Published by Backyard Studio Publishing
Harris, Minnesota (United States of America)

Publisher's Note: This is a work of fiction. Names, characters, places, and incidents are a product of the author's imagination. Locales and public names are sometimes used for atmospheric purposes. Any resemblance to actual people, living or dead, or to businesses, companies, events, institutions, or locales is completely coincidental. Although some real-life iconic places are depicted in settings, all situations and people related to those places are fictional.

Book Editing and Formatting by JeanneFelfe.com

Publisher's Cataloging-in-Publication Data

Names: Schultz, Esther, 1978-.
Title: Roots of the bay / Esther Schultz.
Description: Harris, MN : Backyard Studio Publishing, 2024. | Series: Willow Bay series ; book 3. | Summary: Raina Matson faces hardship and uncovers past family secrets while making a way for herself in the present.
Identifiers: LCCN 2024918310 | ISBN 9781737908678 (pbk.) | ISBN 9781737908661 (ebook)
Subjects: LCSH: Families – Fiction. | Family secrets – Fiction. | Friendship – Fiction. | Resilience (Personality trait) – Fiction. | Women – Fiction. | Minnesota – Fiction. | BISAC: FICTION / Women. | FICTION / Family Life / General. | FICTION / Historical / 20th Century / General.
Classification: LCC PS3619.C48 R68 2024 (print) | PS3619.C48 (ebook) | DDC 813 S38—dc23
LC record available at https://lccn.loc.gov/2024918310

Dedication

To my girls, Bri and Beth, may you always stand firm in your truth and love yourselves fully.

Spring 1948

The dark gray Cadillac slowed to a stop under the reddish-brown stone carport. The driver switched off the ignition and hopped out to open the rear door. The oldest girl bounced off the back seat, pretending not to notice the driver hiding his smile. She stifled a grin as she raced out of the car with her younger sister on her heels. Rushing past the driver, she clipped his elbow as her sister shoved her out of the way, her blond curls flailing around her hat.

"Girls," her grandmother said as she stood upright, her brown chevron coat billowing around her. She adjusted her matching hat and gracefully slid her purse over her gloved hand onto her left wrist. She gave a pointed look at her granddaughters, but winked at the driver. "What would Johnston think of such manners?"

"Sorry, Gramma. Sorry, Johnston," the girls said in unison, halting their race.

"One of you forgot your purse in the back seat."

"It wasn't me. Mine is tucked under my arm," the oldest girl said.

"It's mine," the younger girl said, her shoulders drooping.

Confirming her younger sister was heading back to the car, the older sister giggled before dashing into the house. When she opened the door, she expected to hear a bustling household, but was met with silence.

A shiver ran up her spine. "Mother, Father, we're home."

A stillness settled in the foyer as the girl took off her hat and placed it on the burnished maple entry-way table with the tiny drawers she liked to hide treasures in. She went further into the house, continuing to call for her parents. Still not receiving a greeting, she yelled the housekeeper's name, but no one responded. She jumped at a commotion. Her grandmother and sister were taking their hats and coats off, signaling they had made it into the house.

As she rounded the corner into the library, a piercing scream rang out. She trembled at the sound of her own voice. Her mind had a hard time grasping the scene before her. She spun around, hoping to run out of the room, but slammed into the soft confines of her grandmother's belly.

Her grandmother gasped and placed a hand to the wall. "Quickly, go call for the police."

She obeyed her grandmother and fled the room. As she made her way to the telephone, she caught sight of her sister and yelled, "Go outside. Now!"

"But, what's—"

"Just go!"

Making sure her younger sister followed her instructions, she picked up the telephone and dialed a number, her fingers shaking with every movement. When a voice greeted her on the other end, she took a deep breath. "You must come. There is blood everywhere, and I think my parents are dead."

Chapter One

Spring 1996

Dressed in black, Raina Matson shifted from one foot to the other as she scanned the room filled with what seemed like every single person, known and unknown, from her small community paying their respects. She tugged at her sweater, snagged a piece of white fuzz, and flicked it to the floor. Glancing at her skirt to make sure it was okay after fumbling with her top, she noticed dirt marks on her pumps. Rolling her eyes, Raina tried to focus on the woman talking to her but failed. She straightened her spine to stand taller despite her slight build.

Often told she got her stature from her father's mother, that is where the similarity with her father's side ended. Raina mostly resembled the woman who now rested in the casket next to her. Her grandmother, Gramma Delany Nilsson, had been taller than Raina, but they both had the same blue eyes, cool complexion, and dark hair. There was no denying that they were related.

"It really went so fast, didn't it, dear," the woman said.

Raina blinked, trying to remember who this woman was. *She must be a patron of Gramma D's store.*

"Are you okay, dear?" the woman asked.

"Um, yes. Sorry, I'm just distracted, I guess."

"Of course you are. Such a difficult time, especially after losing your mama in that horrible accident only a few years ago."

Raina tensed at the mention of her mother and wished she could sit on the nearest chair, bury her face in her hands, and cry. Instead, she looked past the woman to the man standing behind her and said, "Thank you for coming."

A sigh escaped Raina's lips when the woman got the hint and walked on. The man didn't linger, and the rest of the line moved quickly. When the last person passed by, the minister motioned for Raina to take her seat. She rushed to sit but slowed when she caught movement at the back.

She positioned herself in her chair and glanced behind her. A tall elderly woman wearing a black dress with matching hat, gloves, and shoes clung tightly to a man younger than Raina, while she found space in the last row. Dark lace hung over part of her face. An ornate cane in her right hand offset a slight limp. Raina lifted her eyebrow at the elegance and grace she exuded with every step forward. Once settled, she began to remove her hat, but Raina's attention was drawn back to the front as the minister began to pray. She was thankful the service wasn't going to be a long one at her grandmother's wishes.

No one needs to fuss over me.

Raina smiled at the memory and forced herself to pay attention. Her mind flitted to the woman in the back. There was something familiar about her. Raina had to fight the urge to turn and stare. As the service was nearing the end, Raina gave into temptation and looked back at the woman, locking eyes with her. A gasp escaped her lips, and she swung her head back around.

Gramma D! But it can't be her, she is lying in the casket in front of me.

The minister started his last prayer and Raina tried to calm her pounding heart.

Who is she? Why does she look so much like Gramma D? Why have I never seen her before?

"Amen," the minister said, drawing Raina back. "Raina has requested that those not joining her at the graveside service, meet her in an hour at the Nilsson's store for refreshments and visiting. Now, the ushers will dismiss each row to pay their final respects to Delaney Nilsson."

Each guest filed past her grandmother and Raina hoped to catch a glimpse of the mystery woman, but she didn't pass with the rest of the mourners. When the last person in line walked away, Raina stood but couldn't move. She tried lifting her foot, but found it was too heavy, and froze.

The clunk of a cane sounded behind her, and Raina spun around. She watched the woman—her hat now firmly in place—walk toward the casket. The woman stopped short of it, as though to gather courage, before taking the final two steps.

She shoved a tissue under the lace and wiped her cheek, then turned and peered at Raina briefly. She moved toward her, but the minister called to Raina, and the woman paused. He advised the casket would be closed soon and encouraged Raina to say a few words before they had to carry Gramma D to the waiting car. He asked a couple of questions regarding the graveside service and Raina answered them impatiently. All she could think of was the old woman and finding out who she was, but when Raina turned back toward her, she was gone.

Raina's shoulders drooped as a wave of annoyance washed through her. Forcing the mysterious woman out of her mind, she continued her earlier quest to see her grandmother's face one last time.

The wind picked up as the procession of cars stopped along the curb next to where Delany Nilsson was to be laid to rest. Raina moved the gear shift to park, watched others climb out of their vehicles, and wished none of them were there. She shut the car off, took a deep breath, and climbed out.

The guests moved gingerly across the grass to avoid the piles of snow that still held on even though it was April. A small canopy encompassed the burial site, and Raina feared it might fall over as the walls flapped in the breeze. The small group huddled together while the minister said a few words and prayed. After the prayer, the mourners sang "Amazing Grace" and the minister dismissed the group.

Raina caught a black gown swishing out of the corner of her eye. The elderly woman stood at the edge of the crowd, talking with the young gentleman from before. He nodded and looked over in Raina's direction. The elder bobbed her head toward Raina. Taking a step forward, the minister stopped her.

"It's time to say your final goodbye, Raina."

Releasing a frustrated breath, Raina turned toward the casket and hesitated, making sure no one else was around. She filled her lungs with air and blew it out slowly through pursed lips, something she had learned from her grandmother.

"It's hard to believe you were only diagnosed a few months ago, Gramma D. But you always said your smoking would take you. I'll never forget all that you taught me about life. Love you always."

Tears filled the corners of her eyes as she kissed her hand and placed it on the casket. "Goodbye."

Straightening her spine, Raina moved toward the few people still milling about. She was hoping to catch the mysterious woman. A sigh escaped her lips, realizing she'd missed her again.

"Just as well, I suppose."

"What's that?" the minister asked.

"Nothing. We should head back to Gramma's shop."

The minister nodded and they wound their way to their cars. The drive didn't take long and Raina settled in to hosting the well-wishers. Raina had been dreading the reception and hoped the next couple of hours would go by quickly. The idea that the unknown woman might show eased her apprehension some. Every time the door to the shop opened, Raina craned her neck, hoping to catch a black lace hat, but the woman never made an appearance. It wasn't long before the crowd dispersed, and she said goodbye to the last guest. Disappointment flooded through Raina as she tried to put the lady out of her mind.

She closed the shop and walked to the apartment entrance, stifling a yawn. The climb up the stairs was slow and Raina's feet grew heavier and her shoulders slumped forward more with each step. Raina swiped at the tears on her cheek as she peered out the window of the stairwell and then stopped in awe. She watched the sun dip behind the horizon as the sky blazed orange.

"Ah, Gramma D. Your favorite type of sunset."

The shop was located on the edge of town, so the apartment looked out over trees and the beginning of farmland. Gramma D, or her mother, could often be found sitting on the steps in the stairwell, peering out the window at the most amazing sunsets.

Raina shoved the door to the apartment open and let out the breath she didn't realize she was holding. She switched on the light and shut the door behind her.

My safe space.

The apartment was a small three-bedroom, two-bathroom with a living area and kitchen combination. Small, but it was home.

Raina picked up a picture of Gramma D. "I can't believe so many people came to visit after the services."

Setting the frame back in its place, she poured herself a glass of her favorite cabernet while the funeral crowded her mind. Gramma D really didn't know the townspeople that well as she had always kept her distance, but they claimed to know her today. Her café and shop had been a staple of the town for many years. What surprised Raina was how caring everyone sounded since most had judged her grandmother, mother, and even her at times.

Gramma D had come to Grand Meadow, Minnesota with no husband and a baby girl years ago. She raised her daughter there and worked her way through several jobs until she could afford to buy the building that now housed Nilsson's Sip and Shop. It was a combination bookstore, gift shop, and café—the only place like it in town. She eventually remodeled the upstairs to create the existing apartment they all lived in.

Raina's mother had gone to college with her high school sweetheart. During her second semester, she became pregnant with Raina. When her boyfriend found out about the pregnancy, he said he couldn't be held responsible and didn't want to have anything to do with either one of them. Not having any other choice, she dropped out of college and went back home to Gramma D.

Giving Raina the name Matson, Raina's mother hoped her boyfriend would return to her, but it was pointless. Raina was told she met her father one time when she was a baby during a summer break from school. After college, he moved out east somewhere, and they never heard from him again.

Both women in Raina's little family had followed the same path of not finishing college. Determined not to repeat it, Raina went to college, got a business degree, and went on to get a master's in marketing. She moved to Minneapolis and worked at a good-paying job for several years, but when her mother died, she returned to Grand Meadow. Gramma D refused to retire, but struggled with managing everything on her own, so Raina believed she didn't have a choice but to stay.

Raina struggled to embrace her role as it was difficult coming back to live in her hometown and the urge to leave never went away. She always dreamed of what she would do if ever given the opportunity to go, but now that her mother and grandmother were gone, she surprisingly had no direction. Thankfully, she didn't have to decide what was next right now. She poured herself a second glass of wine and went to her bedroom to change out of her funeral clothes.

Raina yanked on her favorite sweatshirt while flashes of the mysterious woman jumped to mind. *Who was that?*

Raina slipped on her lounge pants, picked up her wine goblet, and settled on her bed. She grabbed the remote off the nightstand and was swept away by the doctors caring for patients on the television screen. After draining the dark liquid, she set her glass on the table beside her and curled into a ball under the covers. Feeling the weight of her eyelids, she gave in to the pull of sleep.

Her eyes flew open. "No, it couldn't be her. I thought she was dead."

Raina threw back her covers, and rushed into her grandmother's room. She rummaged around, but not finding what she sought, she grabbed the keys to the store and ran downstairs. She paused in the breezeway between the apartment entrance and the store while she fumbled with the lock. Dropping the keys, she bent down to pick them up, but paused at the movement across the street.

Air rushed through her lips as Raina stood. It was her. The lady with the lace hat was standing across the street bathed in the streetlight. The young gentleman handed her a cane and they strode toward the shop. Raina went out to the sidewalk and waited until they stopped short of her. She lifted a hand to her chest and hoped the older woman couldn't hear her pounding heart as they sized each other up. She hardly noticed the young man run back to the car.

Raina tried to speak but paused when she heard a voice so much like Gramma D's.

"You are Raina," the older woman said.

"I am, but who are you?"

"Hmm. I see she really did try to bury everything."

"I don't understand."

"If you don't know who I am then she didn't want any part of her past in her life here." The woman paused and shoved the black lace out of her face. "My name is Katarina Nilsson. I'm your great-aunt. Your grandmother's younger sister."

Raina's forehead creased and her eyebrows lifted. "I wondered if…" She paused. "I wondered if you were her, but I always thought you were dead."

Katarina nodded. "That would make sense. I doubt you even remember us meeting. But it was years ago, and you were only about three at the time."

Raina shook her head. "I don't remember. I don't even know if my mom knew you. If she did, she never talked about it. That is one thing us Nilsson women are good at—keeping things to ourselves."

"Sadly, that has been the way it has been for me, too."

Frowning, Raina contemplated what she meant. "Please, I was about to go into the shop. Won't you come in?"

"Yes, I believe I will, thank you."

They walked in together. Raina flipped on the light, locked the door behind her, and made sure the closed sign still showed in the window.

"Don't want anyone thinking I'm suddenly open and walking in on us."

Raina crossed to the café area and asked if her great-aunt wanted a beverage.

"A hot tea would be lovely. Thank you."

Raina bobbed her head, made a hot tea for Katarina and a latte for herself. She could feel the woman watching her and tried to push away her unease.

"Have you always worked here?" Katarina asked while Raina poured foamy milk into a paper cup.

Securing a tea bag in another cup, Raina said, "Yes and no. I worked here in high school until college. I actually lived in Minneapolis for a while until Mom died, then I moved back home and helped Gramma D again."

"I was sorry to hear about your mother."

This last statement was said with such sadness, Raina ruminated on the relationship between the two women. Gramma D had obviously shared bits and pieces with

Katarina, but Raina was told nothing about her great-aunt or her grandmother's past.

"Did you write or talk often?" Raina asked.

"I wrote often, but I rarely heard from Del. I stopped calling her years ago. She said it was too hard for her to talk to me and keep that line to her past open. I was so angry at her for running away all those years ago, but then I couldn't imagine what it must have been like for her. My anger eventually grew into sadness for her. I never lost the ache in my heart for what could have been." Katarina cleared her throat. "Enough about sad times. Tell me about you. Tell me what you're thinking about for your next steps in life."

Placing the tea in front of her great-aunt, Raina considered how to answer.

"If you don't want to talk about it, that's fine," Katarina said.

"No, I mean, it's okay. I'm just not sure what to say," Raina said. "I guess I'll stay here long enough to figure out what to do with this place. I don't want to keep it or stay in Grand Meadow, that's for sure. I know that probably sounds awful or harsh, but this has never been my store, or my life. It was always hers."

"It doesn't sound harsh at all. I can understand why you would feel the way you do based on the few pieces of information Del gave me over the years."

Raina sat next to the elderly woman and sipped her latte. The conversation grew quiet, and Raina fiddled with her cup, trying to figure out what to say next. She had so many questions but didn't know where to start. She looked around the store and noticed a spot on a shelf that needed dusting and resisted the urge to go clean it. She'd never been good at sitting in uncomfortable silence and always responded to it by finding something to do. But she forced herself to stay planted in her chair.

"Would you be open to a proposition?" Katarina asked.

Trying to hide her surprise, Raina said, "I guess it would depend on what it is."

"Based on our interaction here today, I'm going to assume you really don't know about my sister's history. Your history. So, if you would indulge me, I'll explain a few details."

"I would like that."

Katarina took a sip of her tea. "Our family settled along a small bay on the shores of Lake Superior in the 1850s during what my father called the copper run. It was just my great-great-grandfather, his young wife, his parents, and his two younger siblings. They never found copper, but instead of fleeing the land like many did during that time, our family stuck it out. They opened an overnight boarding house and traded goods, encouraged others to settle in the bay, and eventually founded a small town. My great-great-grandfather was not only the primary financier, but he was also the landlord to most of the tenants who ran businesses there. When he passed away, my great-great-grandmother Tuva became the matriarch and ran things along with her son until he passed away. Her grandson, my grandfather, took over."

"I had no idea that I came from such a place," Raina said.

Katarina's lips curled up. "You do, and it's a grand place to be sure. My Gramma Melia came to our little town and stole my grandfather's heart. They had a great love. He died before tragedy struck my family and he didn't have to go through what my grandmother did. I'm sure it would have broken him after everything else life had thrown at him."

"What tragedy?"

"Ah, well that is another story all together, for another time." Katarina paused. "My grandparents had one son, my father, and together they built our tiny little town into what it is today."

"This is all so interesting, but what does it have to do with your proposition?" Raina asked.

"I suppose I should get on with it then. Our distant relatives have since moved on to different parts or didn't want to be involved in the running of our little town, so that left my grandfather's family. I was married briefly, but my husband became ill and died shortly after. I never remarried and I never had children. Gramma Melia has passed away, so you and I are the only ones left. I injured my leg in a minor boating accident about ten years ago, and as you can see, I'm no spring chicken."

Raina studied the older woman and tried to make sense of everything. *What did she mean by they were the only ones left?*

"I know what I've shared is a lot to digest," Katarina said. "I also know asking you to come and help me is probably more than I have the right to ask, but I'm getting old and tired and would love for this to stay in the family."

"What is it that you want to stay in the family?" Raina asked.

"Our legacy."

"What legacy?"

"Willow Bay."

"I don't understand."

"It's easier for me to show you. I hope you'll at least come and see it. If not, I'll learn to live with the legacy ending with me. But I ask you to think about it." Katarina pulled a card out of her purse and laid it on the table between them. "Here is my information. Please, think about it."

Picking up the card, Raina studied it while everything swirled around in her head.

Katarina shifted in her seat. "I really must be going. It was delightful finally getting to see you again. Even under such sad circumstances."

Raina stood and escorted the elderly woman out.

Katarina took a deep breath, started to say something, paused, and tried again. "I don't expect you to drop everything tomorrow. All I ask is for you to come, visit for a couple of weeks, and let me share how things are firsthand."

"I promise to think about it."

"That's something at least. I hope to hear from you soon."

Katarina gave Raina a stiff hug, said her goodbyes, and made her way across the street. The young gentleman helped her get settled in the car before hopping in and driving away.

Raina watched until the vehicle disappeared around the corner. Their conversation swirled in her head until she yawned. Despite drinking a latte, fatigue washed over her. She locked up the shop and went back up to her apartment. She curled up in bed where she fell asleep dreaming about waves of water and small towns.

Chapter Two

T he first day Raina opened the shop since the funeral she hoped it would be slow, but there was an on-slaught of patrons. She wondered if it was the town being their typical nosy selves or if they actually cared. After lunch Raina tried to take a small break, but the stream of people picked up, so she cut it short.

"Goodness, what a crazy day," Patsy Anderson said while pouring a cup of steaming coffee.

Raina leaned against the counter. "It really is baffling how busy we are. It's midweek, but this feels more like a Saturday rush."

"I agree," Patsy said, pausing to hand the dark liquid to a waiting customer. When they wandered away, she bent toward Raina. "You think more about your aunt's offer?"

Trying to push her irritation aside, Raina shrugged. Patsy took every opportunity to ask about it, and Raina regretted mentioning it to her. Raina had grown up with Patsy working at the store and she was one of the few people in town she considered to be a friend. She knew Patsy cared, so she hated that the question annoyed her.

"I have, but does the offer sound crazy to you?" Raina asked.

"Maybe a little, especially not having heard from her before, but your grandmother didn't talk much about her past, so I guess it's not surprising. I do know you would love it up there, though."

"I've been leaning more toward going, but then I'm not sure what to do with this place," Raina said, sweeping her arms around.

"Yes, well about that."

"What is it?"

"Well. We. Joe and I. We were thinking we might buy it from you."

"Wait, what?"

"I know it's probably a shock, but we want to buy it, if you will sell it to us."

"Wow, I don't know what to say."

"Delany knew you didn't like it here, and she planted it in our minds when she got sick. You don't have to make any rash decisions. Just think about it."

"I will think about it, and I'll try to have a decision soon."

A clang over the shop entrance announced the beginning of another rush, tabling the conversation for now. Raina forced herself to focus on the next person in line, but her aunt's invitation swirled in her mind along with Patsy's offer.

Thankfully the rest of the afternoon went by quickly, and after closing the shop, Raina decided to go see if the offer on the store was real.

As she pulled into Patsy's driveway, it dawned on her that it had been several years since she had been there. She couldn't imagine Patsy wanting to move from such a beautiful home into the apartment over the shop. Raina knocked on the door and it was opened by a surprised Joe.

"Raina? How are you? Haven't seen you since the funeral."

"I'm doing okay considering everything. I was curious if you and Patsy would have some time to talk."

"Sure, come on it. We're about to sit down for dinner, but would love to have you join us."

"Oh, I didn't even realize the time. I'm sorry."

"Nonsense, we'll add another plate. We're about to have my favorite hot dish and Patsy made an apple pie for dessert."

Raina hoped Joe couldn't hear the rumbling in her stomach at the mention of food. "That sounds heavenly. Thank you."

Joe stepped back to allow Raina to enter the house and took her jacket from her.

"Go on into the kitchen. Patsy just poured herself a glass of that new Minnesota wine we've been reading about in the paper. Her friend from college gave her a couple of bottles, but I'm sure she has enough."

"Thanks, Joe."

Raina wound her way through the small house to the kitchen in the rear and was immediately enveloped in the smell of cinnamon and apples being pulled out of the oven.

"Why, Raina, this is a pleasant surprise," Patsy said while putting plates on the island. "Come sit on a stool. Do you want some wine? It's that Frontenac I was telling you about."

"Yes, please, thank you. I was telling Joe I wanted to talk with you two and he invited me to dinner."

"Of course, and yes, we would love to chat about anything you need. I would wager a guess you're here about our offer."

"You know me well."

Joe entered the kitchen and Patsy piled creamy vegetables with cheesy tater tots onto Raina's plate. Patsy and Joe settled on their own seats while Joe explained to Raina they usually just ate at the island since the kids were grown and gone. He told Raina to dig in and she obliged. Food and wine disappeared while they discussed the weather.

Raina struggled to join the conversation, for all she could think about was why she was there. Swallowing her latest bite and washing it down with Frontenac, she said, "I think I want to go. But I want to iron out the details of the shop to make sure what is decided will work for both of us. I don't care so much about myself. I just want everything to be fair for you."

Patsy snagged a pad of paper, scribbled something on it, and placed it between them. Raina wasn't sure why this made her giggle, but she stifled her laughter and tried to act like they were negotiating something more important than the sale of her shop.

Raina's mouth fell open when she read the note. "You can't be serious."

"We believe this is the right offer. We discussed it with our finance guys, and they helped us come to that," Joe said, pointing to the paper.

"I guess I didn't realize Gramma D's place was worth this much," Raina said.

"Well, you have the shop, but don't forget the apartment, and the nice lot it sits on," Patsy said.

"Right, all of it together makes up that price," Joe said.

"Okay then," Raina said. "I guess what's left is to have someone draw up the paperwork. But only if you're sure."

"We're sure," Patsy said.

"If you don't have anyone to help with the paperwork, we can use our guy," Joe said.

"Sounds good to me," Raina said, and took another bite of hot dish.

Patsy held up her wine. "Here's to the future and new beginnings."

Raina swallowed and picked up her glass. "To new beginnings."

The conversation shifted to what Raina knew about her great-aunt, which wasn't a lot. After she was unable to answer the last two questions, Patsy expressed her excitement over Raina's move. She appreciated the encouragement since Patsy was aware of how much she struggled with being back in Grand Meadow.

Growing quiet, Raina gathered her dishes and helped clean the kitchen. They talked about lighter things until Raina said goodbye. As she drove, her mind danced around the dinner conversation. She stopped at the stop sign just before her street and studied the shops on either side of her. She wished she had some sort of nostalgic feeling, but she felt nothing for the town. It was always a reminder of her humble and scandalous beginning.

After the intersection was clear, Raina drove on, and waved at the group of ladies sitting outside the quilt shop. She wasn't close to any of them, but that's just what you did in Grand Meadow. Always nice to your face, but these same women had said some awful things about her mother and even her grandmother over the years. They were the cliché ladies in a small town and could make or break your reputation. Unfortunately, the life Raina and her little family led was apparently too much of a threat to the wholesomeness the ladies of Grand Meadow thought they should live.

It never mattered to them that Raina had gotten her master's degree and had a successful career. The only thing the town saw was a young woman born out of wedlock to a mother who dropped out of college. It didn't help that her grandmother had Raina's mother in her late teens and had never married either.

The sun was beginning to slide behind the trees at the edge of town and Raina drew in a sharp breath. This was the moment nostalgia washed over her. She realized she may never see that sunset again, and her eyes grew misty. It was strange to be sad over leaving a place she didn't really care about, but perhaps the memories of Gramma D and Mom brought it on.

Raina parked her car in her designated spot and wound her way up to her apartment. When she pushed the door open, all feelings of sadness melted away. She rummaged around the kitchen until she found the card her aunt had left. Raina quickly punched in the number and waited for a voice to answer.

"Willow Bay Manor."

Raina studied her aunt's card. "Um, this is Raina Matson. Could I speak with Katarina Nilsson please?"

"Oh, of course, right away, Miss Matson," the voice excitedly explained.

"Thank you."

Several minutes passed before there was rustling in the receiver.

"Raina, I'm so delighted you called."

"Hello, um, Miss Katar—"

"Come now, you must call me Aunt Kat."

"Okay, hello, Aunt Kat," Raina said. "I wanted to call and let you know I decided to take you up on your offer. That is, if the offer still stands."

"Of course, it does," Aunt Kat said. "Do you have any plans yet for when you'll arrive here?"

"I already have a buyer for the shop, but with packing and sorting, I would say it'll be sometime in May before I can get there."

"That's perfect, my dear. I'll have Celia mail you the details on how to get here."

"Is it difficult to find?" Raina asked.

"I don't believe so, but I always like to give extra details to be on the safe side. Wouldn't want you to get lost. Although anyone from here will know how to find Willow Bay Manor."

"I'm starting to get the impression my simple life doesn't compare with the world I'm about to enter," Raina said.

"Nonsense. You're a Nilsson."

"Okay. I'll watch out for the information from Celia, and I'll keep you posted on when I plan to arrive."

"That sounds wonderful. Do you plan to stay only for a few weeks?"

"I haven't totally decided that yet, but I don't have a plan for what happens next, so I may stay longer than what we originally discussed. If that's okay?"

"Of course, stay as long as you like. Hopefully I can convince you to stay permanently."

Excitement bubbled inside of Raina, and she started to say goodbye when Aunt Kat asked if Patsy was the one buying the shop.

"Del mentioned Patsy occasionally in her letters, and when she told me she was dying, it was one of the few times we talked on the phone. She told me she worried about you, but hoped Patsy would buy the place so you could leave," Aunt Kat said.

"I don't know what to say."

"That surprises you? That she talked about your future with me."

"Yes, but I can't help but feel like this is just the beginning of things I'll be surprised to learn."

"There is more you have to learn, that's true," Aunt Kat said. "I have a meeting I must get to. I look forward to hearing the details of your arrival, my dear. Goodbye for now."

Raina's head spun at how quickly the conversation changed and important topics were dismissed. "Um, okay. Goodbye for now, Aunt Kat."

Raina stared at the phone before putting it back on the cradle and questioned whether she was making the right decision. She looked out the window at the glowing sky. "Okay, Gramma D, I'm going. Not sure what I'm getting into, but I'm going."

The excitement of leaving Grand Meadow took the place of her hesitation and she went searching for empty boxes.

Chapter Three

Leaving later than planned, Raina had been on the road for several hours. She had to finish moving some of her things into storage that morning but still hoped to get to Willow Bay before dinner. It was only about a four and a half-hour drive from Grand Meadow, but she wanted to take her time as she heard the north shore of Lake Superior was beautiful and wanted to stop along the way if she felt like it.

As Raina crested the hill, she gasped at the view before her. A honk startled her, and she yanked the car back into her own lane. She sneaked peeks while struggling to keep her eyes on the road.

Duluth lay nestled at the bottom of the hill with a backdrop of the bluest water she had ever seen, far more beautiful than how it had been described to her. The rugged coastline stretched for miles, disappearing into the horizon. Directly below her, the lake narrowed between pockets of green trees, with several bridges connecting the land. Large ships and small boats, resting comfortably, or gliding about the harbor, were scattered as far as she could see. Another honk brought Raina back to the task of driving, and she focused on the road. She continued to sneak glimpses of the view as she drove down into the city, following Celia's instructions.

As she drove past downtown, she decided she would have to come back to this place and take a closer look. She went north along the scenic drive of Highway 61 and was immediately drawn to Kitchi-Gammi Park. She wanted to touch the blue of the water. When her car came to a stop along the rocky shoreline, Raina barely got it switched off before she jumped out.

She ran down the stone beach until she came to the water's edge, surprised that there weren't many people. A woman with her young son of about six stood with their arms open wide toward Lake Superior. The woman glanced in Raina's direction, locked eyes with her, and the spirit of the lake passed between them. Raina was forever changed.

Studying the mixture of blues, Raina enjoyed the rush of water crashing against the boulders along the beach. She closed her eyes and breathed in the misty air, mimicking the woman and her son. All the stress and heartache of the past couple of years melted away and floated off with the wind.

"Come along now, Jay," the woman said.

Mother and son walked hand in hand toward a gray car and Raina understood the light shining from their faces because the same brightness illuminated her soul. Raina moved her gaze back toward the water and watched the waves for a while longer. She knew she'd never seen anything more beautiful in her life and hoped her new home would be just as magical. Checking her watch, she forced herself to leave the park.

Stealing looks at the lake as she drove along, Raina found the scenic highway was everything Aunt Kat said it would be. Patches of blue would pop up between trees causing goose bumps all over her body. Her brightened spirit dimmed a little as she realized her grandmother had left here, never to return.

What could have happened to keep her away from such a place?

Raina yawned so wide her eyes watered. As excited as she was, it had been a long day. She spotted the Mocha Moose and turned into the parking lot.

As she entered the shop, Raina was greeted with various items for sale from local artisans. She picked up a beautiful frame which held the shape of Lake Superior with swirls of blue paint which reminded her of waves of water. She glanced at the price and decided to purchase it along with her coffee.

Her intentions when stopping were to order her drink and a pastry to go, but she was drawn to a beautiful melody coming from a piano in the main dining area. Raina found a cozy chair next to a wood burning stove and sipped her creamy latte in between bites of raspberry white chocolate scone. When a shiver went up her spine, she huddled closer to the fire. Although it was spring, that didn't mean it was warm yet on the north shore of Lake Superior.

The white-haired man appeared to be another patron as he played in between sips of his own coffee, but his talent was undeniable. As she studied him, she questioned if his weathered look came from years on the lake as a fisherman or if it was from the harshness of the land connected to it. Either way she could tell he had spent a lot of time out in its elements.

The song ended and the man smiled at Raina. He picked up his coffee, took another drink, and played a tune she had never heard before. He sang a story about a fisherman who died during the great white hurricane of 1913 and how a love was lost forever to the spirit of the lake.

Moved by the haunting song, Raina swiped at the tears running down her cheeks. She choked down the last few bites of her scone and took a large gulp of her latte, hoping to gain control of her emotions. As she swallowed another sip of the creamy liquid, the song came to an end and Raina rushed to put her cup down to clap.

The man turned in her direction, nodded a thank you, and went back to play a livelier tune. Raina checked the time on the old clock hanging on the wall above the piano. She'd stayed longer than she had planned and wanted to get back on the road. She gathered her things, mouthed a goodbye to the pianist, and thanked the barista as she went out the door.

As Raina drove, the haunting song of a white hurricane flooded through her. She tried to drown it out by listening to the radio, but eventually gave up and switched it off. She shuddered and caught another glimpse of the lake out the passenger window. Her lips curled into a smile, and her spirits lifted. She focused on the water, hoping it would push notions of dead fisherman and lost loves out of her head.

For the rest of the trip, Raina continued to see glimpses of various hues of the blue water. The trees surrounding the highway made her feel like she was driving through a dense forest. Soon she passed an inn on the right with green trim which signaled she was almost there.

Raina's stomach flip-flopped as she glanced at a small restaurant and realized her turn was just after it. Her heart beat faster, and she laughed at herself for being so nervous. The thick trees gave the impression she was in the middle of nowhere, but as the road sloped further down toward the direction of the water, she caught glimpses of houses. Raina rounded a corner and gasped at the beautiful coastal town. It reminded her of similar towns along the ocean. Raina slowed her car to match a sign's demand for reduced speed.

The downtown area was built to match the slope to the water's edge with each street running parallel to the shore. The road Raina traveled led past downtown to a marina with boats and empty docks scattered about and several large buildings surrounding it. Past the marina were a few houses before the road disappeared around a corner into the trees.

Raina passed several streets on the left lined with houses before coming to the business area. She followed Celia's written instructions and turned left onto Shore Drive. It ran along the length of the water with a row of buildings on one side and a boardwalk on the other. Large boulders nestled behind the boardwalk with a pebbled beach that slanted down into the water. She continued to follow the directions given, but when she turned right, she scanned the area, trying not to panic.

Did I make a wrong turn somewhere?

To the left was a large playground, a bandstand, several covered gazebos, flower- and tree-lined paths with benches, and several picnic tables with grills scattered along the ridge. It sloped down to a grassy area with slanted parking spaces. On the other side of the road was more parking, a walking path, and a beautiful view of the bay.

She traveled at an incline along the point until she reached a dead end with a large turnaround area. Upon closer inspection, she noticed a black iron gate with empty vines growing all over it. Slowing to a stop, Raina fumbled with the letter and tried to locate the address scrawled on it. After confirming she was in the right place, she inched her car forward. To her surprise the gate opened.

"I was not expecting this."

She continued along the drive by the bay until it veered left then right again, reaching the top of the point where the house came into view. Slamming on her brakes, Raina leaned forward to get a better look.

"What?" In her amazement, she turned the word into multiple syllables.

The house—which looked more like a castle than a house—loomed above her with grand windows and a massive stone wrap-around porch disappearing around the front. She could see a tower rising above the front of the house with a pointed roof top which looked like a witch's hat.

The building was made of a darkened red stone, but it didn't appear cold like she expected. It was inviting and beckoned her to come closer. The Dutch gabled roof added an extra layer of intricate architecture. Her lack of knowledge about these types of homes made it difficult for her to determine when it was built, but it reminded her of a mansion in Superior, Wisconsin she had read about in a magazine article.

There were a few paths leading to various areas of the grounds, but they all disappeared into the dense trees surrounding the home. The back porch connected to a greenhouse on the left which matched the exterior of the house, and the drive ahead led to a carport on the right. Raina assumed she should park there so eased her foot off the brake and rolled forward until she was under it.

She turned off her car and sucked in her breath. The trees opened in front of the house to the best view of the lake she had seen so far. There was a flower-lined path leading to a rocky cliff. The path jutted to the right to a circle of chairs with a large fire pit in the center and to the left it led to a gazebo with benches. Raina couldn't wait to see the rest of the grounds and could only imagine how grand the house was on the inside.

As Raina climbed out of her car, a side door to the house flung open and a young man came running out to greet her. "Welcome to Willow Bay Manor, Miss Matson."

"Oh goodness, please, call me Raina."

"Well, my name is Johnston, Johnston Smith," the young man said.

He was the same man who escorted her aunt at Gramma D's funeral, but up close he appeared to be a teenager. How could he have the job of driving her Aunt Kat around?

"You're the driver that brought Aunt Kat to the funeral, right?"

"Yes," Johnston said. "And I know what you're thinking. I look younger than I am. I'm twenty-two though, so not that young. Besides that, I have been working here at the manor doing odd jobs for a long time. My grandfather drove for the Nilssons before me and so did his father before him. I was named after them. I believe there has been a Johnston Smith driving for the Nilssons since before your great grandfather was even born. I learned how to drive on a Nilsson car, so when my grandfather decided to retire, he passed the reins on to me, with Kat's blessing, of course."

Raina chuckled, and reached back into her car to gather her purse and one of her bags. She paused when Johnston said, "Oh, I'll get those. If that's okay with you. Kat insisted I help you bring your things in."

"I'd at least like to grab my purse and the bag in my front seat."

"Sure, go ahead, and if you leave the keys with me, I'll move your car to the garage," Johnston said.

Raina looked past the car to where the driveway curved to the right, stopping at a building she had not noticed before. It looked like it had been a barn in a previous life.

Raina shifted her bag, flung her purse over her shoulder, and stepped toward the house. "So now what should I do?"

"Oh, go on in there. Celia is waiting for you and will take you to Kat."

Raina tried to steady the butterflies fluttering in her stomach as she entered the house. She could hear her suitcases being plopped onto the pavement as she shut the door behind her. The foyer was smaller than she expected but of course, this was just a side entrance and not the main one. But the size didn't diminish the finery exuding from the walls and fixtures. Even the small coat closet and table to the left looked fancy.

Perhaps this was a mistake. How on earth can I fit in here?

"Oh, there you are," an older woman said.

Raina jumped as the woman appeared out of nowhere. She looked to be about her mother's age before she died. She was shorter than Raina and had a rounded figure, but she looked ready to take on anything that came her way.

Raina stepped forward. "Hello, I'm—"

"Raina, of course. Or would you rather I call you Miss Matson. Oh, we can figure that out later. I'm Celia. How was the drive? What do you think of our little town? We're so excited you're here. Blessed be, I could talk all day, but you didn't come to see me. Come, let's take you to your aunt."

Raina followed Celia through the house while she continued to prattle on about the weather. She asked again about her drive and told her not to mind the grandeur of the place because it was just a house. Raina giggled and knew she would enjoy Celia's company.

They walked along a small hallway which led to the main area of the home. The grand entrance at the front of the home put the small foyer, for all its refinement, to shame. Directly across the front entrance of the house was a large staircase with a landing at the top where one could turn right or left, and a giant window bringing in light.

Off the main area was a hallway and Raina caught a glimpse of a dining room through open doors which was opposite a living room. She noticed more doors further down and she itched to investigate where they led but that would have to wait. On either side of the grand staircase ornate built-in benches stood guard over glass doors leading to a small room which she assumed must connect to the porch Raina noticed driving in.

Taking it all in, Raina twirled around until Celia brought her back by explaining something about the chandelier hanging above them. Raina was about to ask a question, but Celia cut her off. "Come along now, we mustn't keep your aunt waiting."

"Of course," Raina said and followed Celia into the living room.

Celia stopped inside the entrance. "She's here, Kat."

"Wonderful. It truly is a delight you decided to come."

Raina glanced around the room. "Thank you for inviting me."

Intimidation crept in and she couldn't shake her nerves. Aunt Kat sat on a chair by a large fireplace with a family portrait hanging above it. Across from her aunt was a matching chair. Closer to Raina were two couches evenly spaced with side tables. The furniture came from another era, but nothing was worn like one would expect. It was almost surprising that Aunt Kat was wearing dark pants and a maroon sweater instead of a dress matching the room.

Floor to ceiling windows flanked large glass doors connecting to a covered porch overlooking the front grounds and lake beyond. To the left, doors lead to the hallway. A large area rug, which matched the drapes, covered the wooden floor.

"Did you have a pleasant trip, Raina?" Aunt Kat asked, pulling Raina's attention from her study.

"Yes, it wasn't too bad. The drive along the lake was gorgeous."

"Why don't you come sit while Johnston and Celia take your things up to your rooms," Aunt Kat said, dismissing Celia with a wink and nod.

"Rooms?" Raina asked, moving to sit as directed.

"Yes, your room has a small sitting room and bathroom attached. I picked it especially for you. You get a spectacular view of the water and the grounds. It's on the second floor, quite a bit down from me, but I thought it was the perfect one for you."

"Thank you," Raina said, studying her aunt. "I don't know what to say. The house, or mansion, or manor, well, it's beautiful and the grounds are lovely."

"It's just home to me, but thank you. Take all the time you need to get settled and familiar with the place. I want you to feel comfortable here and hopefully in time it will feel like home for you, too."

"Thank you again, Aunt Kat."

"Raina," Aunt Kat said, taking a deep breath.

"Is everything okay?"

"Please don't worry about me. I want you to take a couple of days to get settled, but I eventually want us to discuss the estate and the town and how it's managed. I believe the sooner you learn about everything the better."

"Of course. Anything you want."

"Have you thought anymore on how long you might stay?"

"As I mentioned before, I intend to stay for now. I brought most of my things with me. Minus a couple pieces of furniture and some boxes I left behind. Beyond getting to know more about you and the town and the family legacy, I don't have a plan."

The crease on Aunt Kat's forehead smoothed out before she said, "Good. That's a start. Can I get you some tea, some coffee, or water, anything?"

"No, I'm good for now."

"Please let me or Celia know if you need anything. You will eventually meet the rest of the staff and any one of them can help you as well."

"The rest of the staff?"

"Goodness child, you don't expect an old lady like me to keep up with a house like this," Aunt Kat said while the corners of her mouth lifted into a half laugh.

Raina giggled and was about to ask a question when another woman appeared at the doorway. She had an air of seriousness about her and a stern look on her narrow face. She wore all brown as though she didn't want to draw attention to herself.

"Yes, Stacia?" Aunt Kat asked, smiling at the woman.

"Celia asked me to come fetch Miss Matson."

"You're all so quick," Aunt Kat said.

"Always wanting to please," Stacia said with a slight smile, but it quickly disappeared, leaving Raina to question if it was truly a smile or not.

"Raina, this is our fabulous housekeeper, Stacia Mays, she has been with us for a really long time," Aunt Kat said.

Raina stood. "Nice to meet you, Stacia."

"The pleasure is mine," Stacia said. "If you'd follow me, I'll show you to your room, Miss Matson."

"You don't need to be so formal with me. Please, call me Raina."

"Thank you, miss, but I will stick with Miss Matson if it's okay with you," the housekeeper said.

"Stacia believes in formality and tradition. Her family has served us a long time and was trained in the proper way to manage a home like this," Aunt Kat explained with a wink at Raina.

"I wouldn't want to change that I guess," Raina said. "Will I see you later, Aunt Kat?"

"Yes, dinner is at six this evening in the dining room. It won't be formal, but it will be nice to have you join me."

"Sounds great," Raina said, crossing the room.

"In the meantime, rest up. I have a couple of phone calls and a meeting which will keep me busy for a bit, so I'll see you at dinner," Aunt Kat said.

Raina followed the housekeeper up the staircase to her rooms, where Stacia excused herself to allow Raina to get settled. She started to unpack but was drawn to explore instead. The sitting room had a small fireplace on one wall with a couple of chairs flanking either side. A small desk nestled under a large window overlooked the front of the house and the lake beyond. There was a door to her own private bathroom with a large, tiled shower and the biggest claw foot tub Raina had ever seen. It sat under a small window overlooking the side yard, and she caught glimpses of the lake through the trees whenever the wind blew.

A second door off the bathroom connected to a large walk-in closet. She went through it, opened a door on the opposite wall, and found herself in the bedroom area. A large four-poster bed with matching side tables stood tall against the left side of the room. On one side of the bed was a window but on the other side was a door leading out to a small stone-covered balcony.

One patio chair and matching chaise lounge rested against the outside wall with a small table between them. She leaned over the stone railing, and looked to the left. A small path leaving the house disappeared into the forest, in the direction of another building peeking through the trees. It looked like a smaller version of the manor house without the tower.

Guest house?

Raina moved away, making a mental note to check out the other building later. She went back inside to continue her investigation of her room. Two large windows with a door in between connected to a second balcony which overlooked the front grounds. Raina gasped at the uninterrupted view of the water. Forcing her gaze away from the lake, she glanced at the two matching dressers lining another wall, then grinned at the fireplace cozily sitting directly opposite her bed. A single high-back chair and small table were arranged perfectly in front of it. The sitting room was through an open door to the left of the fireplace making a full circle.

All the furnishings were more modern than those downstairs. The bathroom had been updated as well, despite having a hint of the old. She investigated the dressers and found them empty. The lack of décor in the rooms outside of the made bed and its flowered bedspread intrigued her.

Perhaps Aunt Kat left it to me to make my own.

Wrapping her arms around herself, Raina's mind raced to her Gramma D. What could have possibly drawn her away from this place? A rush of sadness coursed through her so Raina pushed thoughts of her grandmother aside and went back to unpacking.

Chapter Four

Raina opened the door, let her eyes adjust, and scanned the area. She discovered a rusted blue bike with a wicker basket and a rack on the back. She rummaged around the garage until she found an air pump and blew up the tires. After wheeling it outside, she hopped on and rode around to make sure nothing else was wrong with it besides a layer of dust. It handled beautifully.

Stopping in front of the garage, she found a semi-clean rag and wiped down the bike. A thorough washing would be good, but a quick dust off would work for now. Raina flung her purse across her body and set off down the driveway toward town.

She had explored the grounds and house over the past two days, but now she wanted to check out Willow Bay. It wasn't every day she visited a place her ancestors built from nothing, and as intimidating as it was, she was excited as she glided down the hill.

Raina shielded her eyes as the sun streamed down from a brilliant blue cloudless sky. She pulled her beige sweater tight over her T-shirt and jeans, against the still-damp air. Her tennis shoes had seen better days, but she wanted to be able to walk along the water and not worry about ruining them. She made a mental note to buy a pair of waterproof boots. Even if she decided not to stay, it would be nice to have something she could wear to walk or hike along the shoreline.

Raina stopped along Shore Drive at stone steps she hadn't noticed on her first drive through town. She rested her bike against the wall, skipped down the stairs, and jogged to the pebbled beach at the water's edge. She reached down to press her hand into the cold water and closed her eyes.

Warmth rushed through her despite its icy temperature, and the song of ships and love lost to the lake flitted through her mind. Flashes of giant waves and old boats came to life, and she smiled despite the tears filling her eyes. Sucking in air, she opened her eyes and stared at the sparkles of sunlight dancing across the blue bay and tried to tamp down the rush of embarrassment at becoming so emotional.

A horn brought Raina back and she stood to see where it was coming from. It blew a second time and Raina squinted against the sun. A weather-worn boat was on the way out of the bay. A longing to be with whomever was on the boat overwhelmed her.

The idea of gliding across the water excited Raina and she hoped she would have the chance to do it someday soon. She sighed and moved back toward her waiting bike. Reaching the road, her mouth watered as the smell of coffee wafted toward her. A hot latte sounded perfect to ward off the chill of the day.

Raina rode her bike the short distance to the café. She rested it against a tree and climbed a flight of wooden stairs jutting out the side of a deck connecting several business-es along Shore Drive. She wandered across the wooden boards, glancing over the two rows of tables along the railing in front of the café and restaurant. Benches and flowerpots scattered about gave the space a welcoming feel. Trio Pub was scrawled on a wooden sign above one door and a second door had a matching sign with Trio Café. To the left of the entrance, the deck narrowed to the size of a wide sidewalk stretching along the rest of the businesses.

The café door opened, and a gray-haired man with a dark green stocking cap strolled out with a steaming cup and a white paper bag. Raina breathed in the nutty aroma as he went past and she bobbed a greeting. He smiled and raised his cup in return and started whistling a lively tune as he walked away.

Raina walked into the café with a clang over the door announcing her arrival as a young woman came flying through a door off to the left.

"I'll be right with you if you care to wait. I need to help my customer next door."

Raina nodded. "I'm fine. Take your time."

The woman disappeared as a door shut in the distance prompting her immediate return. "I guess I'll help you now. It seems my customer left. What can I get for you?"

Raina followed the woman to the counter. "A small latte."

"Can I get you anything else?"

"No, that should do it."

Noise behind the counter caught Raina's attention as a man appeared from the back. He held a resemblance to the woman putting together the ingredients for Raina's drink.

"There you are. It's about time," the woman said.

"Sorry. I told you I had to get that done before I could do anything else," the man said.

"Maybe you're running yourself too thin."

"Or maybe I'm not and helping your brother every now and again isn't that big a deal."

"Or maybe—"

"Geez, Annie," the man said. "We can't be arguing in front of customers."

Annie's face turned red as she looked over at Raina. "I'm so sorry. I'll have that latte for you soon. And I'm sorry my brother is blind and started into me without noticing you."

Raina laughed. "Actually, this made my day. I don't have any siblings, so watching this made me thankful I don't."

Blank stares registered on both of the siblings' faces.

Clearing her throat, Raina said, "Kidding. I'm just kidding. People always tell me I'm bad at jokes. And I can be a bit awkward when meeting new people."

They all laughed, and Raina stretched out her hand across the counter. "Raina Matson."

"Well of course you are. I'm Annie," the woman said, elbowing her brother in the gut. "And this here's my brother Conrad, but we call him Conie."

They all shook hands as Raina asked, "So small towns, word travels, is that why you know who I am?"

"Something like that," Conie said while he studied Raina.

Raina shifted under his gaze and asked, "Do you both own this place?"

"I own the bookstore next door," Annie said, "Conie owns the café and restaurant. Plus, we have our sister, Murie, who owns the boutique on the corner."

"Oh nice," Raina said. "I'm assuming you know my Aunt Kat."

"Everyone knows Katarina Nilsson," Conie said.

His statement unnerved Raina. He was sizing her up and she couldn't determine how she was faring. She had spent the last couple of days trying to convince herself not to run from the grandeur of the manor. And with this man's study of her, she couldn't shake the wariness of feeling like she didn't fit in.

Raina fumbled with her purse and shifted her feet. "Um, well I should go."

She snagged a five, placed it on the counter, and told Annie to keep the change. She grabbed her hot beverage and left. She was walking across the patio when the door opened behind her.

"Hey, sorry about that," Conie said.

Raina whirled around. "Sorry about what?"

"I could tell you were starting to feel uncomfortable. All of our so-called fighting is purely just for fun, and I didn't mean anything by my last statement about your aunt."

Stunned at how well Conie could read her, Raina said, "I wasn't uncomfortable by the exchange. I'm just not used to small talk with strangers. Especially ones who seem to know more about my family than I do."

"What do you mean?"

"Nothing really. Just the way you said everyone knows my aunt made it sound like everyone knows her and her story well and I don't know anything about either. Plus, it sounded quite protective, like you aren't sure of my intentions. Or you were trying to decide if I belonged."

"I'm sorry for that," Conie said. "I hope in time you can get to know her as me and my family know her. And I can't help but be protective of her to a stranger no one has heard about until recently."

Straightening her spine, Raina said, "I guess I understand."

"I can tell I'm only making you more uncomfortable and I don't mean to."

Raina studied the handsome man in front of her. He was quite a bit taller than her, had dark hair and the prettiest blue eyes she had ever seen—or were they green? They matched his sister's, especially when they were both fired up. His dark gray sweater and blue jeans fit snuggly over his solid build. Raina's heart skipped a beat. Her cheeks flamed and she shifted her gaze. Taking a sip of her hot beverage, she hoped he hadn't noticed her staring.

"I should probably get back to work," he said.

"I'm going to sit here, if that's okay, while I finish my drink before I ride around. I want to get familiar with the town."

Conie cocked his head to the side. "Sure, sit as long as you like. Getting around town won't take long, though."

Raina chuckled. "I noticed that on the drive in."

"Conie, you got my sandwich ready?" a voice called from below.

Conie rolled his eyes. "Always demanding and rude, aren't we?"

"Hey now." A woman bounded onto the deck stopping next to Conie. "Who's this?"

"Like I said, demanding and rude," Conie said with a snicker. "This is Raina Matson. Raina, this is my other sister and pain in the butt, Muriel, but we call her Murie."

"Oh yeah. I was wondering when we would get to meet you," Murie said. "I helped Kat pick out your bedspread. I hope you like it."

"I do, thank you."

"Excellent. Now, brother, where is my sandwich?" Murie asked.

"Stu should have it ready in the back for you."

"Okay. I'm going to grab it and get on to work. Nice to meet you, Raina."

"And you, too."

Changing the subject, Conie said, "They're calling for rain the next couple of days. Lady Superior is going to be introducing herself to you."

"I look forward to it. I do love a good storm."

"We'll see about that. The storms here can be quite something. Downright dangerous."

"I suppose it can be difficult to manage out on the water."

Conie nodded and shifted toward the restaurant. "I should probably get back inside. It was nice meeting you, Raina, and I'm sure we will be chatting more soon."

Delighted with meeting this small family, Raina was disappointed the conversation was ending. "I suppose I should get on with my adventure."

"If you decide to go down by the marina, be careful along pier two. They've been working on it, and I don't think it's ready for people to be walking on it yet."

"Thanks for the warning," Raina said. "Well, goodbye for now."

"See you later," Conie said and went back into the café.

Raina had finished her latte while chatting with Conie, so threw her cup in a garbage can by the door and meandered back to her bike. She looked out at the water and decided to head toward the marina. The boats called her to them.

The sun was still shining, but the breeze was cool, and a shiver ran up Raina's back as she pedaled along. She stopped in front of one of the large buildings and was surprised when she read Nilsson Boatwerks across the top.

"I didn't think there were any more Nilssons besides my aunt living here," Raina said.

"There aren't, but this business was founded by a Nilsson and when my father bought the place, he decided to keep the name."

Raina jolted. "I'm so sorry I didn't see you there."

"That's because I was at the other building in my office."

"I saw you earlier, getting coffee. You were coming out as I was going in."

"Yeah, I suppose that was me."

"I'm Raina Matson." Raina shoved her hand out between them.

The man's gray eyes twinkled as his mouth curled into a grin. "I'm Henry Mays. You probably met my wife at the manor—Stacia Mays."

"I did," Raina said. "She's been very nice."

The man laughed out right. "Now, we both know when Stacia's at work she's as stiff as a board and as stern as an old schoolmarm."

Surprised by this man's candor, Raina laughed. "She does seem serious all the time."

"Yes, that's my Stacia, but don't let her toughness fool you. She's an old softy on the inside."

"Good to know. Thank you, Mr. Mays."

"Please call me Henry. You want me to show you around the place?"

"I would love that."

Henry rushed past Raina while she hurried to settle her bike to catch up with him. He opened an oversized garage door and as her eyes adjusted, she studied the boats in various stages of repair lining each side of the building.

"I keep this area clear to get the boats in and out," Henry said, pointing down the middle of the aisle. "The only time I don't keep it clear is if I'm working on one of the big gals."

Raina looked around, fascinated at the work this man did. She wandered to the nearest boat and looked it over while Henry continued to talk. She nodded or commented when appropriate but kept wondering what it must feel like to sail along on one of them on the big lake.

"Come over here by me, I want to show you something," Henry said and shuffled closer to a workbench. There were several pictures hanging above it and he took one down, handing it to Raina.

"That there is your great-great-grandfather and his twin brother. The brothers really worked hard to build up

Nilsson Boatwerks. Then when the white hurricane hit, taking so many lives, the Nilssons eventually turned the boatwerks over to the town to operate. It had come under some disrepair before my father bought it and built it back up to what you see here."

Raina studied the picture and looked around the space. "I know they would all be proud. This is quite the business you have here."

"Thank you." Henry beamed.

"You mentioned something about a white hurricane?" Raina asked.

"Yeah, but I don't have time to get into all that as I need to be getting on. I hope that's okay."

"Of course," Raina said. "Thank you for showing me around and showing me this picture."

"You have the Nilsson look about you," Henry said, hanging the picture back up.

"Oh wow. Thank you."

Not knowing what else to say, Raina said goodbye and went to retrieve her bike. The mention of the white hurricane intrigued her again as a large gust of wind blew across the water, taking her breath away. She gazed across the bay at the rocks on the edge of the point and couldn't wait to see the waves crash against them during the impending storm.

She could barely see the manor, but finding the roof peeking through the trees, Raina knew it was there. She leaned against a piling and watched boats maneuver around until a car slowed to a stop behind her.

Rained shifted as a female voice shouted from the open driver door window, "Hey, you there. What are you doing here?"

Confused, Raina stepped closer to the car. "I was visiting with Henry for a bit and am now watching the boats."

"We don't like loiterers around here."

Raina tried to see what the woman looked like, but her face was in the shadows. "I was just watching the boats."

"Violet, leave Raina alone," Henry hollered from the boathouse. "She isn't hurting anything,"

"Raina? So, you're old Kat's niece, huh."

"Have you been drinking again?" Henry asked, walking toward them.

"Mind your business, Henry." The window rolled up and the car drove away.

Shaken by the interaction—or was it the cold? Raina decided it was time to head back to the manor.

"Are you okay?" Henry asked. "I hope she didn't upset you."

"I'm fine, just chilled now. Thanks."

She excused herself and pedaled toward home.

Chapter Five

Walking into the living room before dinner, Raina was surprised to see her aunt sitting near the fire with a wine goblet in one hand and a second resting on the table next to her. Raina knew when Aunt Kat noticed her since she stood and handed her the other glass.

"I heard you had quite the day and thought a little sip of something might help take the edge off," she said.

Raina sipped the dark liquid. "Cabernet?"

"My favorite," Aunt Kat said.

"Mine too. But how did you know about my day?"

"I had a scheduled call with Conie, and we discussed your meeting. Then Stacia came to me and told me about your meeting Violet. For her stern demeaner she really has a soft heart. She was upset for you."

"News travels fast." Raina chuckled.

"So, you're okay?"

"I'm okay."

"Glad to hear. Now come sit by the fire and you can tell me about it. Dinner isn't quite ready."

Raina followed her aunt's instructions and told her version of the day's events.

"Oh, those Strands. Sometimes they can be quite mean to us. Well, to most folks, but especially to us."

"Strands?"

"Violet Strand was the woman in the car today. Her rudeness wasn't surprising. Her mother is much the same way," Aunt Kat explained. "Donna was in elementary school when I was graduating high school, so we never hung around in the same circles. Of course, it was more due to age than status, but when she got older, she was downright rude to me and anyone who worked for me. Later, she just kept to herself, but it seems her daughter is much the same way now."

"Did you ever try talking to her about it?"

"I've tried to smooth things over with her, but she either tries to argue or avoids me all together."

"That's so strange," Raina said. "Of course, jealousy could be the root of it."

"I've thought about that before," Aunt Kat said. "They've struggled some over the years. Especially since Donna's father quit working for us and left for a while to take care of his mother. When he came back to town, he refused to come back to the manor, and he struggled with holding a job until he died. But it all seems to run deeper than that. Like they are holding something against us or something."

"Dinner is ready," Stacia announced, interrupting the conversation, and they dropped the subject.

Raina shuddered at the memory of the way the woman had talked to her earlier.

"Are you okay, dear?" Aunt Kat asked, settling in her chair.

"I'm fine. I was just thinking about today."

"Well, let's talk of other things and change how we feel."

"That sounds great."

The wind kicked up outside and the conversation veered toward the ravaging waves and how they could hear them crashing against the rocky cliffs of the point. Raina wanted to run outside to get a better look, but with the lightning now flashing, she knew it was a bad idea.

After dinner, Aunt Kat said she was tired and went to her rooms for the night. Raina sat in the great room to read, but was drawn to the lake and understood now why Conie had mentioned that Lake Superior would be introducing itself to her. The memory of how Conie and his sisters interacted flashed in her mind and she giggled.

When she remembered her conversation with Henry, she sobered as the white hurricane danced in her head. She was saddened at not knowing her great-great-grandfather had a twin or any of the other details of her family history she was just discovering. Raina went to the library to see if she could find any books about the past. She wanted to do research on what the white hurricane could be, but the lights flickered, and she went back to her room. She watched the ferocity of the storm from her sitting room. Her investigation could wait.

Raina woke to light streaming through the window and birds chirping, signaling the storm had passed. She had fallen asleep on the chair, still wearing her clothes from the night before, and was ready for a hot shower to wash off the grunge of sleep.

She made quick work of that chore and dressed in a pair of black jeans, a red T-shirt, and matching flannel. It was cool outside, especially after last night's storm. When Raina finished dressing for the day, she bounded downstairs as the phone rang. Celia's voice answered the call and Raina caught pieces of the conversation about a boat.

Raina went to the dining room where a buffet was sitting on a sideboard. She grabbed a plate and piled it high as the growl from her stomach announced her hunger. Raina settled at the table while Celia and Aunt Kat meandered in, discussing the phone call. They each prepared their own plates and sat at their designated spots at the table.

"What's this about a boat?" Raina asked. "Did one come loose in the storm?"

"On the contrary," Aunt Kat said. "An old fishing boat washed ashore. It appears to be from a wreck many years ago."

"Oh, how interesting," Raina said. Her heart quickened, and she had a hard time containing her excitement. "Can we go look? Where is it?"

"It washed up on Pebble Beach," Celia said.

"Celia, why don't you take her down to see it after breakfast. It might be fun for Raina to see how our coastal town handles such things."

Her lips curved into a smile, but the light didn't quite reach her eyes, and Raina noticed a shadow in them.

Deciding not to mention it, Raina said, "That would be great. Thank you, Celia."

The conversation changed to the weather, followed by Aunt Kat's schedule and when it would work for Raina to sit down with her to discuss the Nilsson Family Enterprises. Agreeing on a time, the women left the dining room, and Celia told Raina she would meet her outside so they could ride down to the beach together.

It didn't take long for them to get into the car with Johnston and Celia rode with a grin on her face all the way into town. But Raina worried over the concern on her aunt's face and why the boat washing ashore would cause it. As they arrived at the beach, Raina was surprised to see only a handful of people gathered.

Seeing a friendly face, Raina went to stand next to Conie. "Good morning."

Turning toward her, he said, "Good morning. Come to check out the wreck?"

"Yes. Is it strange a boat wreck of this size would wash ashore like this?" Raina asked.

"It depends on the waves and how high the tide was," Conie said. "But I don't think I've seen a boat this intact and this big wash ashore here before. Maybe in a bigger bay perhaps."

"Interesting," Raina said. "I'm so intrigued by this. Is anyone investigating it?"

"Yes, we've reached out to a friend of ours from the coast guard station in Grand Marais. They've already come and gone. A few of us are going to meet and see if we have anything to add to the investigation."

"Is the town helping the coast guard a normal thing?"

"It's normal for this town," Conie said. "But we are a tight knit community, and we like to help each other."

"Can I help?" Raina surprised herself by asking. "Maybe there are some old pictures or something Aunt Kat might have."

"Sure, Conie said. "We're going to meet later this evening."

"Where at?"

"If the pub isn't too busy, we're thinking of meeting there."

"Why don't you come to the manor?" Raina blurted out. "It's quiet and we have plenty of space. I'm sure Aunt Kat won't mind."

"If you're sure," Conie said.

"I'm sure," Raina said. "It'll be fun."

Conie raised his eyebrows. "These types of things rarely end up being fun."

Raina sobered. "I'm so sorry I didn't mean anything—"

"It's okay," Conie said. "Don't feel bad, please. I just meant these things can sometimes end with not finding out anything or finding out too much of something tragic."

"I suppose a wrecked boat means a loss of life," she said.

"You're correct. You still want to help?" he asked.

Raina bit her lower lip. "Absolutely."

"Okay, I'll spread the word to the others. Meet you at the manor after dinner. I'll call you later and let you know for sure how many and what time."

"Sounds great," she said.

Raina studied Conie as he walked away before turning to see what Celia was up to. The older woman wandered around the boat wreck, jotting down a few things on a piece of paper. Raina asked her if she wanted to join the investigation team, but Celia turned her down. Celia studied the mangled boat until a dark cloud blocked the sun, casting a dark shadow across the beach and over the wreckage. Raina shivered and followed Celia back to the car.

Raina sat in the dining room waiting for the rest of the group to arrive. There were only going to be four of them plus any coast guard members who might show. She had requested to have drinks lined up on the cabinet and stared at the array, wondering if she'd gone overboard. A plate of brownies and cookies sat in the middle of the table with laced paper napkins next to it. She wasn't sure if she would ever get used to being able to request anything from the staff and get what she asked for.

Raina clinked her fingernails against her glass of cabernet between sips and tried to steady the butterflies in her stomach. She'd been excited to be a part of the investigation, but after discussing things with Aunt Kat, she realized she should have asked permission first before inviting the team to her house.

Aunt Kat had reassured her all was well, but Raina couldn't shake the feeling her aunt was upset with having them there. Raina jumped when the clang of the doorbell brought her back to the present. Her heart pounded as she stood to receive her guests.

Celia led the group into the dining area. "The team has arrived."

"Thank you, Celia," Raina said. "Are you sure you don't want to join us?"

"I have some things I need to get done before bed, so I'll just get on that. Thank you though," Celia said, winking at Raina. She excused herself and left the room.

"Hello, everyone," Raina said with a shaky voice. "There are several kinds of drinks on the buffet so please help yourself. And of course, Aunt Kat's cook, Milly, insisted everyone needed to have something to munch on."

The group laughed and gathered their refreshments. Conie sat across from Raina, and his sister Murie walked around to sit next to her. Henry Mays and the representative from the coast guard flanked Conie on his side of the table.

Murie asked Raina how she was getting settled, but the conversation between the two wrapped up quickly as Conie stood and cleared his throat. "Thanks for getting together on this. Raina, thanks for hosting." He motioned to the coast guard representative. "This is Oliver Beecham. Oliver, this is Raina."

Raina greeted Oliver and focused her attention back on Conie who was now sharing the few pieces of information they gathered from the boat earlier that day. "I'll let Oliver go into more detail."

"Right," Oliver said while Conie sat in his chair and leaned back. "Apart from the partial letter on the side of the boat and a mangled tin, we really don't have much to identify the boat. Although, based on the craftsmanship and the style, it appears to be a boat from the early 1900s. We found a small trunk anchored to the floor and my team is working on opening it and going through its contents. We hope to stabilize the wreckage and see if we can gather more clues, but it may be a day or two since we are stationed in Grand Marais, and I'm not sure which day we'll get back down here just yet."

"What letter did you find on the side of the boat?" Raina asked.

"We believe it to be an F. And the letter on the tin is an N," Oliver explained.

"Is there anything in the trunk?" Murie asked.

"We are still working on that. It took some effort to open it and once we got into it, the items needed some cleaning up. But I'll bring the items or bring pictures the next time I come," Oliver said.

"Should we make a list of all the boats that went down or went missing during the early 1900s along this area?" Henry asked. "I know the water can carry things a bit, but for a boat that size to wash ashore in our bay it would have gone down close to here."

"That isn't a bad idea. I can pull the list the coast guard has, but some smaller towns may have managed their own records, and we may not have all the information," Oliver said.

"Any boats from around here go missing during that time?" Raina asked.

Henry rested his gaze on Raina. "You remember the picture I showed you?"

"I do," Raina said. "Did they have a couple?"

"Indeed, they did. But let's not get ahead of ourselves now."

"True, but always worth a look," Conie said. "We should check all prospects. So, the next step sounds like stabilizing the wreckage. Would it be okay if we moved it into the boatwerks?"

"Sure, if you're able to secure it and are careful not to damage anything," Oliver said. "Plus, it will keep prying eyes and curiosity at bay."

"I'll get it moved into the warehouse then," Henry said. "My hope will be to get it done by the end of the week."

"Great," Conie said. "After that, Henry and I will work on compiling a list of missing boats or confirmed wrecks, and Oliver will work on gathering the info on what is in the trunk, along with his list."

"Do we want to meet back here, say in two weeks? That way we don't have to rush and miss something?" Raina asked.

"Perfect," Conie said. "Weather should be getting warmer, as we'll be into the first couple of days in June, and we can do it on a Saturday afternoon if we want. Is there a room we could use, do you think, to keep everything together and store it there instead of having it scattered about?"

"Let me discuss it with my aunt," Raina said. "But I'm sure we can come up with something. I'll let you know by tomorrow."

The conversation changed to the severity of the storm and fizzled into general small talk. Raina and Murie hit it off and they agreed Raina should stop by her shop as soon as possible. Raina noticed Oliver watching Murie, and she wondered if there was something between the two of them, even though he lived in Grand Marais.

Refreshments were passed around again, and Raina was giddy as she visited with everyone. It had been a long time since she felt like she was a part of something.

Oliver stood after finishing the last bites of his snack. "I hate to say it, but I have to get back."

Murie seemed disappointed and they exchanged a look. Raina decided she would ask about it later. Raina pushed away from the table and thanked Oliver for coming. Everyone else stood as he left the room, calling their goodbyes to him. Raina looked over at Conie and realized he had been watching her. Her cheeks flushed, and she shifted her feet and looked away.

"Henry, do you need a ride home," Murie asked.

"No, I told Stacia to wait for me, so I'll catch a ride with her. Thanks though."

"Okay. Well, brother, I guess it's just you and me heading out now," Murie said. "I wish we could stay longer, Raina, but I have some things I have to get done for the boutique before I head to bed tonight. We should connect later and hang out sometime."

"I wish we could visit longer as well," Raina said.

"Next time," Murie said.

"Indeed, next time," Raina agreed.

Raina followed the siblings to the door and said goodbye. Murie left, but Conie paused. He opened his mouth like he was going to say something else, but shook his head and left, apparently changing his mind.

Confused, Raina hollered one more goodbye and shut the door.

"I don't think I've ever seen Conie flustered enough not to say what he's thinking," Henry said.

Raina jolted. "I didn't realize you were there. You startled me."

"Sorry about that," Henry said with a sparkle in his eye. "I think Stacia will be about done. Do you want to walk with me to her office?"

"Sure," Raina said and locked arms with the aging man.

"So, Raina, tell me why you joined our little mystery club."

Raina couldn't keep from grinning. "I don't know really. I was caught up in the excitement of it, I guess. I just felt drawn to it."

"Hm, sounds to me like your Nilsson blood kicked in," Henry said with a chuckle.

"Perhaps, but I'm not sure what that means."

"A Nilsson is always drawn to help or fix or take care of anything in this town," Henry explained. "That's the way it's been from the beginning I suppose."

"Interesting," Raina said. "That reminds me, I keep meaning to ask Aunt Kat if there is anything I could dig through, like pictures or old records to see if I can find anything out about other boats."

"It would sure help, but don't be surprised if she hesitates. It isn't anything against you, but she may hesitate."

"Why?"

"That's a question you'll need to ask your aunt. It's her story to tell," Henry said.

"I see."

"There you are, my dear," Henry said to Stacia, as she walked out of her office, followed by the cook. "Hello, Milly."

"Henry, always a pleasure," Milly said and then to Raina, "If you're done in the dining room, I'll tidy up now."

"I am, but I can come help you," Raina said. "Good night, Henry, Stacia. See you later."

"Good night, Raina."

Raina contemplated the match between Henry and Stacia as they left. They were as different as night and day, but one would only need to observe them together to see they loved each other immensely. Molly shuffled into the dining room, so Raina went to help as promised.

Chapter Six

Sitting across the desk from her aunt, Raina was hanging on every word. When there was a pause in her aunt's explanation, Raina said, "I had no idea how much you were involved in the running of the town. Or that Conie helped with things here and there."

"Well, that's how it goes in owning a town," Aunt Kat explained. "You see we have contracts with the different business owners who lease our buildings. We also own most of the land surrounding the town, all the way to the highway. But we are struggling. The businesses are struggling. We were founded on being a town for all and really hoped our tourism would grow. But as the bigger towns grew, fewer people stopped here and most tourists don't even realize we're here any longer."

"That's so sad," Raina said. "Are people leaving?"

"We've stayed at a steady population. We haven't shrunk, but we haven't grown. I fear if something doesn't change soon, the town will crumble. I can't let that happen."

"Maybe we need to amp up our tourist attraction draw. Perhaps a new sign by the highway. Do we have any festivals or anything we could help promote that might bring people in?"

"We have the White Hurricane Festival the first weekend in November every year," Aunt Kat said.

"There it is again," Raina said. "What is the white hurricane?"

"I suppose most don't remember it, but we in Willow Bay will always remember. It's as much a part of our history as the first boarding house being built." Aunt Kat paused and looked out the window. "In November 1913, a storm hit. It rivaled in severity with the one that took the Edmund Fitzgerald. It hit Lake Superior, I believe on the sixth, and spilled into the rest of the great lakes from there. The day dawned like any other November day. The boats went out on the water like normal. Including my grandfather's boat. My great-uncle also went out on another one of our boats. As the storm kicked up, they struggled back into the bay. The storm ravaged the lake, and it took down boats of all sizes including ships. The lake stole close to three hundred souls that day. We called it the white hurricane. We lost quite a few from our own tiny village, including my great-uncle. Most boats were never recovered."

Aunt Kat looked over at Raina. "We honor the lives lost on the lake. Not just from our town but from all over the great lakes. We had it bad here but the worst of it was on the eastern great lakes. The festival was created to honor those lives lost and also those lives forever changed. The festival is also meant to pay homage to those who continue risking their lives as they dance with Lady Superior."

"Is the festival something we could advertise more?"

Aunt Kat chuckled. "Considering we've never advertised it, I would say yes."

Raina giggled and started making a list of ideas to promote the festival.

"I knew bringing you here would be a good idea," Aunt Kat said.

"I'm so glad you invited me," Raina said. Changing the subject, she asked, "Aunt Kat, do you think there might be some old journals or pictures I could look through to see if I can find any clues on the mystery boat?"

Aunt Kat grew pale, and she looked past Raina.

"I'm so sorry," Raina said. "I had no idea asking would upset you so much."

Reaching across the desk, Aunt Kat patted Raina's hand. "Perhaps it's time you and I had a chat. But not here. Come along. Let's go to my rooms."

Raina followed her elder upstairs and into her aunt's room and felt like she was stepping back in time. Where Raina's furnishings and rooms were updated, her aunts were much like the living room, old but refined.

"Go sit by the fireplace. I will join you in a minute," Aunt Kat said while rummaging around a drawer.

Raina obeyed and waited for her aunt to get settled. Aunt Kat lifted the lid of a jewelry box and it tried to play an old tune but haltingly sang warped notes instead.

Aunt Kat grabbed a handful of pictures out of the box and shut the lid. "This has seen better days, as you can tell."

Thumbing through the pictures, Aunt Kat picked one out of the stack and handed it to Raina.

"That is a picture of my family," Aunt Kat said. "It was taken a year before my parents died. We were about to go on a holiday and my grandmother snapped the picture of us. This is my father and mother, and of course, me and your Gramma D."

Aunt Kat paused, selected another picture of her family, and studied it. "Grandfather died a few years before this picture was taken. But despite that, we were happy. Or so I thought. Things in town were going well. Businesses were thriving. We were having so many parties. Life was going well for us."

"It sounds wonderful," Raina said.

"It was a great time in our lives," Aunt Kat said. A flash of pain registered on her face and her smile faded. "Then, in the spring of the following year, Gramma Melia took Del and me to Duluth for some shopping for a couple of days. She said it was good for us to get our summer wardrobe, plus our parents needed some long overdue one-on-one time. When we returned home, Del bounded out of the car first. I was delayed because I had to grab my purse. And when Gramma and I walked into the house we heard Del scream. Gramma told me to stay in the foyer and she ran to see what happened. A few minutes later Del ran to the phone and yelled at me to leave the house."

Flinching at the look in her aunt's eyes, Raina reached across the space and held her hand. "Aunt Kat, if this is too hard to discuss, we don't have to do it now, or ever for that matter."

Aunt Kat took a shaky breath. "Oh no. It's time you know your history. Murder-suicide, is what they determined. Mother apparently stabbed father and then shot herself. They had given the staff a couple of days off, so they were all alone when it happened. The police think they must have been arguing and it occurred in a fit of rage.

I still have a hard time wrapping my head around it. But Del. Poor Del found them laying in a pool of their own blood. She was only eleven years old at the time.”

“Wow, so young. The impact that must have had on her.”

“She withdrew from me, from Gramma Melia, from the town. She started to act out as she got older and got into trouble a lot. And when she turned eighteen, she asked for a couple thousand dollars and left. She never came back.”

“That time you said we met when I was a little girl. That wasn’t here, was it?” Raina asked.

“No. Our other grandparents died and left some money, along with a few items, for Del and me. Gramma wanted to make sure Del got her share. She and I met just south of Duluth so I could give everything to her. I begged her to come home, but she just hugged me and left. It was the last time I saw her alive.”

“Where did she go when she left Willow Bay—before Grand Meadow I mean. Do you know?”

“The only information I ever got about that was in a letter she sent me after we had met that one time. She said she was too ashamed to come home. She said she had done some things not fitting for a Nilsson.”

“Like what?” Raina asked.

"She said when she left Willow Bay, she was hoping it would help with the pain, but when it didn't, she got into drugs. She also drank all the time and was living wherever she could find a place to lay her head down. She was trying desperately to numb the pain and to run away from memories which haunted her dreams." Aunt Kat smiled. "Then she got pregnant with your mom, and she knew she had to do what was best for her sake. She told me she couldn't go home, but she had to make something of herself and create a new home for them. And you know the rest from there."

Raina went to the window to look out at the waves crashing against the rocks. "I don't even know what to say."

"You don't have to say anything," Aunt Kat said. "Everyone in town knows our shame. Our dirty secret. And yet they loved us through it. I just wish Del felt that same love and that it could have helped her. Gramma Melia took over when my parents died and raised Del and me in the family business, but after my sister left, Gramma focused on teaching me how to carry on the legacy. I always planned to have kids and pass it along, but that wasn't meant for me."

Raina looked back at her aunt. "This is why you hesitate when I talk about digging around things in the past."

"Yes," Aunt Kat agreed. "I'm always fearful I'll find out something else."

"Did you ever learn more information about what could have led to your parents' death?" Raina asked.

"We did. Well, we think we did. Gramma discovered in reading through one of Mother's journals that she had been having an affair before she killed my father."

"Oh, how awful," Raina said. "No wonder you're afraid to look in the past."

"Yes, I'm fearful of it. The ghosts of the past have often haunted me over the years. But I'm growing old and tired of running, and perhaps the boat washing ashore is a sign for us to take another look. Even if it hurts."

"Are you sure?"

"Yes. I'm sure."

"Are there more journals, or papers, or pictures, that could help?" Raina asked.

"Come with me." Aunt Kat rose and placed the music box on the table by her chair.

Raina followed her up to the top floor. They went down a long hallway with old servants' quarters lining each side, stopping at a locked door. Raina held her breath while her aunt pulled an old key out of her pocket and fiddled with the lock. The door swung open, and Aunt Kat flinched as light flashed across their faces from a window across the room.

Raina inhaled deeply, following her aunt into the room. It was an old storage room, which appeared to have not been touched in years. There were boxes and chests everywhere with old furniture and suitcases. A bench sat by the window, and Raina knew she would be spending a lot of time there going through everything.

"Gramma Melia didn't go through the rest of Mother's things and never even touched Father's," Aunt Kat said. "She read part of one journal and had everything thrown in boxes or chests and shoved up here to be locked away forever. I really have no idea what we'll find."

"Are you sure you want me to do this, Aunt Kat?"

"Yes. I'm sure. I can't run from ghosts forever."

Raina lifted the flap of the box closest to her and snagged a well-worn journal. She thumbed through the first couple of pages and paused to read.

July 3, 1947

I can't believe I met Him again today. What am I thinking? I have children. And although Stefan no longer notices I'm alive, I do love my husband. I need to stop this before it gets any worse. But oh, the feel of his hand in mine as we walked along the water was heaven. And it was nice to be treated like I was important again. But I can't let this continue. I just can't.

Raina paused and showed what she was reading to her aunt. "It sounds like whatever relationship she had, she felt conflicted, and she did love your father."

"That's something, I guess," Aunt Kat said. "Perhaps what you find won't be all bad. I can always hope even when I already know the horrible ending. I must go now. I have a meeting with Conie. If you don't get too wrapped up in things up here, you should join us. It would be good for you to see what our meetings are like."

"Sure," Raina agreed. "Let me grab a couple things that I want to start with, and I'll be down."

Raina watched her aunt leave and turned back to the boxes. She knew if she didn't pull away now, she would spend hours up there and didn't want to miss the meeting with Conie and her aunt. She grabbed a somewhat empty box and dumped the journal she'd started reading into it. She rummaged around to see what else she wanted to add.

She found some old ledgers which had to do with the Nilsson Boatwerks along with another journal and stack of pictures. Raina plopped it all into the box as a picture slipped out of the stack and floated to the floor. She stooped down to pick it up. It was a picture like the one Henry had shown her of her great-great-grandfather and his twin brother, only this time they were standing next to an old fishing boat.

Raina grinned. *I wonder.*

Hoping to dig further into the mystery of the boat, Raina grabbed the first journal out of the box that her fingers touched. As she read, she realized it was the first one she had found earlier. Not wanting to stop, she decided the boat wreck investigation and her aunt could wait, and dove into her great-grandmother's private thoughts.

Chapter Seven

July 4, 1947

I've done it now. But oh, was it wonderful to be held and comforted and made to feel precious and beautiful. Stefan got word about an emergency in Duluth and had to leave halfway through the day. The girls were being rambunctious, and I just grew tired of it all. I told Melia I was going to head back to the house with the girls, but she offered to keep them for me so they could see the fireworks. She knew I was upset about Stefan and tried to encourage me before I left, but my spirits couldn't be lifted.

When I got back to the house, I decided to go down by the cliff near the gazebo Stefan put up for me last year. As I meandered around to the front of the house, I ran into *him* again. He startled me and I started laughing. Then I smacked him on the arm. It was such an intimate gesture and I immediately looked around.

He assured me no one was there and there was fluttering in my stomach. He asked me where I was headed, and when I told him, he grabbed my hand and walked with me. We didn't talk about it. I didn't even try to pull away, we just walked hand in hand in the growing darkness.

When we neared the water, he told me how much he loved the sound of the waves crashing against the point and I told him I loved hearing him talk about the lake. Then he kissed me. He crushed his lips against mine and I don't think I've ever been kissed so passionately. All the stolen glances. All the small conversations. All the walks along the beach and the grounds, hidden from view, have led to this moment. We wanted to take it further. I wanted to take it further, but he stopped us. Not here and not now he said. But soon. When will it be soon?

July 5, 1947

He winked at me as he passed by me on the path. I had to fight so hard not to smile and turn to watch him leave. Melia would have suspected something for sure if I had. I didn't see him the rest of the day, but I know he watches me when I don't always see him, and that sends shivers through my body. What is wrong with me?

July 6, 1947

Stefan returned today. He was in a foul mood. We fought and I cried. He apologized, but I left him standing in the hallway and rushed outside. All I wanted was to be held by *him*.

When I found *him*, he was working by the tree line that dips out of view of the house. I was never so thankful in my life. When he saw me, he rushed to my side and led me further into the trees before he wrapped his arms around me. He held me until I finished crying. He never asked me what was wrong. It was like he knew.

As my crying slowed, he pulled me into a passionate kiss. It had the same heat as it did the other day. I think it would have gone further if Stefan hadn't called for me in the distance. I kissed him one last time and ran off toward the beach so I could regain my composure.

Stefan finally found me on the beach on the far side of the point, but I buried my head in my lap and begged him to go away. He obliged, and I was left to think about stolen kisses with another man.

Chapter Eight

The rain eased as Raina looked out the window, so she decided to ride her bike into town. She wanted to check in on Conie as she had a couple of questions for him, but she also wanted to see how Henry was coming along on securing the boat. They had one week before meeting again and she was getting anxious to find out if anyone had discovered anything.

The bright yellow of her rain gear made her laugh as she pedaled down the driveway. It was something Stacia had found for her, but the raincoat enveloped Raina and the hat hung low over her face. When Raina tried it on, she was sure Stacia had a smirk on her face, but it was quickly replaced with a stern look in true Stacia fashion.

A sliver of sunlight pushed through the rain clouds, temporarily blinding Raina's already half-covered eyes and she almost lost her balance. She slammed on the brakes and flung her foot to the ground. She tried to catch her breath while she calmed her pounding heart and looked at the view. The sunlight poked through the darkness and sparkled across the waves as they crashed against the shimmering pebbles on the beach.

Raina sucked in air and her hand flew to her chest. The lake never ceased to provide wonderment for her, and she knew she would never leave this place. This was hers.

The rain picked up again, drawing Raina out of her reverie and she rode on. She parked her bike by a tree and rushed into the pub, slamming the door behind her. She shook off the dampness and took off her hat and jacket. Laughter rang through the air as she hung up her gear. It started low but grew louder as she meandered toward the bar. Conie was doubled over.

Raina cocked her head, put her hand on her hip and narrowed her eyes. "I can't believe you're laughing at me, Conrad."

Conie took gulping breaths of air and wiped at his face. "I'm sorry, Raina, but you looked ridiculous. And I needed a good laugh."

Raina tried to show anger but couldn't resist his humor and joined in. She sidled closer. "I'm glad I could brighten your day."

Conie reached across the bar and grabbed her hand. "You always brighten my day, but this was the best moment yet."

Raina knew he was trying to tease her, but the heat flashing between them told a different story.

They both jerked their hands away and Raina looked past Conie. "What do you have on tap that will warm me up a bit."

Conie appeared confused and made a noise in his throat. "I would recommend a good stout. It's the best on a day like today, I think."

"A good stout then," Raina said and sat on the nearest stool. She looked around the room and realized they had just put on a show for several tables in the pub. The patrons avoided eye contact with her, and heat rose in her cheeks.

"Why didn't you tell me I was making a spectacle of myself," Raina said while Conie put her beverage in front of her.

Conie glanced around and blinked. "I forgot they were there. Hm."

Raina stared at the dark liquid in front of her and tried to steady her hand as she lifted it to her lips. She took a couple more sips before trusting herself to speak without sounding awkward.

"Have you found anything out yet. Has the list been completed, I mean for the boat wreck?" Raina asked.

Conie leaned against the bar and said, "I've heard back from a few people but haven't received all the information I was hoping to get. I know Henry has the boat stabilized but hasn't had the chance to really look it over yet, and neither has Oliver."

Raina perked up. "Oh, we should go over there. Take a look at it."

Conie grinned. "Let me see if I can pull Stu away to watch the bar for a bit. It's a slow day, so I imagine he is ahead of the game in the kitchen. Besides those two tables are about to leave and Shelly will be coming back from her break in a few minutes."

"That sounds great. It will give me time to finish my beer."

"I suppose you'll want to ride with me in my car since you rode your bike down?"

"That was pretty silly of me."

Conie's eyes twinkled and he tried to stifle a smirk. "You have no idea. I was wiping a table by the window, and I saw this yellow streak coming down from the point. The yellow bounced around, almost falling. I hope you're okay. But it really did make my day."

Raina laughed outright. "Yes, I know I looked ridiculous. The coat is obviously way too big for me. It even got a response from Stacia."

"See, if you got a rise out of Stacia then it must have been silly."

"Okay, teasing aside. I would appreciate the drive, but the sun keeps trying to come out, so I hope when it's time for me to go home I can just ride my bike back. I love the sound of the waves while I ride."

Conie's grin widened, and Raina made a snort before he disappeared into the kitchen. She took another sip of her beer, and her heart skipped a beat as Conie's face, full of delight, danced in her mind.

I don't have time for nonsense. Perhaps it's best to keep my distance.

The kitchen door swung open and upon seeing Conie, any thoughts of keeping her distance flew out of her mind.

"Ready to go?" Conie asked, eyeing Raina strangely.

Raina gulped down the last of her beverage, contemplated grabbing her rain gear, changed her mind, and followed Conie to the rear entrance of the pub. They rode the short distance in silence and Raina was intimately aware of the man sitting next to her. If it was the same for him, he didn't let on. She watched the passing scenery and hoped he didn't feel the same awkward tension she did.

Conie stopped his truck in front of the boatwerks and Raina climbed out just as Henry opened a side door. When Henry spotted them, he made a motion to follow and went back inside. Raina trailed Conie and allowed her eyes to adjust before moving too far into the building. The boat was bigger than she remembered, and was being held up by chains and pulleys while the bottom was nestled in a cradle of wood.

Raina could see several planks of wood sticking out here and there bracing various parts. A platform with stairs leading up was nestled on the right side and she asked, "Are we allowed to go on it."

"Don't know why not," Henry said. "But be careful. I tried to get it as stable as possible to rummage around in, but this was beat up pretty bad in the water."

"How can you tell what year it's from," Raina asked.

"Oh, the shape of it. How it was made. Those sorts of things."

"There are parts of the boat missing, I see."

"Yes, there used to be an enclosed room on the stern, but the only thing left is a partial bench," Henry explained. "A wooden covering ran from the bridge to the room on the stern and it's gone. The bridge is partially gone. I think that is where they found the chest anchored to the floor. And there are large holes in the upper deck. We haven't been down in the hull yet, so not sure what we'll find there."

"Do you know what we would find if this wasn't damaged?" Raina asked.

"I suppose a galley, a bunkroom or two, and the fish hold," Henry said.

Raina trudged up the stairs to climb aboard, examining the large cracks and gaping holes on the side of the boat. "Are these from being battered in the water?" Raina asked.

"That or the waves on the night it claimed its victims," Henry said.

Conie followed Raina as she looked through holes and finally made her way to the upper deck. She checked the pressure of each step before moving about. Conie stepped gingerly wherever Raina walked. They continued to move single file until Raina found the ladder down into the hull.

Conie grasped her arm. "I think Henry was going to cut a hole in the side of the boat and brace it so we can climb through the side to check things below, so best not to go down the ladder now."

"Probably a better idea," Raina said.

They continued to walk around, hoping to find anything, but found nothing. Raina tried to hide her disappointment as she went back to steady ground.

"I suppose finding some huge clue and declaring we know all the answers is a wishful thought," Raina said.

"You never know what secrets the Lady will let us find as we dig around," Henry said.

"The lady? As in the boat or the lake?" Raina asked.

"Both," Henry and Conie said in unison.

A shiver ran up Raina's spine as a wave crashed against the rocks outside.

"You cold?" Conie asked.

"No, just felt strange crawling around the boat," Raina said.

"When do you think you'll have the hole put into the side Henry?" Conie asked.

"Hope to have it done by the time Oliver comes next. Thought we could all meet here next time to check things out, then discuss everything in detail. "

"That should work for me," Raina said. "I did discuss with Aunt Kat the idea of using the library if we need to have future meetings. She said she could have a table put in there if it's necessary."

Conie studied Raina, "Is she really okay with us doing it there? This isn't something Kat would usually be so involved in."

"Of course, she was happy to help."

"But still, it isn't like her to help with something like this. Are you sure you're not misreading the situation?" Conie asked.

Raina's eyes widened. "It feels like you're doubting me."

"No, it's just she distances herself from anything that could hurt her or her family, so it's hard for me to believe she's on board with this."

"So, you don't believe me."

"That's not really what I meant," Conie said.

"What did you mean?"

"I think Conie is just trying to watch out for Kat," Henry said.

"From the stranger who is pushing her agenda, no doubt."

"No, well, yes. It's just that she's usually very private about her life and her family and her past. And although we knew she had a sister, we were still all surprised when she announced you were coming here. To have her so open to being involved with an investigation that could affect her family goes against how she normally acts. As hands-on as she is with everything that goes on in this town, when it comes to anything that could negatively impact her family, she tends to shrink back and let others take the lead until she absolutely has to get involved."

"Oh, I see. The woman who claims to be her niece is also pushing her own agenda," Raina said, shifting her feet to get some distance from Conie.

Conie opened his mouth. Shut it.

"Look, I know I'm a stranger, but she sought me out. Not the other way around. I didn't even know she was still alive until she showed up at my Gramma D's funeral. And I don't know how things were before I got here, but I assure you, I'm doing everything with her blessing."

"We don't mean any offense," Henry said.

Raina repositioned her purse and cleared her throat. "I have some other things I need to get done today, so I think I'm going to head home. Sorry, I mean to my aunt's house."

"But it's raining," Conie said.

"I won't melt. Now if you'll excuse me, I'll see myself out." Raina spun around, ducking her head to hide her flaming cheeks, and marched out of the building. She didn't want them to see her embarrassment, and she especially didn't want them to see her cry.

Once out in the rain, she allowed the tears to slide down her cheeks. She wished she had her ridiculous yellow raincoat after all. She wrapped her arms around herself and continued on toward the pub. She wasn't looking forward to going back there, but she at least wanted to grab her bike. Memories of being misjudged and being made to feel out of place in Grand Meadow flashed through her mind and she shivered. She was about to round the corner onto

Shore Drive when splashing tires behind her forced her to pause.

The truck stopped and a window rolled down. "Raina, please get in."

Raina stepped closer. "I'm fine. Really, I am. Besides, I don't have much further until I can get my bike and ride it back ho—I mean to my aunt's."

"Don't be ridiculous. Get in the car. Please. I'm sorry for what I said and how I said it. I wish you would allow me to explain," Conie said.

Raina brushed at her wet face and shivered again. "Fine, but only because I'm getting cold."

Conie let out a laugh. "You're so much like her, you know."

Settling into the passenger seat, the window now closed, Raina glanced at Conie. "I'm sorry for my behavior."

"No need to say that. I'm the only one who should be apologizing."

"Maybe we can call it a truce."

"I would like that, but I would still like the opportunity to explain."

"I'm all ears."

"It could take a bit and after I take you home, I need to get back to the pub. Would you mind coming by the café in the morning so we can talk?"

Raina nodded. "Sure."

"Okay, let's grab your bike, and that goofy coat of yours," Conie said with a smirk.

Raina's shoulders relaxed but she looked out the window instead of responding. Conie made quick work of securing her bike in the back of his truck and retrieving her gear, and it wasn't long before they were parking under the carport at Willow Bay Manor. Conie jumped out to get her bike down just as Johnston appeared.

"You look a bit soaked, Raina, but your aunt would like to talk with you," Johnston said.

"I'm pretty wet, yes. I'm going to run upstairs and get cleaned up before I meet with Aunt Kat. Can you make sure she knows?"

"Of course."

As Raina disappeared into the house, Conie hollered a farewell, but she didn't stop. Her embarrassment over their exchange at the Nilsson Boatwerks and how she handled herself made her want to hide. Plus, the idea anyone would question her integrity stung, especially after deciding she wanted to make a go of it in Willow Bay. She couldn't stay if people in the town believed she was only there to take advantage of her aunt. The idea anyone would question her presence hadn't even crossed her mind until today.

Perhaps I should tread carefully and make sure this is really where I am wanted before I make this my permanent home.

Chapter Nine

S ipping the hot creamy liquid, Raina watched Conie over the rim of her mug. He was finishing up with the last customer before his sister Annie took over so he could talk with her. Raina mulled over their dispute and was embarrassed at how strongly she'd reacted to his questions. Conie poured coffee into his own cup and crossed the room to sit with her. Raina straightened her spine and waited for him to say something first. But when he didn't speak, Raina's discomfort grew.

"I can only guess how this must look to some people," Raina said.

"We were surprised to hear about you, yes, but I haven't doubted you, because I would never doubt Kat," Conie said.

"Then why the questions and doubts yesterday?"

"I can't help but be protective of Kat. She helped me and my sisters after our parents died and when the time came, she made sure we each had the building space for our businesses."

"That was kind of her."

"That's Kat. She takes care of her own."

"Are you related somehow?"

"No, my father owned a store for many years, as did his father before him and so on. Our ancestors were one of the first to settle here who weren't a part of the Nilsson family. Spencer and Marcy Olsen were their names."

"So, your loyalty runs deep. I can't imagine belonging to a place with such deep roots," Raina said.

"But you do belong to a place with such deep roots. You may not have been born and raised here, but you're a Nilsson. Your roots here are very deep."

"I suppose they are."

"It isn't just my loyalty from having lived here my whole life though. Our parents died in a car accident during a blizzard when I was eighteen. I had been working for my parents and graduated high school that following spring. Murie was a sophomore in college, and Annie was a sophomore in high school. Kat stepped in when they died and made sure we all went to college. She helped us so we wouldn't lose our family home. After college she said if we wanted to come home, we were all promised prime real estate for businesses. Murie wanted her clothing and home décor store, Annie wanted to sell books, and I wanted my restaurant and café. The name Trio represents all three of us and we all adopted the name for our own businesses."

"So, Annie and Murie's places are called Trio too?" Raina asked.

"Well sort of. Annie's bookstore is called Trilogy. And Murie's store is called Le Tercet Boutique."

"I love those names. I'm not sure why I never noticed them before. I guess because I still haven't made it by their stores. I know I promised Murie I would stop by a couple weeks ago, but I haven't found the time."

"You should stop by after this. All of our businesses are connected inside, or you can walk along the deck to get to them."

"I think I will."

Conie studied Raina and an awkward silence fell over the two. Raina took a long drink, hoping he would stop looking at her so intently.

"So, that's it then, she gave so much you feel indebted to her," Raina said, breaking the tension.

"It's not like I feel I owe her anything. She's like family to me, to us. Just so you know, we're not the only ones she has helped over the years. She has kept this town going even when times have been hard, because as she has said, that's the Nilsson way."

"That sounds like her. That also sounds like Gramma D too."

"Your grandmother is a legend around here. Some knew her back then, and some feel like it's been so long since she lived here, she couldn't possibly have been real. I think everyone understands why she left, though."

Raina studied her mug while she contemplated once again what it must have been like for her grandmother to walk in on her dead parents. She shifted in her chair and took another sip, trying to hold back her tears.

"Are you okay?" Conie asked.

Raina nodded, set the mug on the table, and looked out the window to the water beyond.

"You look so much like Kat," Conie said. "The first time I saw you I knew who you were without you even saying it."

"The sisters look so much alike, and I look like my Gramma D."

"Yes, you have the Nilsson look about you, that's for sure."

"Henry said the same thing to me the first time I met him."

"Raina, there is no denying you are who you are. Anyone just has to look at you to know it's true. And I'm sorry if I, or anyone else, have made you feel like you came here under false pretenses. I know she invited you. She told me she was going to go get you when she found out her sister had died."

"Really?"

"I was with Kat when she got the phone call from her lawyer. She was devastated. She looked at me and said she had to go get Raina. It was time for you to come home. At the time I had no idea who she was talking about."

"Why do you help with the running of the town?"

Conie's face registered surprise at the sudden question. "She asked me to. My father helped with a few things here and there. And she asked me to help once I got my business up and running. She likes having someone help check her work, and also do some of the grunt work for her."

"How much control do you have?"

"None. I had hoped she would do more to help build up the town, but she wasn't ready to take that on. I think she was waiting for you."

"And by grunt work, you mean reaching out to those who miss payments, etc?"

"Yes, that's part of it, but also making sure people received their bills in the first place. And if they haven't paid, she has me find out why. It's easier for them to talk to me sometimes instead of Kat because she is so generous, and we are a proud bunch here in Willow Bay. We don't like admitting we need help."

"Sounds about right," Raina said, smiling into her now empty mug.

"What do mean?"

"That was Gramma D, too."

"Why did you change the subject so abruptly a minute ago?" Conie asked.

"You noticed that."

"I did."

"It's hard for me to think about how much Gramma D and Aunt Kat must have been hurting all this time, but instead of coming together, they stayed apart. I missed out on so much, which I'm not mad about. It just makes me sad there was so much pain. I can't bear to think of that for her. On top of it, my mom missed it all."

"I'm sorry if this conversation is too hard."

"It's okay. The conversation isn't too hard. It's just hard to really think about everything that's happened and how much we all missed out on."

Conie reached across the table and grabbed Raina's hand. She stared at their fingers intertwined for a second before jerking away as though she'd been stung.

Gathering her things, Raina stood to leave. "I think I understand now. Thank you for sharing it with me. It makes sense you would be weary of a stranger coming in and poking around into things that could hurt Aunt Kat. But you can trust me."

"I do."

"I believe you do. Or at least I hope you do," Raina said.

"Look, Raina—"

"I'm going to head to your sister's store now. Thanks for chatting with me, Conie," Raina said, walking away, not giving him time to respond. She knew he was watching her, but she wasn't ready to consider any possible attraction she felt toward him.

Forcing their conversation aside, Raina dove into the enjoyment of visiting the bookstore and boutique and engaged in a fun interaction with Conie's sisters. Raina really liked them both and hoped they would all become good friends. By the time she left to go home, her sides hurt from laughter, her arms were full of purchases she had been excited to buy, and all thoughts of Conie were gone. At least that's what she told herself.

Chapter Ten

The group huddled around the boat listening to what Henry had to say about the structure. Raina had a hard time staying focused because Conie stood only inches from her, and they hadn't seen each other since their conversation. As Raina shifted from one foot to the other, Murie glanced at her oddly before smiling at her brother.

Conie mouthed something to his sister, but Raina pushed it out of her mind when Oliver wandered in with a box in tow. He moved to the center of the group, putting the box down in front of Raina.

"We found some things that might belong to you," Oliver said.

"To me?" Raina asked.

"To the Nilsson family at least," Oliver said, pulling items out of the box. "Here is a pea coat with the initials N. N. sewn into it, and a picture of a woman. It's torn up a bit, but you can make out who it is."

Raina grabbed the picture, and to her surprise, she instantly recognized who it was. She studied the woman in the photo who was the exact image of her great-great-grandmother—a younger version of the image in the large painting which hung on the wall opposite the grand staircase, which she had studied often.

"Do you know who it is, Raina?" Murie asked.

"I do. This is Amelia Nilsson," Raina said wistfully while stroking the picture and imagined the sea wind whipping through Melia's hair.

"I knew it. This has to be the *Vide Fjärd*," Henry said.

"Was that a boat of the Nilssons?" Murie asked.

"It was, it went down during the white hurricane," Henry said.

"We agree with your assessment, so my superior is stating the mystery is solved," Oliver said.

"But you want to make sure it really is the *Vide Fjärd*, right?" Conie asked.

"Because it's Kat. I want to make sure," Oliver said.

"Then we shouldn't tell her yet," Conie said.

"Is everyone in agreement?" Henry asked, glancing around as the group nodded in agreement.

"I won't take everything out of the box, as there are only a few other small things, but I'll hand it off to you, Raina.

Keep it in a safe place in your house for now, and we can talk more the next time we meet," Oliver said.

"So, we'll continue to meet, including you, Oliver?" Raina asked.

"Yes, I've been told I can still work on it during my off time."

"Perfect," Murie said with a grin.

Slapping his hands together, Henry said, "Who wants to climb aboard and see if we can find any other clues?"

Raina put the peacoat back into the box and tucked the picture of her great-great-grandmother in her pocket before following everyone else toward the boat. Conie waited at the bottom of the platform and as Raina approached, he smiled at her and asked if she was okay.

"Yes, it just seems so bizarre to discover parts of my history in such a way. Two months ago, I didn't even know who this woman was, or that this place existed, now it's starting to feel like such a part of me, and I'm engulfed in a mystery that has to do with a past I know nothing about. But strange enough, I recognized Amelia."

"See, deep roots," Conie said.

"Deep roots."

"After you," Conie said, stepping back from the platform.

Raina climbed the stairs and as she stepped into the belly of the boat, her hand skimmed Conie's. Her cheeks flamed. She jerked her hand away and stumbled.

Conie caught her from behind. "You got it?"

"Yes, just clumsy," Raina said, avoiding his gaze.

Steadier now, Raina rambled around. Her jitters changed to disappointment on finding this section of the boat empty. There were still partial walls where rooms once were. A partial bedframe stood in a corner bolted to the boards. As she inspected where the fish hold had been, she was thankful Henry did such a good job of cleaning out the remnants from being in the water.

Murie crossed to stand next to Raina and frowned. "It's disappointing finding nothing."

"It is, but it also feels surreal knowing my ancestors owned this."

"Oh, I didn't think of it like that."

Raina looked over at her friend to ask another question, but Murie's cheeks were bright red as she watched Oliver walk toward the exit of the boat.

"Is there something between the two of you?" Raina asked.

"We're moving in that direction I think."

"I hope it works out for you. He seems like a really great guy."

"He is. He's originally from here you know. We went to high school together but lost touch after my parents died. Then he showed up in my store one day. He said he was looking to buy something for his mom who lives in Lutsen now and heard about my store from her. We talked for a long time just catching up and have kept in touch ever since. He lives in Grand Marais right now, but we try to get together as often as we can. It's no coincidence he's helping us with this project."

"It sounds like things are going well."

"I think so, too."

They climbed out of the boat and down the stairs of the platform, leaving Conie and Henry behind.

Raina went to pick up the box to carry it to the car but paused when Murie asked, "So, how do you feel about my brother?"

"What do you mean?"

"I've watched the two of you interact. There's a spark or something there."

"I think you're seeing things," Raina said with a laugh.

"No, I see something. The question is, are you ready for there to be something?"

"That's the question isn't it. And I can't answer it right now."

"Fair enough," Murie said, smiling at Raina.

"I'm going to take this to my car. I'll be right back," Raina said and went outside.

It didn't take long for her to nestle the box securely on the backseat. Raina shut her car door as footsteps approached.

"I came out to see if you needed help," Conie said from behind.

Raina whirled around. "Nope. I'm good."

"I know you're trying not to let your feelings show, but this has to be exciting and yet unnerving for you."

"You read me so well," Raina said.

"I do? Sometimes I feel like I'm way off."

"No, you get it right most of the time. I'm fine right now. But there are times I think I'm going to wake up from a dream. Gramma D died, and I was sure I was going to be all alone in the world and then my great-aunt, who I believed to be dead, shows up and invites me to come here. I get here and realize my history is much bigger than I could ever have imagined."

"That's a lot."

"It's a lot."

Raina glanced in the direction of giggling across the parking lot. She caught Murie and Oliver holding hands as they ducked behind his truck. Raina grinned and focused on kicking the rocks at her feet.

"I can't decide if I'm okay with the idea of the two of them yet," Conie said.

"They're cute together."

"Perhaps, but there's the brother part of me who wants to be protective."

"I believe she knows her own mind and doesn't need her brother to protect her."

"I agree she knows her own mind."

Conie stepped closer to Raina and started to say something, but paused and took a step back when a car slowed to a stop next to them. The driver's window rolled down and Raina recognized the scowl coming from the woman in the driver's seat.

"What are you all doing, Conie?" Violet asked, her words slurring.

"Should you be driving?" Conie asked.

"That's none of your business. I just got off work and was heading home when I saw your little party here. Thought I would stop by and join the fun, but if you're gonna be rude, I'll head on home."

"We don't mean any offense. Besides, it's not a party. We're working on a project," Raina said.

Violet opened her car door and stumbled over to Raina, stopping inches from her face. Violet weaved and the smell of alcohol engulfed Raina as she took a step back.

"Get back in the car, Vi," a voice called from the backseat of the car. "I need to get home. You promised straight home."

"I know I did, Ginny. But I want to check out what was going on."

"Ginny, are any of you sober?" Conie asked.

"Why you questioning us, Conie?" Violet asked, crossing to him, and stumbling into his arms. He caught her before she could hit the ground, steadied her, and let go.

"Geez, Violet, let me call your mom to come pick you up," Conie said.

"Don't you dare. I'm not a child," Violet said, pressing against Conie and running a finger down his cheek.

Conie steadied Violet as he pushed her away from him. "Not going to happen and you know it."

"Why?" Violet asked.

"You know why," Conie said.

"That's right. She tried to hop in bed with him on their first date," Ginny said.

"That's not why, but it's part of it," Conie said.

"First date? You used to date?" Raina asked.

"Oh god no. We went out once, shortly after my parents died. It was a mistake, and it never happened again," Conie said.

"How dare you," Violet said with a screech.

"Come on, Violet, let me call your mom," Murie said, joining the scene.

"Stay out of it, Murrrieeal," Violet said and burst into laughter.

"At least let someone else drive you home," Conie said.

"You can drive me home," Violet said, inching closer to Conie.

Conie moved to stand next to Raina. "I think the conversation needs to be over. If you won't let me call your mom, I'll have to call Jenks."

"You wouldn't dare. I can't have another DUI."

"Then let me call your mother and let's be done with this," Murie said.

"Zip it, Muriel."

"That's enough rudeness now," Oliver said.

"Well, if it isn't Oliver Stephens. You back in town?" Violet asked.

"Enough now. Murie call Donna," Conie said and leaned closer to Raina like he was going to whisper something but was cut off by Violet's laughter.

"Are you hooking up with old Kat's trashy offspring?" Violet asked.

"Okay, I've heard enough," Conie said. He turned his back on Violet and steered Raina toward the boatwerks.

"How dare you turn your back on me!"

"Your mom is on her way, Violet," Murie said, walking back from the office.

"You called my mom? I can't believe you called my mom," Violet said as she stumbled back toward her car.

Raina spun around just as Murie moved to position herself between Violet and the car.

"Can't let you get back behind the wheel," Murie said.

"Conie, you might need to help your sister," Raina said.

"Oliver has her," Conie said while Oliver moved to stand next to Murie.

"Still, I think we should wait and make sure Murie is okay."

"Okay, but we'll stay back here."

Henry sauntered out of the boatwerks as another car drove into the parking lot.

"Everything okay?" Henry asked as a woman got out of the car and waved in Henry's direction.

"Violet has had a little too much to drink," Conie said.

"I see that now," Henry said. "You mind following behind me so I can take Donna's car back for her?"

"Sure can," Conie said. Turning to Raina, he asked, "Raina, you going to be here when I get back?"

"Probably not. I'm going to head home I think," Raina said.

Disappointment washed over Conie's face. "Call you tomorrow to confirm when we meet next?"

"I'll do you one better. I'll pop by the café for some coffee," Raina said with a smile.

Conie brightened and said his goodbyes. He explained to Murie what he was doing and told her he would see her at home. He lowered his voice, but tossed his head in Raina's direction, so she knew he was talking about her.

Donna must have overheard Conie's conversation with Murie for she looked around the parking lot asking, "Raina? Who is Raina?"

Recognizing the second Donna saw her, Raina took a step back as Donna's expression changed from a worried frown to surprise followed by anger. Raina considered going into the building but paused when Henry jumped to her defense.

"Donna, come on now. Raina is Delaney's granddaughter. You knew she was in town and it's not her fault what happened, no more than it was Kat's or Del's," Henry said.

"Always taking the Nilsson's side. Everyone in this town always takes their side," Donna said.

"That's water under the bridge," Henry said. "Now come on, let's get your girl home before she falls over."

"Leave Violet out of this. You know she's had a hard time of it."

"Fine, but let's get her home just the same."

Donna glared at Raina and turned to help Violet get settled into the passenger seat. She tossed another scowl at Raina before getting into the car. A shiver went up Raina's spine, but she waved at Conie who was backing out of the parking lot. Once he waved back, she left to go get the rest of her things to head home. Murie and Oliver followed Raina inside and they both apologized for what happened.

"None of this was your fault," Raina said.

"No, but we feel bad just the same," Murie said.

"It's unfortunate Donna and Violet have such hard feelings toward your family," Oliver said.

"Why do they? Aunt Kat doesn't really talk about it," Raina said.

"I'm not sure I know every part of it. Something about Donna's dad used to work for the Manor, but had to leave town due to an ailing mother. When he got back, he no longer worked there, and had a hard time holding a job after that," Muriel said.

"There has to be more to the story," Raina said.

"I suppose there is, but no one really knows," Oliver said. "The Strands have just always hated your family."

"Oliver," Murie said.

"Sorry, but it's true."

"But you didn't have to be so blunt."

"Okay, sorry if I was rude," Oliver said.

"You're fine. I think I'm going to head on home now though. It's been a strange night," Raina said.

Raina said goodbye and left. As she drove to the other side of the bay, the exchange with Violet and Donna played in her mind. She wanted to know how much her aunt knew about it or if there were more family secrets she needed to uncover.

Chapter Eleven

Aunt Kat and Raina walked arm in arm across the café and waved at Conie. Raina hoped her blush went unnoticed as they found a seat close to the counter.

"Tea, Aunt Kat?"

"Actually, I think I'll take one of those fancy drinks you like."

"Okay, I'll go order," Raina said.

"Here I have cash."

"My treat," Raina said, stepping to the counter before her aunt could argue.

Annie rounded the corner from the back carrying a tray full of pastries, hollered a hello at Aunt Kat and turned to Raina. "You sure have brightened my brother's mood."

"Hello, Annie," Raina said.

"Hya," Annie said with a wink. Turning to her brother, she said, "You going to just gawk at the pretty lady or you going to help me unload this tray?"

Conie ducked his head but not before Raina registered the look he sent his sister. Raina stifled a nervous laugh while studying the menu board which hung on the wall behind the counter.

Annie finished placing the last pastry into the display case and asked, "So what can we get you today?"

"Is the bookstore not open?" Raina asked.

"It will be in about thirty minutes," Annie said. "I open a little later Monday through Wednesday. It's supposed to be so I can get some things done at home or in the back office, but somehow Conie always ropes me into helping him around here."

"I don't rope anyone. You and Murie always offer to help. Like I could get either of you two to do anything anyway."

"Good point," Annie said with a snicker.

Raina joined her but pretended to sober when she caught Conie's look of feigned disappointment.

"Does Kat want a tea?" Annie asked.

"Actually, she asked for a fancy drink. I was thinking a London Fog for the both of us if you can make them."

"We can make them," Conie said.

"We should add it to the menu," Annie said.

"Get on it while I make the drinks," Conie said.

"Or you make the drinks, and *you* can add it to the menu later. I have things to do before I open," Annie said.

"Aunt Kat and I will pop in for a visit when we are done here," Raina said.

"Looking forward to it. I always enjoy our conversations."

"None of those conversations better be about me," Conie said.

Annie put her hand on her hip. "Why on earth would we talk about you?"

"Because I'm so delightful and charming."

"That is debatable, brother."

"Ha, not nice."

"What do you think, Raina? Is my brother delightful or charming?"

Raina's cheeks flamed. "Um, I suppose so."

Annie's teasing expression softened as she studied Raina. She looked over at her brother whose cheeks were also pink, and she smiled, looking back at Raina. "Well, well."

"I think I'll wait for my beverages over at the table," Raina said.

"Let me ring you up first," Annie said.

Raina dug in her purse and plopped some cash on the counter. "This should cover it."

"Do you want some chan—"

"Keep the change," Raina said, rushing back to sit next to Aunt Kat.

As Raina settled in her chair, she glanced over at Conie who was focused on making two London Fogs. She studied him until her aunt shifted in her chair.

"Sorry, Aunt Kat. I was lost in thought. Did you say something?" Raina asked.

"I didn't, but I do have some questions for you."

Raina noticed the twinkle in her aunt's eye, and she wanted to bury her face.

"Come now, dear, they will be quick and easy questions."

"Okay."

"Is there something between you and Conrad?"

"No."

"Do you wish there was?"

"Aunt Kat!"

"Do you want there to be?"

"I don't know."

The twinkle in Kat's eyes faded. "Do you have feelings for him?"

"Can we talk about this somewhere else?"

"Best not to lead him on, dear."

"I'm not leading him on. We're just friends. I doubt he's attracted to me. And I'm not sure I'm ready for anything anyway."

"Two London Fogs," Conie said, placing steaming mugs in front of Raina.

The heat traveled up Raina's neck and set fire to her cheeks. She refused to make eye contact with Conie as she mumbled her thanks. She glanced at her aunt while picking up her mug and creamy liquid sloshed over the side from the trembling in her hand. She plopped the mug back onto the table and more foam slid over the rim. Raina attempted to clean it up with her napkin, which ended up a soggy mess. She spun around to rush to the counter and slammed into Conie.

He reached out to steady her, while she sucked in her breath. Her eyes met green ones, sparkling with amusement, and it took her a few seconds to realize he still held her.

"I. Um. I," Raina said, moving away from Conie. "Napkins."

Raina rushed to the counter and reached for the napkin holder. Conie's hand rested over hers.

"No need. I'll grab the sanitizer from the back. You go and enjoy your drink before it gets cold."

Raina slid her hand away from Conie's and avoided making eye contact again. The jumble of feelings made her stomach turn over, so she went to the restroom instead of going back to her seat. She had to get a hold of herself, and couldn't do it under her aunt's scrutiny. It took several minutes of pacing back and forth across the floor to steady her shaking hands. She took calming breaths until the pounding in her chest slowed.

What must he think of me? What must any of these people think of me? Clumsy. Silly. Foolish. What is happening to me?

Raina took one more lap around the bathroom and stopped. She peered in the mirror to make sure the red in her face had faded and went back out to join her aunt. She scanned the room, and not seeing Conie, she sighed in relief.

Settling into her chair, Raina took a sip of her tea latte and closed her eyes, willing her aunt not to say anything.

"Are you okay, dear? That was quite something to watch," Aunt Kat said with a chuckle.

"I'm so embarrassed," Raina said.

"Don't be. I doubt he heard everything you said."

"Just most of it. Then I slammed into him. Not just bumped into him. I literally almost knocked us both over. What the hell is wrong with me?"

"I have my own theory, but you probably don't want to hear it."

"You would be right," Raina said, checking again for Conie.

"He cleaned up the spill and went in the back," Aunt Kat said.

"Should we finish our drinks and just leave?"

"Nonsense, we are going to sit here with our heads held high and enjoy these delicious beverages and when Conie returns, we will have a pleasant conversation with him."

"And pretend nothing happened?"

"And pretend nothing happened," Aunt Kat said.

Conie appeared from the back, stopped to pour himself a cup of coffee, and went to sit next to Raina. He peeked at her as he settled into his chair, but turned his attention to Kat.

"Did you hear about last night?" Conie asked.

"Raina mentioned a couple of things, but Stacia filled me in on most of it," Aunt Kat said.

"Is this something we need to address with them? After all, you own the building Donna's hair salon is in. She can't treat people that way," Conie said.

"No. We won't do a thing. I can't help how they feel about me. Gramma Melia always refused to stoop to their level, and neither will I," Aunt Kat said.

"Has it always been like this?" Raina asked.

"Yes, however, Violet seems to be really stirring the pot these days," Conie said.

"Did we do something?" Raina asked.

"Donny Strand used to work for us," her aunt said, "but he had to take a leave to care for his mother. Gramma Melia told me when he returned home, she tried to contact him to give him his job back, but he refused to talk to her. He wouldn't return her calls or letters, so she stopped reaching out and gave the job to someone else. Donny went around town telling people he lost his job because he had to miss work to take care of his sick mother."

"He outright lied?" Raina asked.

"He absolutely did, and to make it worse this was only a few months after my parents' death. Gramma Melia was devastated at the treatment and how his lies compounded the family scandal."

"How awful," Raina said.

"It's terrible," Conie said.

"No one seems to believe it now though," Raina said.

"Time can heal. Some people forgot. Some people saw how the Strand family represented themselves in the community and made up their own minds on the matter. But some people were not sure what to believe and chose not to think about it or discuss it. And we all got on with life."

"It feels like the elephant in the room, so to speak," Conie said.

"Perhaps," Aunt Kat said, "but there is nothing I can do about it."

"Maybe I'll find something in the journals," Raina said.

"I doubt it, but you are welcome to look through all of them."

"Are you sure?" Raina asked.

"It's your legacy as much as it's mine. Read away."

Raina stood and hugged her aunt.

Aunt Kat patted her arm. "Thank you. It feels so good to have a family member give me a hug. I just might shed a few tears."

"We have a lull in business so cry away," Conie said.

Aunt Kat laughed. "I'm feeling less weepy now. But thank you."

The conversation veered to business as Conie had a few questions about some missed payments by one of Aunt Kat's tenants. Raina added a little to the conversation but mostly just watched the two. She loved this woman. She missed her mom and grandmother terribly, but she was so thankful her Aunt Kat had come and urged her home.

Home. This place is more of a home than Grand Meadow ever was.

"Raina, you appear to be lost in thought. Is everything okay?" Aunt Kat asked.

"Yes, sorry I was just thinking. Um, Aunt Kat, I have a couple of ideas and since you're both here, I believe now would be a good opportunity to go over them."

"A couple of ideas on marketing and building the town back up?" Conie asked.

"Yes, based on my last conversation on business with Aunt Kat, I did some digging. The community garden has gone by the wayside, but I think we should build it back up. It may be too late to plant some things now, but we could figure out what we could plant and get it going. Add some trees and flowers to it and a walking path."

"You want to bring Tuva's Garden back to life?" Aunt Kat asked.

"I do," Raina said. "Anyone who works it can have however much produce they want. We sell the rest in a farmers market every weekend in the parking lot right outside the garden. We could have additional booths available for anyone who would like to rent one. And if we have a lot of people who want booths, we can have them spill into the park grounds right next to the garden. The proceeds from the booth rentals and community garden produce sales can go to the Willow Bay Festival—that I want to bring back to life—and the White Hurricane Festival. We could market the festivals and try to get more tourists to come. I have other ideas, but it's a starting point. Oh, and we should also do a Fourth of July celebration."

"These are great ideas," Conie said.

"Thank you. We should get several planning committees together on each of the events too so it's not all the same people volunteering their time. Less chance of people getting burned out."

"It makes me happy you have given this so much thought and are actively trying to help," Aunt Kat said.

"It's my legacy too," Raina said, glancing at Conie. "My deep roots."

Conie grinned at her and sat back in his chair. The clang over the door announced a new customer so he excused himself, and his smile widened as he sauntered to the counter.

"Aunt Kat, who is Tuva again?"

"Ah, well. Tuva Nilsson was a great woman. She helped her husband build the town. She was the matriarch of our town, if you will."

"I see."

"You know the drawing of the family that hangs in the foyer next to the carport?"

"Yes, I've studied it several times."

"That is Tuva and her sister and parents. The story goes she brought it with her from Sweden. It survived a fire, the battering of the lake, and more. It held a special place in Gramma Melia's heart too."

Raina drained her mug and stared at her hands.

"Penny for your thoughts?" Aunt Kat asked.

"I went from the tiniest family and knowing absolutely nothing about my lineage to having a town and heritage deeply rooted in history. It boggles the mind."

"I suppose it does. Shall we go next door to find some books, then head over to visit with Murie?"

"Your plan sounds fun. Let's do it."

Raina followed her aunt to the bookstore entrance but paused to say bye to Conie. He was busy making a drink and didn't seem to notice her staring at him until he smiled, and she realized he had been watching her the whole time. She waved and went in search of her next read.

Chapter Twelve

The wind whipped Raina's hair around her face as she stared out at the open water. Henry had finally agreed to take her out on one of his boats so she could see what it was like to be on the lake. She had rarely been on a speed boat or pontoon in the lakes near Grand Meadow, so she wasn't sure what to expect when on the great lake.

Conie moved to stand next to her. "Well, what do you think?"

"It's the most magical thing I've ever done," Raina said turning her beaming face toward Conie.

Sucking in his breath, Conie gazed into Raina's eyes before turning back to focus on the water. Heat radiated in the pit of her stomach and spread to the rest of her body. She shifted her feet and tried to focus on the beauty of the day instead of the sparks flying between them.

"Raina, come look here," Henry said.

Moving to stand next to him, Raina looked in the direction he was pointing at a large fishing boat sailing out of the bay.

"That is a beautiful fishing boat," Raina said.

"It's yours."

"Mine? You mean it's my aunt's."

"It's a Nilsson fishing boat."

"Is it the only one Aunt Kat has?"

"Goodness no. The Nilsson Fishing and Boating branch of the business has a whole fleet of boats. The day-to-day business is run by a president over the whole outfit, but your aunt owns the whole thing."

"I had no idea," Raina said.

"If you plan to stay, you should dig into all the fingers of the Nilsson Family Enterprises," Conie said, joining the conversation.

"I've been to several meetings with you and my aunt, but I've been focusing on the Fourth of July celebration and putting together planning committees for the two festivals later this year."

"No one is saying you're not doing your part, but if you're going to stay and take over the day-to-day operations, you should get to know all parts of the business," Henry said.

"I suppose you're right," Raina said.

Raina grew quiet and moved closer to the rail to think on Conie and Henry's words. She kept telling herself she was staying, but she had been acting like being here was temporary. She hadn't taken on any ownership even in the planning of her events. She had relied heavily on her aunt's authority and input to help her make some of the bigger decisions, even though she knew what to do.

"You chew any harder on that lip you just might bleed," Conie said.

"I'm just thinking about what you said is all," Raina said.

"I hope it didn't put a damper on our day."

"No, it's still a beautiful afternoon and I'm enjoying being on the water so much," Raina said, smiling at Conie before turning back toward the water.

"You should have Henry show you Kat's father's boat. It's quite something. It needs some restoration, but it could be back on the water in no time."

Raina focused on the gentle bounce of the water below them. "I just had a thought. I wonder if we could get it ready to sail by the fireworks show for the Fourth of July celebration."

"I would have to look at the boat first before deciding because it's been a while since I've seen it, but although it might be cutting it close, with the right crew, it might be possible."

"It would be great to give her such a beautiful gift. She has done so much for me."

"I love that. Let's see what we can do to make it happen. Even if I have to join the work too."

"You know about boats?" Raina asked looking back at Conie.

Conie's eyes twinkled. "Something like that."

"Well let's do it. And I'll help however I can."

"What are we doing?" Henry asked.

"Restoring the *Mäktig Våg*," Conie said.

"Ha. You think I have time for that?" Henry asked.

"If we hired you an extra crew, I bet we could," Conie said.

"Let's look when we get back to port," Henry said. "For now, though, how's about we have some lunch. I've been looking forward to Milly's sandwiches and homemade chips all day."

Raina giggled. "I'm glad I could oblige in bringing the food."

"I could have brought food from the pub," Conie said.

"Your pub has excellent food, but it isn't Milly's sandwiches and homemade chips," Henry said.

"I guess I've never had them," Conie said.

"Of all the time you've spent at the manor, I'm surprised," Henry said.

"We've always had other food, or it wasn't around a meal."

Raina selected a sandwich from the insulated picnic basket. She handed it over to Conie with a bag of chips and he eyed it carefully like he was memorizing the ingredients. He sniffed the sandwich and took a bite.

His shoulders drooped and he sat down in the nearest chair. "This has got to be the best sandwich I've ever tasted. I have to ask Milly how she makes this."

Henry and Raina laughed while Raina passed out the rest of the food and drinks. She studied Conie out of the corner of her eye. She found she enjoyed watching him work no matter what he was doing. The meticulous way in which he made fancy coffee drinks, or crafted a delicious meal or drinks at the pub, or now studying ingredients on a simple sandwich to up his menu. He was dedicated to his work, to his sisters, to Aunt Kat, and to Willow Bay. And Raina knew she was falling hard for him.

As the meal ended, dark clouds rolled into the bay and a cool breeze slid across the deck of the boat. Raina packed up the picnic basket and grabbed her jacket.

"Are you cold?" Conie asked.

"The wind has turned chilly is all."

"It does that here."

"I'm figuring that out."

"Looks like rain is going to be over top of us in a moment. We're heading back in," Henry said.

"It was such a glorious day, Henry. Thank you for taking me out on your boat," Raina said.

"It was my pleasure."

The boat flew across the water and slid easily into its space at the dock. Disappointment flooded through Raina. She didn't want to disembark and couldn't wait to be back out on the water again. She asked Henry to show her the Nilsson boats and he obliged while Conie went to the office to call and check on things at the pub and café.

When the fleet inspection was over, Conie joined them, and Raina meandered with him to the parking lot. The rain had passed on and the sun was out again. Raina tucked her things into the backseat of her car and turned to Conie as Violet drove by. She rolled down the window, made eye contact with Raina and scowled. She rolled her window back up and sped away.

"What is her deal? I mean, I know bits and pieces of the story, but why does she hate me specifically?"

"It's not you. It's me. She wanted to date me all through high school and she really went after me when my parents died. In a moment of loneliness, I went out with her. It was the worst date I ever experienced."

"You been on a lot of dates?"

"You curious about my dating life?"

"Maybe," Raina said as heat crept between them for the second time that day. Shifting her body, Raina asked, "So you only went out with her the one time?"

"Only the one time. I took her to dinner where she complained about all the people in her life. She said some awful things about Kat and criticized the town. We went to see a movie and she kept trying to hold my hand and, um, things. I told her I wasn't interested, but she didn't get the hint and I eventually moved a seat away from her to give us some distance. When that didn't work, I went out into the lobby. I thought about leaving her there. But being the nice guy I am, I stuck around until she came out and I took her home."

"It sounds like she has some struggles in her own life and needs some help."

"That is a very generous way of looking at the situation."

"People are generally good. We all have struggles or go through hard times, and if we are not taught how to navigate it, or find a way to heal from the hurt, we tend to take it out on everyone else around us. This can lead to hate, resentment, and bitterness, and hurting others can become a way of life."

"I've never looked at it that way before."

"Hurt people, hurt people. It's what my mother used to say," Raina said, swallowing the lump in her throat at the mention of her mother. Surprised by the sudden emotion, she took a step back and shifted to look toward the lake, hoping Conie couldn't see her face.

"You don't have to hide your tears from me, Raina. It's only natural for you to have feelings of sadness. I cry too sometimes at the memory of my parents. That never changes no matter how much time goes by."

"It's nice talking to someone who understands."

Raina peeked at her watch, and realizing how late it was, said she had to get going. As she climbed into her car, Conie stopped her.

"Raina, you have a friend in me. I hope you know that," Conie said.

"I do," Raina said and slid into the driver's seat. She started the car but before driving away she rolled down the window. "Thanks for making this such a fun day."

"Anytime."

Raina drove to the manor, rolling the day's conversations around in her head. By the time she parked under the carport, she had made up her mind on her next move. She got out of the driver's seat, bobbed a greeting to Johnston, and went in search of Aunt Kat, who was hunched over some paperwork reading intently.

"We need to set up a meeting, Aunt Kat," Raina said.

"Oh, what for?"

"I know we have discussed some parts and I've been given a flyover view on things, but it's time I learned absolutely everything there is to know about the family business."

Chapter Thirteen

T ugging her dress over her head, Raina stuffed her arms in the sleeves and smoothed the blue linen down around her frame. She grabbed her sandals and, taking one quick glance in the mirror, went in search of Aunt Kat to see if she was ready to go.

The festivities of the Fourth of July celebration had been a huge success in bringing tourists in and promoting the town, but they had one more hurdle to jump—the fireworks display. It had taken a lot of work to get to this day from her first conversation about it in the café, and Raina was proud of what she'd done in a short time. Moving forward with her plans for the two festivals coming up in August and November, stemmed from how well this event went.

Crowds lined Shore Drive for a parade, then meandered through food tents, picking their favorite treats and devouring local foods at the picnic tables while several local bands played. The farmers market provided special offerings for the day. The downtown businesses offered discounts and the café and pub had specials. It was too soon to call it a total triumph, but based on preliminary reports, the day had been everything Raina had hoped it would be.

Finding Aunt Kat standing at the glass doors in the living room, Raina cleared her throat hoping not to scare her. Despite her best efforts, her aunt flinched when Raina asked if she was ready to go.

"I'm so sorry, Aunt Kat. I didn't mean to scare you."

"It's okay. I was just deep in thought."

Raina went to stand next to her and looked at the view. The rocky point, the water glistening from the sun as it began to lower in the sky, and the lush green of the trees around it was her favorite view.

"I often wonder what my father would say about how the town has turned out. I did the best I could over the years, but I often feel like I've failed," Aunt Kat said.

"Do you think perhaps instead of looking at it as failing him, he might actually be proud of what you've done, especially after all you were faced with?"

"You think he would be proud?"

"I wanted to wait to share anything until I've read more, but in your mother's journals she writes about how she believed he sometimes struggled with the business."

"I had no idea Gramma Melia did so much. When she handed me the reins, things were going well again."

"We all face difficulties just as you have, but you've never given up."

Aunt Kat put her arm around Raina. "You're a treasure to me."

Raina hugged her aunt when Johnston appeared at the doorway announcing the car was ready. Aunt Kat and Raina linked arms, went outside, and climbed into their seats. Once they were settled, Johnston announced he'd heard from Conie and everything was ready.

"Ready for what?" Aunt Kat asked.

"It's a surprise," Raina said.

"This day has already been wonderful, what other fun things do you have up your sleeve?"

"You'll just have to wait and see."

Johnston pulled out of the carport and drove into town, but instead of stopping at the pub as was the original plan, he continued on toward the other side of the bay. Raina's heart pounded, her stomach flip-flopped, and a grin spread across her face. She studied Aunt Kat, who looked about in confusion.

"Raina, where are we going?"

Giggling, Raina said, "Okay, wait for it. Now, take a look out your window."

Aunt Kat gasped and Raina leaned closer to get a better look. She had missed most of the restoration, so seeing it finished was as much of a surprise for her as it was for her aunt.

"My father's boat."

"Yes, we had the *Mäktig Våg* restored. It wasn't in as much disrepair as we originally thought and Henry had all the supplies. We hired an extra team to help finish it in time, but yep, it's your father's boat. We'll be going out on her to watch the fireworks."

"I don't know what to say," Aunt Kat said.

"Well, ever since Henry took me out for a small ride around the bay, I've been dying to get back out there, so this is as much for me as it is for you," Raina said with a grin.

"You sound like Gramma Melia. She loved the water."

"Really?"

"Oh yes. Henry has *Song of the Lake* in storage somewhere. She was Gramma Melia's, and she was out on her every chance she got."

Raina shook her head and sat back in her seat. Although Gramma D's shop had done well enough, they had times of struggle. And with the added stigma of being a child out of wedlock, she felt poor and out of place most of her life. But now she was here and a part of a family who owned a town, a fleet of boats, and lacked nothing. The idea of it all was still overwhelming even though she had immersed herself in helping Aunt Kat with the family business and settled into being a part of the community.

"Are you mad at her?" Aunt Kat asked.

"Mad at who?"

"My sister, your grandmother."

"I have moments where I'm angry at her because I feel like my mom and I missed out on so much. But then I remember the circumstances in which she left and my heart breaks for her."

"I feel the same."

"We're here," Johnston said, stopping in front of the ramp to the dock.

Conie opened Aunt Kat's door and helped her out while Johnston opened Raina's.

"I don't think I'll ever get used to this, but thank you, Johnston," Raina said.

"Here to serve."

"Raina, you look so lovely," Annie said, coming to hug her.

"You look so festive," Raina said, eyeing her friend's outfit of red, white, and blue, with a glowing star necklace draped around her neck.

"You should see Murie. She looks as adorable as I do," Annie said.

Laughing, Raina went around to the other side of the car and linked arms with Murie who matched her sister, just as Annie said. Henry motioned to Conie to come along, so he led Aunt Kat across the dock with everyone else trailing behind.

Once on board, Raina took in the small party of people joining them on the maiden voyage of the restored vessel. All the staff who worked at the manor had been invited, but only a few had confirmed coming along. Still, Raina wanted to make sure they were all there.

Conie sidled up beside her. "You look beautiful tonight."

Raina sucked in her breath and shifted toward him. "Thank you. I. Um. Well. Thank you."

"You're cute when you get flustered."

"You always seem to knock me off kilter."

"We should investigate that sometime," Conie said.

"Maybe."

"I'll take the maybe." Conie squeezed Raina's hand and sauntered away.

Annie rushed over to her. "What was that about?"

"Your brother. I don't know."

"He cares about you, you know."

"Does he?" Raina asked. "I knew he liked me, but saying he cares for me makes this different somehow. We've been spending so much time together with planning and business meetings and restoring this boat and I sometimes feel like he is interested, but then I second guess it."

"*Are* you interested?" Annie asked.

"I suppose I am. It's just. Well. I'm still trying to get my bearings and get settled into the idea that I'm a Nilsson of Willow Bay."

"Have you talked to him about it?"

"No."

"You should. I think he is waiting for you. He doesn't want to scare you off, so he's moving at an unbelievably slow-for-him snail's pace. He is waiting for you to give him a sign that you want the same things as he does. This isn't like him, so you're special I think."

"What are we talking about?" Murie asked.

"The fact that our brother is falling for our friend," Annie said.

"Oh duh. I saw that coming a mile away."

"See, you should talk to him," Annie said.

Raina looked across the deck at the man helping her aunt get settled and her heart skipped a beat. She had never been in a real relationship with anyone and the idea scared but excited her. She'd gone on a few dates in college and dated a guy on and off when she lived in Minneapolis but nothing serious. She excused herself from her friends and went to see if Aunt Kat needed anything. As she approached, her aunt was asking Conie when he was going to talk to Raina.

"Talk to me about what?" Raina asked.

"Nothing. It's nothing," Conie said. "Can I get you a beverage of some kind."

Raina started to respond but was interrupted by Violet screeching from the boat next to them.

"You can't be serious taking that old thing out on the water. Why, you'll all drown," Violet said, roaring with laughter.

"You just can't show kindness can you," Raina said.

"I don't have to be nice to you just because you're rich," Violet said.

"Stop it, Vi," Ginny said, yanking on her friend's arm. "You're going to get us kicked off.

"Nah, they think we're too cute," Violet said.

"Don't be so sure," Ginny said.

"I see you were invited to join the group who rented my boat," Conie said.

"Your boat?" Raina asked.

"Yep, the *O'Duchess*. Dad named it for my mom, who he used to call his duchess. We rent it out to people who want to boat the bay," Conie said.

"There's still so much I need to know about you."

"Is that an invitation?" Conie asked, stepping closer to Raina.

"We were invited, but Vi is being Vi, and I fear we'll get kicked off before we even leave the dock," Ginny said, interrupting Raina's response.

"Perhaps you should take her back to the party guests, and leave us alone," Conie said.

As the boat nudged away from the dock, they turned their backs on Violet and Ginny and ignored Violet's shouts. They went to make sure Aunt Kat was okay and settled before Conie went off to get their drinks.

"This is such a nice boat, and much bigger than I remembered from when I looked at it in storage," Raina said.

"How did you come by all of this, anyway?" Aunt Kat asked.

"Henry. The day we went out on his boat, he showed me all your boats in the fleet. And then we looked at this one. He said it was your father's favorite, but also your favorite. It just needed some repairs. We decided to have it restored in the hopes we could take it out for the fireworks tonight. And we made it happen."

"You're such a gem, Raina. This is truly a wonderful gift and surprise."

Hugging her aunt, Raina changed the subject to the gentleness of the water. They visited for a while and Raina settled into the euphoria of the evening as she looked around at the guests again. The evening was running as smooth as she'd hoped for her aunt's sake. The sun sank behind the trees, giving way to stars, and as much as Raina was enjoying it all, she wished they would start the fireworks soon. She was about to comment on it when the first light shot up and bloomed into bright sparkles in the sky.

Celia moved to join them and helped Raina ensure her aunt was warm enough as the next one flew up into a different design. Sounds of enjoyment echoed across the boat deck as everyone else settled in to enjoy the show. Conie sat next to Raina as the sky glittered with hues of blue and white. He asked her if she needed anything. She whispered everything was just perfect, and the shimmery display drew her into a trance.

Grabbing Raina's hand, Conie held it gently and she leaned closer to him. She decided to ignore the butterflies of fear dancing in her belly and enjoy the beauty of the moment.

The fireworks were half over when a bright light flickered in the corner of Raina's eye, and she pulled her gaze from the sky.

"Fire!"

Conie looked in the direction Raina was pointing, and she recognized the second he knew his boat was up in flames. People were jumping into the water, others were running to the other side of the vessel, and most were screaming. Raina rushed to the cockpit to give instructions to the captain to help, but as she reached the helm, he was already turning the boat.

"Miss Raina," the captain said, "perhaps help gather supplies for when people get on board. Some may be injured. I'm having my crew make ready to help pull people out of the water."

"Good thinking," Raina said and gathered the first aid supplies, blankets, and bottles of water.

She rushed to the side of the boat that was easing alongside the people in the water and waited. Raina looked around to make sure her aunt was okay. She mouthed a thank you to Annie—sitting next to Aunt Kat—who nodded. Raina scanned the area for Conie just as he and Oliver jumped into the water with a couple of the other crewmen.

It didn't take long for people to be rescued and Raina rushed to assist along with Murie and Stacia. Raina became caught up in helping, and she lost track of time. She turned to assist another victim when Conie trudged up asking if she had a towel. She snagged one from her bag lying close by and handed it to him.

"Did we get everyone?" Raina asked.

"Yes, I think so," Conie said. "It was a small party of only about ten to fifteen people based on the reservation, and a quick count of the captain confirmed we have everyone."

Murie rushed over to Conie. "It's sinking."

Raina stepped closer to him as they watched his boat pitch into the dark water. Flames sizzled out with every inch the boat slipped into the bay.

"Oh, Conie, I'm so sorry," Raina said, studying his face. She wanted to wrap her arms around him but stood with her arms at her side instead.

"It's only a boat. I'm just glad we got everyone off of it and no one was seriously hurt," Conie said.

"What happened?" Raina asked.

"That's a question I'll be asking the captain. But first I'm going to watch her sink."

Raina rested her hand in Conie's and squeezed it. Surprise registered on his face as he swayed toward her. He wrapped his arms around her, and she held onto him until the last of the *O'Duchess* slid into its watery grave.

Sirens rang out from the marina as the captain of the *O'Duchess* rushed over to Conie.

"What happened?" Conie asked.

"I'm still piecing it together, but from what I understand, Violet brought firecrackers and sparklers on board. People were drinking, alcohol was spilled, and a fire broke out."

"Were the actual renters out of control?" Conie asked.

"Nope, just the people they invited."

"You mean Violet and Ginny and her friends," Raina said.

"Yes."

"I want a full investigation done," Conie said. "We need to call Jenks."

"Already done. He is meeting us at the marina. He and a couple of his deputies have taken over a space in the boatwerks offices and will be conducting interviews before anyone leaves tonight."

"Okay. Thank you for your help."

"Will my aunt need to give a statement?" Raina asked.

"I'll talk to Jenks and see if you and her can stay out of it," Conie said. "Or see if you can give your statement tomorrow so you can get Kat home."

Raina peered at her aunt who had a gaunt look on her face. She knew this was bringing up memories of other traumatic times. She moved to sit with her the rest of the way to the marina and as they disembarked, Conie rushed to help get Aunt Kat to the waiting car.

Conie confirmed Raina could leave with Kat, explaining Jenks would be by in the morning to get her statement, and he would stop by too to give her his own update. Raina went to climb into the back seat, but Conie caught her arm and gently pulled her to him. He kissed her forehead and took a step back. She moved closer to kiss him on the lips, but hesitated and slid into her seat instead.

"Chicken," he teased and shut the car door.

Chapter Fourteen

The doorbell rang and Raina flinched. She was standing in the living room staring at the lake waiting for Conie to stop by. He had called her that morning, giving her an update on what time he would get there, but he was a few minutes late. She was still at the window when Celia led Conie into the room followed by an older man who commanded respect but with kind eyes and a belly that looked like he enjoyed delicious meals.

"Raina, this is Sheriff Jenks," Conie said after saying hello.

"Call me Jenks."

"Nice to meet you," Raina said, offering her out-stretched hand.

"It's nice to finally put a face with the name, but I guess I should have known it would be the same as Kats," Jenks said.

Raina giggled and asked if she could get anything for either of them. After she directed Celia to get water for the guests, she motioned for them to sit by the fireplace. She sat in her own chair and waited for the questions to come.

"So, you saw the fire first from your boat, correct?" Jenks asked.

"Yes, that's right." Raina remembered the moment she noticed it, but all she could think about from the night before was the feel of Conie's hand in hers, and her cheeks warmed. She glanced at Conie, who hid the grin spreading across his face, and she knew he was remembering the same thing.

"Was the fire already out of control?" Jenks asked.

"Yes, I saw flames shooting up from the deck and spreading rapidly. Some people were jumping into the water. And some were trying to run to the far side of the boat to get away from it."

"So, you didn't see anything of what happened that lead to the fire, correct?"

"I didn't."

"Did anyone say anything to you while you were helping them get settled once they were aboard the *Mäktig Våg?*"

"No, I think they were mostly in shock and just thankful they were alive and safe on board my aunt's boat."

"Okay, that about does it. Do you have any questions for me?" Jenks asked.

"I don't have any questions. Well, I have lots of questions, but I have a statement from my aunt to give to you. I hope it's okay we do her interview like this?" Raina asked.

"Of course. Is she okay?"

"Yes, just resting. It was a traumatic night for her and a late one. She's really tired so I told her to rest today, and I would manage things for her."

Raina handed the statement to Jenks who quickly glanced over it. He jotted a few more things in his notebook and snapped it shut. Celia appeared with water and handed the glasses to the men and left.

"You can ask what happened," Conie said.

"Okay. What happened?"

"Violet and Ginny were charged last night for reckless endangerment," Conie said.

"I'm going to take my leave now since I have all I need," Jenks said, cutting into Conie's explanation.

Raina and Conie followed Jenks to the door and said their goodbyes. Instead of going back to the living room, Raina asked Conie if he would like to walk to the gazebo and talk there. Agreeing, they went out the front door and strolled along the sidewalk in silence. Birds flew overhead chirping, and small waves rushed the boulders at the end of the point. Raina smiled at the symphony of noise and glanced at Conie.

"You don't look like you're okay," Raina said, her smile fading.

Running his fingers through his hair, Conie paused at the doorway of the gazebo, motioning for Raina to go first. As she moved past him, he caught her hand, squeezed it gently, and let go. When they were settled across from each other, Raina urged Conie to share whenever he was ready.

"Apparently the group who rented the boat had run into Ginny and Violet in town earlier in the day at the parade. They had hit it off and hung out for part of the day. When they parted ways one of them invited Ginny and Violet to join the group on my boat for the fireworks. Violet brought several types of firecrackers and sparklers on board."

"Let me guess, she had too much to drink and played with the firecrackers."

"That's about the gist of it. I guess Ginny was lighting sparklers and handing them to everybody when Violet got out the firecrackers and lit some. After the first round of them had finished, the captain came out and said to stop as it was a fire hazard. They put out the sparklers and went back to drinking, listening to music, and talking. Ginny said Violet was trying to get the attention of one of the guys in the group, but he was ignoring her at this point, so she grabbed several firecrackers and lit them.

Ginny laughed and lit a couple of sparklers to hand out to people again. Violet stumbled and dropped her drink and knocked over her bag. More firecrackers fell out, ignited and all hell broke loose. We didn't hear it over the noise of the fireworks show. But everything went up in flames and then you saw the fire."

"What a disaster of a night. I'm sorry, Conie."

"I have insurance, and the people who rented the boat have a hefty fine they have to pay based on the contract they signed. I could sue Violet, but I know it would only cause Donna's business to go under and I'd hate to do that."

"What a kind way of approaching it, Conie," Raina said, moving to the door of the gazebo.

"Are you okay?" Conie asked.

"That should be my question for you," Raina said.

Conie moved slowly toward Raina, stopping inches from her face. Her heart pounded, and she couldn't stop her racing thoughts.

"You have no idea how badly I want to kiss you right now," Conie said.

"I can imagine."

Conie shortened the distance between them, kissed her on the lips while she wound her arms around his neck.

A moan escaped from him before he jerked back. "Raina, I..."

When he didn't continue, Raina asked, "Did I do something wrong?"

"Oh god, no. We should just talk about this. Us."

"Is there an us?" Raina asked.

"I would like there to be an us," Conie said. "I also know you're not ready for an us."

"How do you know that?" Raina asked.

"Because I see you floundering your way around while you try to find your footing and your place here in Willow Bay and the Nilsson Family Enterprises. I know you're trying to decide if you even want to stay here for good."

"How do you know all this?"

"Because I see you. I see you struggling. I can't imagine what it was like for you to find out you had this whole family lineage your grandmother never told you about. You lost everyone dear to you. You're still grieving. A great-aunt shows up and tells you that you're not alone, but you still feel alone. I can tell. Kat shared with me her proposal in having you come here, and although you've mentioned here and there that you would like to stay, and you've helped with things, you haven't made any permanent moves to solidify you're staying."

"I'm not searching for another place to go."

"That's good to know."

"But you don't want to start something with me until I make up my mind," she said.

"I think it's too late for that," he said.

"What if I told you I've decided to stay?"

"I think you have to a point, but there is still a part of you that has one foot out the door just in case, which I have no doubt is how you lived in Grand Meadow. You're not used to a community of people loving you and supporting you. You had your grandmother and mother, yes, but your father abandoned you. Your mother died and then your grandmother died. You feel alone in the world despite having a family and community who love you."

"You're so perceptive. I don't even know if I've been able to define all this for myself yet."

"It's as I said before. I see you, Raina."

"So, what do we do now?"

"Let's just spend time together. Go slow. I'm not going anywhere while you work through all of this."

Raina leaned across the space between them and kissed Conie. She deepened the kiss but broke free before taking it too far. Conie hugged her and she settled into his embrace. As she started to pull away, she stopped inches from his ear. "I'm not going anywhere either." And ran toward the house.

Chapter Fifteen

The rain settled into the bay and brought a chill in the air. It had been several weeks since the Fourth of July incident. Ginny and Violet were out on bail with Ginny's family helping to cover fees for both. The boat wreck investigation had stalled since no new clues had been discovered. Raina hated that they hadn't told Aunt Kat the truth about the *Vide Fjard* yet. The festival plans were well on their way, despite the mishap during the fireworks show, and she didn't have anything pressing at the moment. Conie was searching for a replacement boat, so he had gone to Duluth for a couple of days and Annie and Murie were busy covering the café and pub.

Raina tugged on a sweater as she climbed the stairs to the attic. Now was as good as a time as any to really dig into uncovering the secrets she believed lay buried in the boxes and trunks scattered around the storage room. She had read a couple of diaries but hadn't spent a lot of time on them, and something inside her told her this had to change.

She started with the trunk sitting to her left and flipped the lid open. She rummaged through its contents until her fingers found a stack of leather-bound journals. Pulling them out, she studied them closely as she settled on the floor. Putting the stack in her lap, she opened the first one. A pencil drawing of a woman slid onto the floor, and she carefully picked it up.

She had the same eyes as Raina, only this woman's eyes were full of fire and determination. This was the picture of someone strong and fierce, and it made her even more beautiful. Glancing over at her reflection in an old dusty mirror, Raina didn't see fire. She saw fear and a weariness which always clouded her.

No wonder Conie doesn't want to move things forward with me. He has seen the line of women I come from. They are mighty. I am not.

Raina turned the picture over and in the upper right-hand corner it said Tuva. Gasping, Raina flipped it back over so she could study the face once more. She slid her fingers across the picture and tucked it into the back of the journal. She flipped open the first page and began reading.

It's been a couple of weeks since I've written anything. I finished my last journal but couldn't find the words to write anything for a while. I thought my heart was going to burst into a thousand pieces when Isak saw Bill's arm around me. The pain was so intense. I love my husband so much and I wish I could get him to understand Bill was just there for me as a friend after my attack. I can't help that Bill has feelings for me. But I don't care for Bill in that way. Why does this all have to be so complicated? Why can't we catch a break here? Sometimes I wish I could pack up and go home to my parents. But the idea of living my life without my Isak stops me every time. I could never leave him. And I could never leave my beautiful home on the great water.

Raina stopped reading and looked out the window at the waves billowing. *The women of my family always find themselves spellbound by this place and they never leave. Could I actually leave here? Could I pack up my belongings, put them into my car, and drive away? No, I don't think I could. Staying and being vulnerable terrifies me, but I really don't think I could.*

Thumbing through the rest of the diary, Raina read bits and pieces before closing it. She looked through the rest of them and decided these would have to wait for a later investigation. She loved learning about Tuva, but she needed to dig for clues from a different time.

Closing the trunk, Raina moved on to the box next to it. She dug through it but found nothing of interest.

She continued rummaging for several hours. She looked at pictures and read journal entries, but didn't find what she was looking for. She decided to look at one more trunk before going downstairs to look through the few journals she already had again.

When the trunk popped open, Raina's hand flew over her mouth. There was a stack of journals matching the ones from Aunt Kat's mother. There was also a jewelry box, a hat box full of pictures, and a shoe box full of mementos. Raina looked through the items and decided this was what she was looking for. She would have Milly's husband, John, who was also the groundskeeper, help her bring this down to her room.

Raina looked around to make sure she didn't want anything else brought to her room and stumbled on another box full of items around the time the *Vide Fjärd* had gone down. Grinning, Raina slapped her hands together and went in search of John. She needed help with two boxes now. It didn't take long for Raina to fetch him, and he helped her bring the items to her room. As he left, Aunt Kat rambled in.

"What's all this?" Aunt Kat asked.

"This is the stuff from the attic I plan to dig further into. That is, if you're still okay with it."

"Of course."

"I found a picture of Tuva. It was a pencil drawing of just her. It was tucked inside one of her journals. She looked incredibly um..."

"Strong. Mighty. Fierce. Beautiful."

"Yes. You've seen it?"

"Oh yes. Gramma Melia used to talk about her all the time, and she would bring the picture out. When Gramma Melia died, I had it tucked in with the journals so it would stay with the memories of Tuva."

"That sounds so poetic and beautiful. The memories of Tuva."

"She was a great lady."

"I would argue, you're a great lady."

"You flatter me. But I'm old and tired."

"Who was Bill?" Raina asked.

"Gramma Melia told me the story only once, right after I got married. I was having second thoughts about my marriage, and she told me the love story of Tuva and Isak. It helped me decide to go ahead and stay with my husband and we had a beautiful marriage until he died."

"Your story sounds lovely even with its hardships."

"Not as lovely as Tuva and Isak. I think I've shared before, but what they had was a great love, almost destroyed by the hardships of founding this place and a man named Bill. Tuva had been attacked while Isak was preparing the homestead. Some wonderful people who would become Tuva's friends stumbled upon the attack and brought Tuva to Bill. Bill was a good friend of Isak's and because she was attacked, he felt obligated to make sure she was okay. He fell in love with her. Tuva grew to love him as a friend loves another. She had a bond with him through the attack, but it was different than the bond she had with her husband. Isak and Tuva had to work through it amongst other things, but in the end, they founded the town, grew a family of love, and created the legacy which is now ours. Yours."

"What a story."

"Yes. What a story. It's part of your story too, Raina."

"Hmmm, I love that notion."

"Have you heard from Conie?" Aunt Kat asked, changing the subject.

"No, not for a few days. He is keeping his distance, I think, to give me time and space to decide what I want. To figure out my footing as he put it."

"What can I do?"

"Nothing really. I want to dig in and learn more about my history, my story. I've never felt like I belonged anywhere, but this place gives me hope that I've found my home."

"Dig away. Let me know what you find. I'm anxious to figure out the secrets that lay buried so they may lay to rest, and we can get on with building Willow Bay back to what it once was when Gramma Melia married Grandad Nick."

"Aunt Kat, the wrecked boat," Raina said but paused. "I don't know why we aren't telling you what we've found yet."

"It's the *Vide Fjärd* isn't it?"

"How did you know?"

"I knew as soon as I heard about it showing up. It was a feeling I had. Gramma Melia and Grandad Nick were devastated by that loss. And she passed on some of that pain to me I suppose. They loved each other and they had a strong marriage, but they felt the loss of Nathanial for the rest of their lives. They loved him dearly."

"I have some things that came off the boat if you want to look at them."

Aunt Kats eyes danced with excitement, and she had a lift in her spirits Raina hadn't seen in days. Raina was sorry she went along with the decision to keep things from her. She knew deciding to do so came from a good place, but now she questioned if they had been wrong.

Raina retrieved the box from her closet and set it in front of the fireplace. Aunt Kat sat in the chair closest to it while Raina grabbed the first item. It was the picture of Amelia.

She carefully handed it to her aunt, as tears sprang in Aunt Kat's eyes.

"Should we not do this?" Raina asked.

"I'm only shedding a few tears of love and joy at seeing my Gramma's beautiful face. Let's keep going."

Raina selected a tin box and opened it. Inside was a knife, a compass, and pocket watch. They all had the initials N.N. on them.

Handing it to Aunt Kat, Raina asked, "Was this our Uncle Nathanial's?"

"No, the *Vide Fjärd* was always led by Grandad Nick. These would be his things. Nathanial volunteered to go help another one of our boats. He insisted Grandad Nick take over his boat so he could get Gramma Melia home safely."

"So, I'm assuming this pea coat was Grandfather Nicks?"

"It may have actually been our uncle's."

Raina fumbled through the pockets, checking to see if anything was in them. She held up the coat to get a better look at it and noticed a hidden pocket in the lining of the coat. Inside was a small leather journal bound together with a tiny rope. Raina studied it and handed the coat to Aunt Kat.

"What do you have there?" Aunt Kat asked.

"One thing is for certain, everyone in our family liked to write down their story."

Aunt Kat laughed while Raina opened it. The words were smudged on most of the pages, but Raina could make out bits and pieces as she carefully turned any page that didn't fall apart.

"How is this not completely ruined?"

"I would guess because it was inside the pocket of the pea coat inside of a trunk. Somehow it survived just as the picture of your aunt did. Oliver and his friends did a great job of cleaning these items."

Raina gingerly turned another page. "Look at this, it's an entry just days before the storm. Here let me read it to you.

"I've decided to release Amelia from any promises she has made to me. She loves Nick. I have always known it. I just hadn't allowed myself to see it until now. It breaks my heart she won't be mine, but she would never be mine even if we continued on together. I will always love her and perhaps one day I'll find someone who loves me as she does Nick."

Lowering the journal, Raina asked. "What is it with this family and love triangles?"

Aunt Kat giggled, which slowly grew into a full belly laugh with tears streaming down her face. Raina joined in and leaned on her aunt. Aunt Kat patted her arm, and Raina straightened as Stacia appeared, announcing it was dinnertime.

Raina escorted her aunt to the dining room and beamed with joy. Aunt Kat settled into her chair and as Raina went to sit in hers, her aunt dissolved into laughter once more and Raina couldn't help but follow her lead. Dinner was delicious and Raina enjoyed the company. It was more carefree than it had been since she had arrived.

When they were done eating and going their separate ways for the night, Raina promised herself she would dive back into the history of her family right away. It seemed like just talking through things released her aunt from the weight of carrying it all.

Making a quick chore of getting ready for bed, Raina settled under the covers with a stack of journals. She picked up the first one and began to read. She closed it and went to grab the other two journals from her desk. Nestling under her quilt, she flipped through a few pages before looking at the new one again.

Looks like I stumbled onto the beginning.

Chapter Sixteen

March 8, 1947

I did something really stupid today. Stefan has been gone for a couple of weeks on business, the girls are busy with their studies, and I just had to get out of the house.

As I walked along the path toward Melia's house, I ran into one of our workers. He was clearing the path, and he stopped to let me walk past, but as I went by him, I stumbled, and he caught me. For a split second, I truly believed he held me a little too long. I tried to push that notion away but the excitement I felt at being held...It's been far too long.

I thanked him for his kindness and turned to walk away. Then I saw a clump of snow and feeling young and foolish I made a snowball and threw it at him. He was surprised, but he must have read my face because he picked up his own and threw it at me. A snowball fight ensued until I stumbled and fell into the snow. When he helped me up, this time he did hold me too long, long enough for our laughter to die down and the only thing between us was our breath.

The girls' laughter telling me they had come out to play brought me back to reality. But I didn't jerk away. I stepped back slowly, and he did the same. I mumbled a farewell and ran back toward the house. Now I can't stop thinking about it. And I don't know what to do about it.

March 9, 1947

I saw *him* today. I wanted to try and speak to him, but I couldn't find a way. I know he was watching me too. Did he have a hard time sleeping last night like I did?

March 10, 1947

I had a letter from Stefan today. He sounded tired and weary and expressed how much he is missing me and the girls. His work bores me, but sometimes I wonder if things are harder for him right now. And yet all I could think about today was *him*. What kind of person am I that I'm pining over another man when my husband is working hard and missing me?

March 11, 1947

I ran into *him* again. I tried to explain that what had happened before couldn't happen again, and he thanked me for giving him a reason to laugh. Even if it was just for that moment. He was thankful for that. He told me his name. I told him of course I knew his name, which was a lie, but I felt bad for not knowing everyone's names who work here. How superficial am I?

So, I tracked down Mavis and asked her to give me a list of all the people who worked here and what their jobs were. I'm sure she was confused by my request, but I don't want to be a superficial person. She gave me more than the list of names. She gave me their titles and how much everyone earned. I was embarrassed to not realize how little he made compared to how much money I have just in jewelry from my childhood. Is this a game to him? Am I only fooling myself?

March 12, 1947

I suppose you could say we had our first fight. I told *him* we couldn't possibly flirt any longer and if I had initiated anything inappropriate, I was sorry. He told me, not here, and instructed me to meet him at the beach on the far side of the point. So, in my foolishness, I did. I met him.

I told him meeting him was too risky and he asked me why I did it. And I couldn't come up with a better answer other than I wanted to. I wanted to see him. I wanted to talk to him. He said it was good enough for him. I asked him if it was because I had money. A flash of anger sparked in his eyes, but he controlled it and told me to never mention money ever again.

We walked along the beach, and he talked about his work. I talked about the girls. We didn't talk about his wife or my husband. We talked about everything else. When it was time for me to leave, he helped me over a boulder and held my hand for a moment longer than he had to. This is just the beginning, he whispered. It's the beginning, I whispered back. And I left.

Chapter Seventeen

Raina lifted the banner up to John, who was helping decorate the bandstand in the park. The Founders Day Festival was only a few days away and there was still so much to do. The original bandstand had needed to be brought back to life, so Raina donated some of her own money for its refurbishment. The point of the festivals was to bring in tourists to help jumpstart the town's economy, but she was hoping she could also revive a sense of pride and love for the town, which was fizzling out. And the bandstand was as good a place as any to start revitalizing things.

Feeling like she was behind, Raina barely let the paint dry before roping John into assisting her today. Raina grabbed the ribbon which would hang above the banner and handed it up the ladder when Conie hopped onto the stage.

"You startled me," Raina said.

"Sorry, about that. You're so focused on your work I'm surprised you heard me at all," Conie said, looking around the space. "You've outdone yourself. This looks great. It looks like the original, just a brand-new version of it."

"Thanks. I want to help breathe life back into existing things."

"It shows. It's giving me ideas on how I can give my restaurant a facelift."

"Raina, can you hand me the other side of the ribbon?" John asked. "It's getting caught on the banner and won't let me hang it up the way I want."

Raina yanked it away from the ladder, helping John untangle it, and passed it on to him. He secured it and climbed off the ladder.

"How'd we do?" John asked.

"Looks great," Conie said.

Raina helped John pick up the supplies. Conie asked if he could have a word with her. She said she wanted to finish, but John waved her off. Promising to be back shortly, she followed Conie toward the path winding around the park. They ambled along in silence until Raina started to ring her hands.

"I'm making you nervous, and I don't mean to," Conie said.

"We've hardly talked alone since the day in the gazebo. It seems like you've been keeping your distance, so now out of the blue you track me down to specifically talk to me about something. So yes, I'm a bit nervous."

Conie chuckled. "I'm sorry."

"It's not funny. I was starting to think you were mad at me, or you weren't being genuine that day."

Sobering, Conie stopped and gently touched Raina's arm. "Believe me, my feelings for you are genuine."

Raina sucked in her breath at the heat in Conie's eyes. She moved closer to him, her lips hovering above his, but the pounding of a hammer across the park reminded her they were not alone. She stepped back and sauntered away while Conie's hand slid down her arm and snagged her hand, but he only squeezed it and let go.

"Your aunt told me you've been meeting with her weekly to study all things Nilsson Family Enterprises."

"I have."

"And?"

"And what? Conie, you're holding back because you want me to find my place without the distraction of a relationship. I get it. But I don't know what you want me to say. It's like you're expecting some magic words from me confirming I'll never leave."

"That's not what I meant when I said 'and' Raina."

"What did you mean?"

"I was curious what you thought about everything. The magnitude of it. It's multiple fingers in so many different directions."

"Oh," Raina's cheeks burned, and she went to sit on the closest bench.

Conie sat next to her. "Don't be embarrassed."

"I completely misunderstood you."

"That happens."

"But you see me and read me so well."

"It's not a competition. Besides I can be a master at hiding what I'm thinking if I want to. And I don't think you could hide your thoughts even if you tried. It's actually one of the things I love about you."

The word—love—singed the air between them, and Conie jumped up, running his hands through his hair. Raina stood but kept her distance. She watched him wearily until he turned her way.

"Did you find a boat?" Raina asked.

"What?"

"Did you find a boat when you were in Duluth?"

"Oh, yes, it's to be delivered at the end of the month. Did I not tell you?"

"We haven't spent a lot of time together. And the time we have spent together has been centered around conversations about the festival, business, and how your sisters are pests."

Conie burst out laughing, which is what Raina was hoping for. She reached over and squeezed his hand. "We don't have to make this complicated, Conie. We don't have to force things. Let's just see where things take us."

"You seem different," Conie said.

"The more I learn about my past, the more grounded I feel. I'm starting to feel more confident in myself."

"Ah, I see. Your deep roots are showing."

"Hah!"

Conie tugged Raina closer to him and kissed her on the cheek before they walked hand in hand back toward the bandstand. The walkway curved and they stumbled onto a group of people doing community service. Conie tried to guide Raina off the path, and she chastised him for avoiding the workers before she made eye contact with Violet. The anger there made Raina take a step back like she had been slapped.

As Raina trudged away, Violet yelled for her to come back because she had more things to say to her. Not turning around, Raina jogged across the grass.

"Stay off the grass, Raina!" Violet yelled.

The deputy leading the community service project stepped in and told Violet to stop or she would be forced to sit this one out and start over on her hours for the day. Raina didn't stick around to find out Violet's response.

"She won't ever stop, will she?" Raina asked.

"I suppose not," Conie said.

"It's like something is fueling her anger and hate right now."

"I know. I wonder what it could be?"

"Is her mother like this?" Raina asked.

"No, at least not that I could ever tell. She may have been at one time, but lately she's always seemed indifferent toward Kat and me. She has never been outright hostile, though. But with Violet, it's like she is blaming all of her problems on what happened between her family and yours."

"What are all her problems?"

"Her father left them when she was about ten. He went south somewhere, I think. She had a steady dating life in high school but it fizzled out. Murie thinks it's because she always hoped I would get together with her. Which won't ever happen. She works at the restaurant and bar up by the highway but spends a lot of time after her shifts getting drunk. She has had several DUI's and was arrested once for drug possession when she was twenty."

"Wow, small town gossip really does know everything."

"It's not gossip, she proclaims her issues to anyone who will listen when she gets drunk enough."

"Funny thing is, that could have been me," Raina said, stopping to stare out at the water as it lapped steadily against the rock beach in the bay. She shifted her gaze toward Kat's house, peeking up through the trees past the park grounds.

"That could never have been you."

"Maybe, but I do know what it's like to live paycheck to paycheck, to not have a father, and only have my mother and grandmother in my life."

"She chose a path of bitterness, though, and that's just not who you are."

Raina contemplated Conie's words. John hollered that he was heading back to the house if she wanted a ride. She said she'd be right there and focused back on Conie.

"Thanks for stopping by to check on things and talk to me."

"Oh, I never even mentioned why I popped by."

"Oh?"

"I wanted to ask if you would spend the evenings of the festival with me. I know we both have responsibilities during the day, but I have people who will cover for me at the pub."

"Like a date?"

"Like a couple of dates," Conie said, beaming.

"Sounds fun. I'll meet you at the pub at six on Friday."

"Looking forward to it."

Raina grinned, said goodbye, and walked toward John. Someone hollered her name across the park, and she turned to see the figure of a woman by a clump of trees, but when she looked closer, she was gone. A shiver went up Raina's spine, but thoughts of her dates with Conie shoved her unease aside and she hummed the rest of the way to the truck.

It didn't take long for John to drive Raina back to the house, but it was later in the afternoon and with all the bigger projects almost finished, she took a shower and went over all the plans one more time. She wanted to make sure she wasn't forgetting something.

As she pored over the last of her checklists, she caught her great-grandmother's journals out of the corner of her eye. She told herself she didn't have time, but she was intrigued by the developing story and wanted to read more. Giving up on her chore, she grabbed a few of the journals and curled up on her favorite chair by the fireplace.

She picked up where she left off, but for the rest of the month of March her great-grandmother wrote mostly about her girls and how she and Stefan were arguing.

Occasionally she would write a sentence about how *he* glanced her way or waved at her, but nothing more.

Raina finished March and realized each journal was a different month. She found June and read about visitors and picnics and time at the beach hoping to catch a glimpse of *him*. It was mostly the same happenings and writing as the previous month.

Picking up the month of July, Raina remembered this was the first journal she had read from. She hoped she might find more things, but the rest of the month the writing was mostly uneventful, minus a quick trip to Duluth with Stefan.

At the end of the journal, her great-grandmother poured her heart out, professing she was afraid she was falling out of love with her husband, for he no longer saw her. She described how he rarely even said hello. The pain was evident by her words on paper, and Raina couldn't help but feel sorry for her.

Celia entered her room, bringing Raina back to the present and announced dinner was ready. Raina thanked her and said she would be right down. Tucking the journal safely away, she went down to join her aunt. She tried to focus on the dinner conversation until her aunt commented on Raina's distraction. She waived it off and explained she was just tired and distracted by the festivities coming up.

After dinner, Aunt Kat suggested Raina turn in early and she obliged, but she didn't go to sleep right away. She donned her most comfortable pajamas, crawled into bed, and snuggled into the covers before diving into the August journal.

Chapter Eighteen

August 1, 1947

I've been back from Duluth for several days and I haven't seen *him* yet. I was told he was off doing a special project for the estate. I need to be careful because some of the staff are growing suspicious of my questions. I missed him terribly while I was in Duluth and not being able to see him yet has been awful.

Sometimes I wonder if this is just all in my head. Did we really kiss passionately? Is there a connection between us?

Am I losing it? I'm a married woman with two daughters. Why would any man want me? My own husband doesn't even want me.

August 3, 1947

I saw *him* today. He ignored me. He either must be having second thoughts about us, or this has all just been a game to him. I can't think right now about how this will hurt my heart—if it's true. But maybe it's for the best. After all, we are not free to be with one another.

August 5, 1947

I received a note from *him* telling me to meet him tomorrow at the beach. This is it. He is breaking things off. I just know it. It's just as well. On a positive note, Stefan actually talked to me today. He even told me about his business plan for this new venture he was doing. I must admit it's all so boring to me. I wish I could take an interest in this place as much as Melia has.

I sometimes feel like Stefan is disappointed with me because of it. Maybe that's why there is such a disconnect between us. I hate that I feel so disconnected from this place. It probably has more to do with my upbringing. I have always just been an ornament. No brains. No ideas. Just good for marrying, bringing out for social engagements, and having babies. I've done all of it, so now what? What do I get out of all of this?

Him. I get *him*. At least I hope I still do.

August 6, 1947

How do I write these words? Should I write them? Mama used to tell me, "Don't say the words out loud, dear, write your thoughts into your journal. It is your private space. It is your place to let it out." So here goes.

I met *him* at the beach today. A storm was rolling in, but I had to go. The girls were visiting with their grandmother and would be gone for hours, and Stefan left this morning for another trip. He said he would be gone for several days, but if it's like last time, it will turn into several weeks.

The wind and waves had just kicked up when I stumbled onto the beach where it has become our spot. *He* was waiting for me. He looked upset and I prepared myself for things to be broken off between us, but a fire sprang in my belly, and I could see the same in his eyes.

He moaned and rushed closer to me. I'm not sure when the rain began to fall, but I noticed it as I fumbled with the front of my dress. He jerked me closer and told me, not here. We looked around and I spotted the old boat house from years ago, which was never used anymore.

Grabbing his hand, we rushed across the sand and rocks until we were safely inside. We stared at each other like wild animals, sizing each other up as the lightning flashed and the rain poured on the roof above.

He said we couldn't keep doing this. I told him I knew we couldn't. He didn't want to have these feelings for me. Neither did I. He couldn't stand being away from me. I said I had missed him so much. He said he wanted to kiss my naked flesh. I asked him what he was waiting for.

We leaped into each other's arms and what we had started on the beach flew unchecked into the most passionate love making I have ever experienced. He held me in his arms long after and as the rain slowed, we quietly dressed. We said we couldn't do this again, but we knew we absolutely would. When we parted ways, we said we were saying goodbye forever, but we knew we were lying.

Chapter Nineteen

Waking with a start, Raina looked over at the beam of light coming in through the window. She sat up as the memory of her dream faded away. She shook her head and rubbed her eyes. It was Sunday morning and so far, the Founders Festival had gone smoothly.

More importantly the time she had spent with Conie had been everything she hoped it would be. There was dancing and laughter and they talked about so many things over stout and fries at the end of each evening. There was hand holding and stolen kisses. She was falling hard for him.

Throwing back her covers, Raina made quick work of her shower and getting ready for the day. Grabbing the tote bag she had prepared the night before, she flung it over shoulder and made her way to the dining room where Aunt Kat was sipping a cup of coffee at the table.

"Good morning, Aunt Kat."

"Good morning. You look quite refreshed and have a spring in your step this morning."

"I do?"

"Don't lead him on if you aren't planning on staying, my dear girl."

Raina frowned at her Aunt Kat's words. "I would've hoped my interest in learning all the things and my involvement in the festivals would have told you I had planned on staying."

"I hoped that was what it meant, but I learned a long time ago, one must never assume anything, and one can't judge one's behavior. People are very good about keeping secrets to themselves."

After fixing her plate from the buffet of food on the sideboard, Raina sat next to her aunt. "Does this theory come from multiple offenses against you or is it because of your parents' situation?"

"What happened to my parents left deep scars. The idea that my mother was having an affair under all our noses, and we didn't have a clue, is hard to process."

"It must have been such a difficult time for you, Aunt Kat. The pain obviously still runs deep. I'm sorry I said anything at all."

Aunt Kat poured a cup of coffee and handed it to Raina. She grabbed the mug and took a sip, contemplating the situation.

"I'm finding it helps to talk about it to someone who wasn't a part of it," Aunt Kat said. "Perhaps if Del and I had talked more about what happened, she may not have ever left. Of course, we wouldn't have you, so maybe it was always meant to happen this way."

"I couldn't possibly be a good replacement for Gramma D."

"Oh Raina, there is no replacing either one of you. I'm just thankful I got to spend time with both of you for a little while."

Raina mulled over her aunt's words. Her comment about her limited time with Raina unnerved her.

"Aunt Kat, I'm going to say the words, so my intentions are absolutely clear. I plan to stay in Willow Bay. I consider this my home now. I'm all in with helping, not only to carry on the legacy, but also building it up and adding to it if I can."

"I think I knew deep down. I just needed to hear you say the words I guess."

"It's understandable with all that's happened in your life," Raina said.

A comfortable quiet settled around the two of them as they finished breakfast. Raina took the last sip of her coffee and looked over at her aunt. She was staring at her coffee mug with a strange expression.

"It still would have been nice to have you both here though," Aunt Kat said.

"It would have been wonderful."

"You know I never saw them. My parents. Only Del did. And Gramma Melia of course. But Del protected me. She even shielded my eyes when they brought out the gurneys. Finding them though, must have haunted Del the rest of her life."

"There was always something there I couldn't quite put my finger on," Raina said. "She was a wonderful grandmother, don't get me wrong, but there was a loving from a distance kind of way she handled things. Occasionally she would let her guard down and I treasured those moments, especially after mom died, but there was just always something. My heart breaks for her. It was from such a horrific tragedy."

"The thing haunting me is the idea my own mother could have killed my father," Aunt Kat said. "None of us saw it coming. They had been getting along for several weeks leading up to that day. It's why they opted not to go to Duluth with us. At least it's what Mother said. She told me she wanted to spend time with Father, just the two of them."

"Do you think he found the journals?" Raina asked.

"I guess it's possible," Aunt Kat said. "Or maybe she was so torn up about all of it, she couldn't handle it, and snapped like they say she did. Maybe she blamed my father's absence for the affair, and she couldn't handle the guilt, or Father forced her hand."

"This doesn't make sense to me."

"It has never made sense to any of us."

"Can you tell me why they ruled it a murder-suicide?"

Celia walked into the room advising Johnston was ready. Thanking Celia, Aunt Kat asked Raina if she wanted a ride. Raina nodded and said she wanted to run to the bathroom.

As Raina left the dining room, Aunt Kat reminded Celia to advise the staff that everyone was to take the rest of the day off again today, so they could all enjoy the festivities. Thinking about her aunt, Raina stared into the mirror as she washed her hands. She was curious what response her aunt would give to the question about her parents' deaths and hoped they would pick up the story on their way into town.

Grabbing her bag, Raina rushed out to the waiting car, worried she was running late, but discovered she'd arrived first. She stared out at the water while she waited instead of climbing into the car. It wasn't long before Aunt Kat joined her.

"Always such a pretty view," Aunt Kat said.

"It is."

"It's why Tuva chose it."

"Gramma Tuva chose this place?"

"Yes, she chose where to make her and Isak's homestead. The rest of the family scattered about, but Tuva claimed this plot as theirs."

"I love that she chose this."

"So do I," Aunt Kat said, settling into her seat.

Raina followed suit and stared out the window as Johnston drove them toward town. There was to be a parade and Aunt Kat was to ride in the first float. She was the current reigning matriarch of the town, and the planning committee believed it to be fitting to include her to kick things off on the last day of the festival.

"I suppose you're wondering what my answer to your question would be," Aunt Kat said.

"Yes, I'm curious." Raina shifted in her seat to make sure she didn't miss anything.

"I was told everything pointed to that, including the bloody scene Del stumbled on. There was no other motive and no witnesses. My father had several stab wounds, with the knife lying next to him. And the gun was laying so close to my mother's hand it was like the gun had fallen out of it when she fell over. They were lying only inches away from each other. The investigator told us he believed she stabbed him and in a fit of remorse or a realization of what she had done, she got the gun and killed herself."

"I'm sorry, Aunt Kat. This is supposed to be a fun day, a joyous day, and I'm having you dredge up painful old memories. I hope I'm not ruining things for you."

Aunt Kat swiped at her cheek. "On the contrary, it feels good to talk about it again. It's somewhat healing for my soul."

"We're here, Kat," Johnston said and ran around to help Kat out of the car.

Thanking Johnston, Aunt Kat moved to climb out but paused and leaned back into the car. "Raina, would you join me on the float?"

"You want me to join you?"

"I do."

"It would be an honor."

It wasn't long before Raina was seated next to her aunt on the float and the parade had begun. She waved at the townspeople and smiled, hoping they would accept her presence next to her aunt. Everyone appeared delighted as they waved and cheered the Nilsson family, and some even called out Raina's name.

As they rounded the first corner, Raina locked eyes with Violet. She was standing next to her mother, but while Donna acted indifferent, Violet stood with her arms across her chest, glaring at her. Raina's smile faltered and she couldn't stop her hand from trembling as she waved at the next person.

"Don't let them get to you, Raina. Their blame and dislike are misplaced. Besides, Gramma Melia always said to rise above and show kindness anyway."

Raina nodded and tried to focus on the excitement and grinning faces of everyone else. She attempted to release some of the unease when cheerful voices called her name. Scanning the crowd, her smile faltered for another reason as she caught Conie's beaming face in the crowd.

Conie was standing next to his sisters along with Oliver and Stu. Raina waved wildly at her friends and laughed. She glanced at Aunt Kat whose spirits had also lifted.

"Now, that's something to be excited about," Aunt Kat said.

"What's that?" Raina asked.

"New love and wonderful friends."

Chapter Twenty

Placing her hand gently into Conie's, Raina wandered across the deck, where she'd had a nice meal with Aunt Kat. Her aunt went next door to get the second book in a series she was reading, and Raina knew she did it to give her and Conie a moment alone.

The parade was long over, a small band was setting up to play on the deck, and tents for vendors selling their wares lined the street below. Raina looked across at the bandstand in the park where it was being made ready for the final band to play later that day. A few food vendors were also setting up for the evening and the final arrangement of extra picnic tables were being lined up. The moveable dance floor was getting a quick cleaning as well.

"Are you sure you're free now?" Conie asked.

"I am. I was just double checking the final arrangements being made."

"It's been a fun weekend. You did a good job?"

"Have you seen a lot of new faces?" Raina asked.

"Yes, there's been an influx of tourism, if that's what you're asking," Conie said.

"Excellent. Now, how long does the band play here at the pub again and when are you off work?" Raina asked.

"They are playing for an hour, which leaves about thirty minutes to get cleaned up and close up shop to get to you in the park."

"You don't want to miss it. Aunt Kat is going to give a speech before the last bit of fun of the weekend."

"I'll try to be there on time. My sisters are closing in twenty minutes, and they plan to help me with the pub and café."

"I love watching you all work together. It would be fun to have a sibling, I think. Or at least cousins or something."

"I would be happy to share my sisters with you," Conie said, picking up trash on a nearby table and throwing it away.

Sobering, Raina studied him. The idea his sisters could be hers had not entered her mind until now. Pondering a life with this man, she attempted to steady her racing heart. As Conie shuffled back toward her, she tried to put a smile back on her face, but he looked at her quizzically.

"You okay?" he asked.

"I'm fine. It's nothing. Just remembered something else I needed to do before tonight."

"Promise to come back. I'll have a stout or a cabernet waiting for you."

"Um. I promise." She kissed Conie on the cheek and fled down the stairs.

She knew she wanted to stay in this town. Her town. Raina knew she wanted to help continue the family legacy. She knew she wanted to make her aunt proud. She knew her feelings for Conie were turning into a love she was not expecting. But what Raina didn't know was how to navigate loving someone like Conie. And it scared her.

Raina strolled past vendors, glancing at their trinkets but not really seeing any of the items. She decided to go to the beach and glanced back toward the pub before going down the stone steps. She caught sight of Conie watching her intently and she hoped she hadn't just made a mistake, but she needed air.

Conie whirled away like someone had called his name, and Raina focused on getting down by the lake. She meandered along the water and allowed the waves of feelings to roll through her. She concentrated on breathing and her body relaxed until Violet stumbled toward her.

"Violet, always a pleasure," Raina said.

"Is it?" Violet asked.

"I'm enjoying getting to know all of the townspeople, including you. Despite our, um, differences."

"You mean you enjoy torturing me."

"How do I torture you, Violet?" Raina asked.

"I watched you with Conie all weekend. Holding hands, kissing, dancing together. That should be me."

"Violet, I'm sorry that he doesn't love you."

"Are you saying he loves you?"

"Well no. But I'm sorry he doesn't have the same feelings for you as he has for me."

"It's not enough your family ruined ours, you have to take away the only man I ever loved," Violet said.

"How can you say you love him? You've never spent time together beyond one date years ago."

"What do you know about it?" Violet spat.

"Why don't you tell me about it then."

"I was getting my shit together before you came along. I knew I just needed to do it, and he would give me another chance. I know he would have."

"You don't know though. You were hoping he would, but you couldn't have possibly known for sure."

"Now we'll never know since you came along and stole him from me."

"He wasn't yours, Violet. He never has been."

"And now because of you, he never will be."

"I'm sorry you feel that way, but I won't apologize for the relationship I have with Conie. It has nothing to do with you."

"It isn't enough your family stole my grandfather away from us, you have to come here and take Conie away too."

"What are you talking about, Violet? My family didn't steal your grandfather away from you or anybody else."

"Of course, you stand up for the Nilsson clan. But I know the truth. I know—"

"Violet, this has got to stop," Conie said, walking toward them.

"Why are you defending her. She isn't from here. I'm from here. I've always been here waiting for you," Violet said.

"You need to hear this, Violet. I'm sorry our one date led you to believe there could ever be a future between us. But that simply has never been and never will be the case. And it was like that before Raina ever came to town, so stop taking it out on her," Conie said.

"Violet, come along now," Donna said, appearing by her daughter's side. She tugged gently on her arm, but Violet jerked away.

"Why do you do this, Mom?" Violet asked. "Grandma told me all the time that the Nilsson family drove Papa away and that's the reason he died."

"Violet, she shouldn't have ever put that on you," Donna said.

"Aren't you mad at them too?" Violet asked.

"I'm mad at the situation, but it isn't Kat's fault, and it especially isn't Raina's fault."

"Grandma would be so disappointed in you," Violet said and stormed off.

Donna let out a sigh and her shoulders drooped. "I'm sorry, Raina. I know we've never actually met, and I know the first time you saw me I was unfriendly. I'm sorry for being unkind and I'm sorry for my daughter."

"That's very generous of you," Conie said.

"Yes, thank you for apologizing. And if it helps, my great-great-grandmother tried to give your father's job back to him."

Donna laughed. "This goes much deeper than that, Raina."

"What do you mean?"

"Too much to get into now. I need to go after Violet," Donna said and walked away.

"You okay?" Conie asked, grabbing Raina's hand.

"I'm okay. But what do you think they meant?"

"What do you mean?"

"It seems like there is more to the story and we are missing something."

"I don't know what it could be. Maybe your aunt knows."

"Maybe," Raina said, staring after Donna.

"Come to the pub, and I'll pour you a glass," Conie said, tugging on Raina's arm.

"A glass of what?"

"Whatever you desire," Conie said with a spark in his eyes.

Heat radiated in her belly, and she stepped closer to him. She would have kissed him right there if they weren't on display for the whole town to see.

"Come along now," Conie said with a catch in his voice.

Walking beside him the earlier feelings of love and desire mixed with fear flooded through Raina, but she knew she couldn't stop them. Conie glanced her way and she tried to smile but she knew it wasn't quite reaching her eyes. She worried he was reading her mind.

Instead of commenting on it, Conie only squeezed her hand. "I'm thinking a nice cabernet will do the trick."

Laughing nervously, Raina only nodded and followed him to the pub.

Chapter
Twenty-One

Aunt Kat was escorted onto the bandstand as Raina turned toward Conie who had just arrived from the pub. Raina had offered to take her aunt, but the leader of the band said he was happy to help her. The microphone was adjusted to her height, and she cleared her throat. The microphone shrieked and Aunt Kat stepped back.

Covering her ears, Raina leaned into the side hug Conie gave her. The crowd died down as Kat tested the microphone to make sure it was at the appropriate volume. Clearing her throat, Kat started into her speech.

"Hello, Willow Bay. It was such an exciting weekend as we honored my ancestors and the founding of this beautiful town. I want to thank the planning committee as they worked tirelessly to make sure everything went smoothly. I also want to thank you, the people of Willow Bay, who have not given up on us as we have navigated a few difficulties in growing our beautiful community."

The crowd cheered and chanted "Willow Bay" with fists pumping in the air. Raina laughed as she and Conie joined in. Raina knew this was a beautiful moment for her aunt after all the hardships of the past. She enjoyed watching the joy on her aunt's face, as she let the town be taken over with excitement.

Kat motioned for everyone to quiet. "I look forward to hearing this amazing band play tonight as we wind down the last of the festivities. But before we listen to them, I must honor someone very special. Someone who I believed I would never get to know. Someone who I have grown to love very much. Her dedication has made me so proud. And I know as life winds down for me, I will be passing the Nilsson legacy on to capable hands. Raina Matson, everybody!"

The town erupted while tears slid unchecked down Raina's face. She blew kisses to her aunt and mouthed "thank you" and "I love you" to her. As the cheers quieted once more, Conie grabbed Raina's hand and held it tightly. She glanced his way, and her heart skipped a beat while he beamed at her with pride.

"I'm sure everyone is tired of this old lady prattling on, so without further ado, let's give a warm welcome to the star attraction for the weekend, our favorite hometown band, The Bay Boys!"

Kat clapped and the crowd went wild again. Conie ran up to help her off the stage and led her to where she was planning to sit during the concert. The rest of the crowd scattered to various picnic tables and chairs to make room for people to dance if they wanted to. Some people went for refreshments while others cozied up to loved ones and sang along.

Raina went to purchase some lemonade and planned to join Conie and her aunt with the refreshments. She was paying when Violet approached from the side.

"Always the center of attention, aren't we?" Violet said with a sneer.

"Violet, enough," Raina said.

"Don't tell me what to do."

"But this is ridiculous. If you got to know me better, you would discover my upbringing wasn't much different than yours."

"Don't patronize me."

"I'm not," Raina said, her shoulders drooping. "Look, I don't have a problem with you. I can't help that you have a problem with me. But what I can do is promise to steer clear of you as much as possible if it would help. Just know I'm not going anywhere. This is my home. This is my town. This is where my roots are. And sooner or later we will have to bump into each other, so I'm offering you a white flag in the hopes you and I can start over."

"Not a chance," Violet said and stormed off.

"This is your home huh, and your town?" Conie asked, coming up from behind.

Raina spun around. "Good, now I don't have to carry all the drinks by myself. And yes, this is my home. I grow more in love with it every day."

"Just the town?" Conie asked, cocking his head to the side.

"That's a different conversation," Raina said, laughing nervously. "Come on, let's head back to sit with Aunt Kat."

"Only if you promise me a dance."

"Absolutely."

Making sure Aunt Kat was settled, Conie led Raina to where people were dancing to a lively tune. They joined in the steps and Raina's laughter bubbled out of her as she twirled around in Conie's arms. She caught Murie dancing with Oliver out of the corner of her eye, while Annie danced with Stu, and she thought her heart would burst.

The people around her were so precious to Raina. She never would've believed she could ever find a place where she belonged or find friends who were like family. But she had, and she was so grateful.

The band slowed the pace with a familiar song, but one Raina hadn't heard since the day she had driven to Willow Bay. The haunting melody filled her, and she shivered. Conie moved closer to her, and asked if she was cold.

"No, I just. This song. I remember it. It's breathtaking. It's haunting."

"It's a Nilsson family song," Conie said.

"What?"

"Yes, I believe it was your great-great-grandmother who wrote this song. It's about the white hurricane. It started as a poem, but someone put music to it. It's one of Kat's favorites, but it's not well known outside these parts, so I'm surprised you know it."

"I heard it when I stopped at a coffee shop on my drive up to Willow Bay. An older man played it on the piano. I've never been able to get it out of my mind."

"I'm not surprised. That song only resonates with those who truly belong here. And you, my love, belong here."

Heat seared through Raina at Conie's words. Throwing caution to the wind, Raina pulled his mouth to hers. Conie moaned and deepened the kiss, stoking the fire between them. Raina shoved her fingers in his hair as his hand slid down her back.

"You guys might want to go find some privacy," Murie said with a chuckle.

Raina jerked away and looked around. The song had stopped, and the band had taken a break. The people around them were pretending not to notice the kiss despite their awkward grins.

"Oh my god, what must Aunt Kat think," Raina said.

"By the looks of her, she is tickled pink. I would say she likes the idea of the two of you together, and so do I. Just not in full make out mode on the dance floor," Murie said with a laugh.

"You two should go for a walk and let the air around us cool down a bit," Annie said with a giggle.

"I'm so embarrassed," Raina said. "What must people think?"

"They think we are a cute couple and are happy for us," Conie said unfazed.

"How does this not affect you?"

"Because I don't care what people think."

"Easy for you to say. You don't own the town, so you don't have skin in the game."

As soon as the words were out of her mouth, she regretted them. A flash of hurt crossed Conie's face before he hid it.

"Conie, I'm sorry."

"No, it's okay. But I need to check on some things at the pub before tomorrow. I'll catch up with you later," Conie said and walked away.

"I've done it now," Raina said, walking toward her aunt.

"He just needs a minute," Annie said, walking beside her.

"I agree with Annie," Murie said, flanking Raina.

"The words just blurted out."

"I know. I could tell by the look on your face." Annie paused to pick a tiny purple violet and handed it to Raina.

Smiling at her friend's sweet gesture, Raina said, "In Grand Meadow, everything I did was judged because I didn't have a father and neither did my mother. My family owned a business though, so although everyone expected the worst from me, they demanded the best. I could never win."

"That's a tough spot to be in," Murie said.

A boat clanging in the distance caught Raina's attention and she looked toward the water. "It was. Now coming here, I'm afraid I'll add to the already scandalous past Aunt Kat has had to endure."

"That's a lot of pressure you're putting on yourself, Raina," Annie said, sidestepping a woman walking past her.

"Too much pressure," Murie said, squeezing Raina's arm gently.

"Maybe, but I don't want to make things worse for her. I want to help her," Raina said.

"You are helping her. And you deserve love and happiness along with the rest of us," Murie said.

Raina flinched as a band member dropped something on stage, and glanced in the direction of the noise. "Maybe, but I need to make things right with Aunt Kat and Conie."

"I don't think you need to make things right with Kat, but an apology will go a long way with our brother," Annie said, tucking her arm in Raina's.

Stepping over a twig, Raina said, "You guys are the best. Thank you for trying to help me feel better even though it was your brother who I hurt."

"We kind of like you a lot and think you would be good for our brother," Murie said.

"It's nice to know I have your approval and didn't offend you just now," Raina said, pausing to let a group of people walk past them.

"What do you feel about him, Raina?" Annie asked.

"Annie!" Murie said.

"No, it's okay," Raina said, walking around a garbage can. "I think I might be falling hard for him. Really, really hard for him."

"Do you love him?" Annie asked.

"The idea of loving any man terrifies me," Raina said.

"The idea of it can be terrifying for anybody, but that doesn't keep someone from loving," Annie said.

Raina contemplated her words, but as much as she wanted to proclaim words of love, she hesitated.

"You don't have to answer," Murie said, patting Raina on the shoulder. "Even though he is our brother, it still isn't our business, especially if you guys haven't worked things out between the two of you."

"Worked what out?" Aunt Kat asked.

"Aunt Kat, I'm so sorry for the inappropriate behavior you had to witness on the dance floor. And I'm sorry if it causes a scandal or creates more gossip for you or hurts you or the family or the legacy."

"Raina, there is nothing to apologize for. You kissed each other. So, what. Besides, this town needs a good jolt of fun gossip every now and again."

"You mean it? I didn't ruin the family name?"

Aunt Kat burst out laughing.

"It's not funny, Aunt Kat. I'm so embarrassed."

Sobering, Kat squeezed Raina's hand. "You, my dear, need to take some time to heal the part of yourself that believes it has to meet some impossible standard. You're carrying the weight of it around with you. I know where it comes from, and I'm sorry for that. But you don't need to carry it with you anymore. Especially here. It's hurting you and will continue to do so until you make peace with it. You are you, and you are loved for it. And you are meant to live your life as you see fit no matter what others say or think."

"Wise words, Kat," Murie said.

"Wise words, I need to apply to myself too, I think. I have my own wounds I need to heal because they are putting additional pressure on my niece," Aunt Kat said.

Raina hugged her aunt. "Perhaps we can work on it together."

"Sounds like a fine plan."

When the band played again, Annie and Murie went off to find their dance partners. Conie didn't return for the rest of the evening. As Aunt Kat and Raina got into the car to head home for the night, Conie appeared and apologized for not returning. Raina tried to talk to him, but he said his sisters were waiting for him and he would reach out soon.

Raina watched him walk away and worried about the hurt he was obviously feeling. She didn't think what she said would have caused this much upset. There had to be more to it, but she would have to wait, since she needed to get her aunt home. As they drove toward the manor, Raina tried not to think about how such a beautiful weekend was ruined by her own insensitivity.

"Aunt Kat," Raina said while walking into the house.

"Yes, Raina?"

"I think it's time I went back to Grand Meadow to figure out the rest of my belongings. I obviously don't need most of the furniture I left behind, but there are a couple of pieces I'd like to bring home, along with the few boxes I'm storing."

"Sounds like a fine plan, Raina. Do you want some help? Do you want me to send Johnston with you?"

"No, I think I can manage."

Beaming, Aunt Kat hugged Raina before heading off to bed. Raina was glad she could at least make her aunt feel better. She was hoping this decision would also help smooth things over with Conie. With her spirits lifted, Raina walked to her room whistling her favorite song while making plans to head back to Grand Meadow one last time.

Chapter Twenty-Two

Raina fumbled with the box as she pushed it into the back seat of her car. She shut the door and went back into the storage unit. Her stomach growled and she checked her watch. She was planning on having dinner with Patsy, but she still had time.

She had arrived in Grand Meadow earlier in the afternoon and stopped by Gramma D's old shop before moving on to the storage unit. It was different being back. This place no longer had a hold over her. Something shifted in her as she had driven through town and she was thankful for it.

All these people had been unkind to her, but none of them could touch her anymore, no matter what they did or said. She was comforted by the knowledge she had of Willow Bay and the people she loved. Grand Meadow's cruelty no longer mattered. The years of hurt blew away in the wind. Now all she had to do was figure out what to do with her things and head back home.

Frowning, Raina looked into another box as Conie's face rolled through her mind. She hadn't gotten a chance to talk with him before she left, but she hoped the distance would give him the time he needed. Bending down, Raina rummaged through the contents and attempted to push all thoughts of Conie out of her head.

Raina picked up a photo album and a picture fell to the ground at her feet. She picked it up and stared at the two smiling faces. It was the only picture her mother had left of her father. Raina had seen it several times before, but it was like she was seeing it with new eyes.

She used to mourn for the man who wasn't there. She used to wonder if she had done something wrong to make him not want her or her mom. She used to daydream about becoming successful and going to find him so he could know the amazing person she had become. But now Raina looked at the stranger who was her father and felt nothing for him.

She was still sad he wasn't the man her mother believed him to be. But she no longer cared that this man missed out on her life. She had an amazing life, and it was only getting better, and that had nothing to do with him.

The sound of a vehicle approaching caused Raina to glance out toward her car, hoping they could fit around her as they passed by. But the truck didn't pass by. It stopped and Conie hopped out.

"Conie!"

"I have something to say to you," Conie said.

"Um. Okay."

"You can't leave. You can't leave because you and I had one small misunderstanding."

"I didn't lea—"

"No, let me finish. I care about you, and I know you care about me too."

"I do."

"And you've been doing so well with learning everything from Kat. You're so close to being able to take things over for her, which means you will have a job. And let's not forget the manor. It's a beautiful home and it's yours. And you have a town that loves you. And you can't forget your deep roots in this town."

"Conie, slow down. What are you talking about?"

"You can't leave us. You can't leave me," he said, stepping closer to her.

"Conie, I didn't leave."

"What? But you're here."

"Yes, I'm here going through my things. I'm getting the rest of my things to take back home."

Laughter bubbled out of Conie, and he bent over. Raina inched closer to him but stepped back when he straightened. He was beaming.

"You thought I left?" Raina asked.

"I thought you left. I went to see you. I thought for sure you would've called me, but you didn't, so I decided to go see you, to explain," Conie said.

"You said you were going to call me the night we had the misunderstanding and when you didn't right away, I wanted to give you the space you needed."

"Oh yeah. I would've done the same for you. I forgot I told you I would call. Anyway, I went to see you and you weren't there. I asked Kat where you were, and she said she was sorry but you had left just that morning for Grand Meadow and she thought I knew."

"She didn't tell you what I was doing?" Raina asked.

"I ran out of there so fast, I didn't give her the chance. I went to see my sisters and told them I was going after you."

Raina laughed this time and found she couldn't stop.

"Are you laughing at me," Conie asked, stepping closer to her with a twinkle in his eye.

"Maybe," Raina said in between laughs.

Conie shortened the distance between the two of them and Raina didn't have time to respond before his mouth was on hers. The photo album fell to the floor and Raina's hands flew around his neck. His hands were frantic on her back before he cupped her bottom and pulled her against his body.

Moaning, Raina's fingers wound through his hair. She realized they were all alone with no one to stop them. She met touch for touch until they were on her old couch toward the back of the storage unit, desire coursing between them.

"I want you," Conie said.

"I want you too. Please don't stop."

Conie paused briefly before lowering his mouth to hers once more.

Tugging her shirt over her head, Raina looked around for her shorts. She found them across the storage unit and giggled. She was fastening them when Conie asked her about the person in the picture he held.

Walking over to see, Raina said, "My father," and rummaged through the box at their feet to see if there was anything else she wanted to take home.

"Wait a minute. This is your father? I thought you didn't know him?"

"I didn't. I don't. That picture was taken of my father and mother during their first week in college. It's the only picture left of the two of them together, and it's the only picture I have of him at all."

"Does it make you sad seeing this picture of him?" Conie asked.

"Not anymore. I used to dream about him coming in and saving us when we were going through a hard time. Or I would dream I would grow up to be this amazing, successful person and he would profess how sorry he was, and how he really always wanted us. But not anymore. I somehow no longer care. Like I'm numb or indifferent to him now."

"I don't know if I should be happy it doesn't hurt, or worry you feel nothing."

"It's not that I don't feel anything. I just don't need him anymore. I don't need him to save me or love me. I had my mother and Gramma D. And I now have Aunt Kat, you, and your sisters. I truly don't feel like I need a man who didn't want me."

Conie wrapped his arms around Raina. "You, my beautiful Raina, don't need him. And how tragic for him, he never had you in his life."

"My sentiments exactly," Raina said, gently pressing her lips to his.

Pulling away from her, Conie said, "Careful woman."

Laughing, Raina stepped away. "We don't have time anyway. We should lock up the unit and head to dinner."

"Why the rush all of sudden?"

"Because we're supposed to be at Patsy's house in five minutes."

"Patsy?"

"Yes, she'll love you."

"Oh wait, is she the woman at your grandmother's old shop?"

"Probably. You stopped there?"

"I did. She told me you were here."

"Ah, so that's how you found me."

Conie kissed her once more. "Yep. Are you sure we can't be late."

"Yes, but I have the most incredible hotel room just outside of town for the night."

Desire flared in Conie's eyes and Raina considered being late for dinner. Deciding against it, she shut the storage door and secured it with her padlock. She offered to drive, and he obliged. As she drove, she let her mind wander to the two of them alone later.

When later came, though, they were too tired and fell into bed. After a full meal, good conversation, and finishing things in the storage unit, they couldn't keep their eyes open. Raina curled up in the arms of the man she knew she was in love with and fell into a peaceful sleep.

Chapter Twenty-Three

Securing the last strap, Raina looked across the bed of the truck now filled with her belongings to make sure Conie was done securing things on his side.

"'I'm so glad you came to get me. I'm actually not sure how I would have gotten all of this home."

"I'm sure you would have managed."

"Maybe, but you being here is so convenient."

"Do you want to follow me home or do you want me to follow you?" Conie asked.

"How about I follow you just in case. I'll flash my lights at you if I need us to stop. Otherwise stop if you need gas, food, or just a kiss," Raina said with a smirk.

"Ha! Don't tempt me. I might just take a break every hour."

Raina rounded the truck to get closer to Conie. He hugged her to him and kissed her on her forehead.

"Did you want to talk about why you were upset by my comment the last night of the festival? I mean besides me being a completely unkind person. It seemed like there was more to it than that."

Conie kissed her temple. "Sure. We can talk, but let's do it over breakfast. I'm starving."

"Hey, you're the one who didn't want to eat the hotel food and wanted to get going."

"I knew we had a few more things to load up here and I wasn't sure how long it would take. Plus, with the long drive ahead of us, I wanted to get on the road as soon as possible. Since things didn't take as long here, I need some food."

Chuckling, Raina squeezed him and moved toward her car. "Meet you at Patsy's. They have the best pastries and breakfast sandwiches in town. Besides, I told her I would stop by before I left."

"Meet you there."

Raina led the way to Gramma D's old Nilsson's Sip and Shop and was surprised at the butterflies in her stomach. As much as she had wanted to leave the town and start a new life, she never believed it would happen for her. The realization that this was probably going to be the last time she would ever set foot in the place made her apprehensive, and she struggled to make sense of it.

The drive to the shop was a short one and Raina parked out front. She studied what had been her home. It looked the same as it did yesterday, but now it was foreign to her. She had let it go and was excited about her future, so why was she sad?

Conie opened her door and smiled. "You coming, or do you need another minute?"

"What do you mean?"

"You look like you might cry. Saying a final goodbye is never easy."

"Yes, but this place is the source of so much hurt from my past."

"But it's also a source of so much joy. For better or worse, it was your home. It was the home and life you and your family created. And saying goodbye is hard."

"Thank you for putting into words what I'm feeling, because I was struggling to make sense of it."

"I knew you were. Do you need another minute?" Conie asked with so much tenderness, Raina struggled to swallow the lump in her throat.

"I don't know."

"If you need to cry, go ahead. Take all the time you need."

Breathing deeply, Raina stepped out of the car, closing the door behind her. "I'm okay walking in with you. Let's go."

As the bell jingled over the door, a few patrons glanced their way. Some paused to stare, others pretended not to notice her at all.

"Just like old times," Raina said under her breath.

"Feels a bit frosty in here," Conie said.

"Raina, Conie, there you are," Patsy said, waving them to the counter.

Looking around the shop as they approached, Raina noticed the few changes Patsy had made that she hadn't seen when she stopped there yesterday.

"This place looks amazing, Patsy," Raina said.

"Oh, it's just a few things we updated. I hope that's okay."

"It's your place. And I love it. How are your tenants working out for you?"

"A little bumpy at first finding the right fit, but we have some great people in there now. They are a young couple who bought the old Treamonts Hardware Store down the street. They were excited to live somewhere close to the business until they found the right home."

"I love that. I'm glad it worked out," Raina said.

"So, what can I get ya?" Patsy asked.

Raina and Conie ordered, said a few more pleasantries and found a quiet place to sit and talk. A few of the other customers waved at Raina and went back to their own conversations. Raina pondered if she was their topic of discussion, realized she didn't care, and focused on the handsome man sitting across from her.

"Let them talk," Conie said.

"Surprisingly, I don't care right now."

"Good job, you."

"So please tell me how I hurt you?" Raina asked.

Conie slid his hand across the table to grab hers. "Diving right in. Okay."

"Is that okay? Or do you want to wait."

"Nope, now is good." Taking a deep breath, Conie said, "When Kat was helping my sisters and I she was also teaching me things about your family business mostly because I think she needed and wanted someone to talk to about it and to share in some of the responsibilities. But a lot of people didn't understand and for a time it was a source of contention with the townspeople."

"How?" Raina asked.

"They believed I was taking advantage of her and trying to weasel my way in to take over. They questioned my loyalty to Willow Bay. It put a lot of pressure on me to show them I was invested in helping only, not taking over.

And it put a lot of pressure on me to be successful in my own business. It took a long time for people to trust me."

"So, you *do* have a vested interest in Willow Bay. And things *do* impact you," Raina said, putting her hands into her lap. She stared at them, realizing how her words must have stung.

"Here is your black coffee, Conie, and a latte for you Raina. Your breakfast sandwiches are just a minute behind. And I'm warming up your scones," Patsy said, putting their drinks on the table.

"Thank you, Patsy," Raina said.

"Is everything okay over here? I can kick people out if they are making you feel uncomfortable," Patsy said.

Raina smiled and looked at her mother's dear friend. "Thank you. But no. We're good. We are just talking about other things."

"Let me know if that changes. I'll be right back with your food."

Watching Patsy walk away, Raina caught someone saying her name as they looked at her table. She chuckled, picked up her latte, and took a sip.

"They don't even care if you can hear them," Conie said.

"Nope. They never did care about that. To them I'm trash. The wrong family. The wrong breeding. To them I'm a nobody, a nothing."

"Should I set the record straight?" Conie asked.

"I thought about doing that myself, but I decided to take the high road. Let them wallow in their own miserable judgements. They no longer affect me like they once did."

Conie sipped his coffee, and Raina shifted in her seat under his gaze. Her mind wandered to their time together in the storage unit and her cheeks warmed. Raina took another sip, trying to hide her face. But she knew by the grin flashing across Conie's face he was thinking about the same thing.

"Stop it," Raina said, taking another drink.

"Only if you do," Conie said.

"I'm sorry I hurt you. I had no idea, but that's no excuse. My words were hurtful, so I'm sorry."

Conie squeezed Raina's hand. "Thank you. You're forgiven. And you're beautiful when you blush while thinking about me."

"Here you go, you two," Patsy said, plopping the food on the table.

"Thanks again, Patsy."

"You heading out right after this?" Patsy asked.

"Yes. We want to get home."

"You sure it's good for you? That place I mean. I know you talked about it last night, but I just want to make sure. I think your mama would have wanted me to do that."

"Yes, thank you, Patsy. And thank you for being a wonderful friend to my mother and grandmother all these years. I don't know what they would have done without you at times."

"They helped me just as much over the years. I will miss you. You have to stay in touch."

"Perhaps you could come visit sometime," Raina said, standing to give Patsy a hug.

"We will just have to do that," Pasty said. "What did you do with your extra items?"

"I made a deal with the owner of the storage unit. He is going to sell the few pieces I left behind."

"Well, that was nice of him."

"I think he is sad to lose such a great tenant, so the extra money is a consolation prize."

Patsy chuckled and went back to work while Raina focused on finishing her breakfast. When done, Conie left to go inspect the items secured in the back of his truck, while Raina went to find Patsy to order a latte and coffee to go and to say one final goodbye. When Raina went out to meet Conie, he was sitting in his truck and advised everything was good to go. She handed him the coffee, kissed him on the lips, and got into her car. She slowly drove behind, while glancing at Nilsson's Sip and Shop in her rearview mirror until she turned the corner up the street.

Swiping at the tears springing from her eyes, Raina focused on the truck in front of her. She let herself be sad for a few more minutes while they sat at the stop light. The light changed to green, and she caught Conie grinning at her in his side mirror before he drove onto the ramp to I-35.

She straightened her spine and smiled. "Let's go home."

Chapter
Twenty-Four

Raina and Conie had been back for a couple of weeks, and she had settled into a nice routine of learning all she could, so when she did take over the reins, she would be prepared. She and Aunt Kat had been going over projections for the rest of the year based on some changes Raina had suggested they implement when the call came in about the fire.

Flying across the yard toward the garage, Raina hoped she would get there in time to help. A fire had broken out at the Marina, and she worried for Henry. Johnston offered to drive her, but Raina asked him to wait in case Aunt Kat decided to come later.

Raina sped toward town and it didn't take long before she was parking along the street a block away from the boatwerks. She rushed to the police line and waited for Jenks.

"Raina, come on over," Jenks said, lifting the police line. "Your aunt coming or is it just you?"

"It's just me for now."

"Let's stand over here out of the way. The volunteer fire department has everything well in hand," Jenks said.

"I think Conie was heading down too. Is it okay if he joins us?" Raina asked.

"Yeah, oh there he is," Jenks said.

Putting a radio to his mouth, Jenks gave his deputy instructions to let Conie in. When he joined them, Jenks explained the events of the evening leading up to the fire.

"What I've gathered so far is that Violet and a few of her friends were having a little get together in the parking lot. There was some alcohol involved and at some point, someone started a fire in the garbage can sitting outside the building. An altercation occurred and someone was shoved into the trash can, knocking it over. Panic ensued and the fire spread, catching the building on fire."

"Did anyone get hurt beyond those in the fight?" Raina asked.

"No one we're aware of. A couple of people took off and we are following up with them. But those who were here when we showed up were not hurt," Jenks said.

"Is it going to be a total loss you think?" Raina asked.

"We won't know for sure until we put it out. The wood on this old building is like dry kindling, and some of the boats are old too."

The blood drained from Raina's face as she stared at the blaze. "Like the wreckage of the *Vide Fjärd*."

"Oh, Raina, she's still in there, isn't she. I'm sorry," Conie said.

"Is Violet still here?" Raina asked.

"Yes, she's sitting over there with her friends. We will be taking them to the station in a few minutes. I wanted to talk with you first before taking care of that."

"I appreciate it. Can I go talk to her?"

"Are you sure that's such a good idea?" Conie asked.

"I want to ask her if she is okay. Show her I don't hold a grudge. Maybe it can help pave the way for us to start over. We both live in this town. I'll be taking things over eventually from Aunt Kat and I need to work on diplomacy with her as much as I can. We may never be friends, but I don't want her as an enemy."

"Okay, but I'm coming with you," Conie said.

As Raina approached, Violet looked gaunt and sad, but when she caught sight of Raina anger flared in her eyes.

"Are you okay, Violet?" Raina asked.

"What do you care?"

"I do care. I care for everyone in my town."

"You act like you own the place. But you don't. You're a nobody like me, and a bastard child. Yes, I know where you come from. Mama told me. So, you don't own anything. Old Kat does."

The sting of Violet's words ripped through Raina, as she realized this woman would never see her as anyone other than an adversary. Her shoulders drooped and she twisted toward Conie, mumbling they should go.

"That's right, run away."

"What is your problem, Violet?" Conie asked.

Jumping to her feet, Violet said, "She is. Her family is. Her family stole everything from my family."

Raina hung her head and sighed. "I'm sorry you believe that, but it simply isn't true."

"Oh yeah! Old Kat's mom was having an affair with my grandfather. And when she went crazy and killed her husband then herself, he was devastated. That's why he lost his job at the manor."

Raina trembled at Violet's words. *Could this be true? Is he the one she had fallen for?*

"You don't know what you're talking about," Conie said.

Tugging on Conie's arm, Raina said, "It doesn't matter. Let's go. We should go."

"You're shivering," Conie said, looking down at Raina's hand.

"Please, let's just go."

"She knows I'm right," Violet said with a smug look.

"Even if they had an affair, it doesn't mean Raina or anyone else in her family took anything from you," Conie said.

"My grandmother was devastated by that whore seducing my grandfather. But he was never okay again and neither were they. Oh, they tried and that's when they had my mama, but that woman ruined my grandfather, which is why he took his own life. So yeah, they have stolen everything from us."

Raina stared at Violet who slid to a puddle of sobs on the ground. Ginny tried to comfort her, but Violet pushed her off. Raina took a step forward, but Violet's flash of hatred in her direction stopped her.

"I'm sorry for your pain." Raina wheeled around and walked away.

Conie rushed to follow her, grabbing her hand while they strode toward Jenks.

"Do you think it's true?" Conie asked.

"I know it's true," Raina said. "I didn't know it was him until this moment, but it makes sense. It all makes sense."

"She can't hold your entire family responsible for the actions of Kat's mom. And she can't hold you responsible for the actions and decisions her grandfather made, or her own father made for that matter. There isn't fault to be had here, and if she wants to blame your great-grandmother, some of the blame has to be at her grandfather's feet too."

"The pain of betrayal is a hard thing to get over, and it can pass on to future generations," Raina said.

"Do you want to leave?" Conie asked.

"No, I need to stay. It's the Nilsson way."

Conie smiled and reached out to her. She let him fold her into his arms and she took several deep breaths. She looked over his shoulder at the fire and her heart broke into pieces. She shifted her gaze and noticed Henry across the parking lot with his hat in his hand while Stacia had her arm around him.

Slipping away from Conie, Raina went to them. Henry reached out his hand to her as she approached. She squeezed it and looked at Stacia questioningly, who nodded her head.

"Henry, I'm so sorry," Raina said.

"We all are," Conie said.

"Thank you," he said.

"Can I do anything? Do you want to leave for a bit? I can keep an eye on things," Raina said.

"No, I have to stay."

"Any word on how bad this is going to be?" Conie asked.

"It's going to be a total loss," Henry said.

"Have they said?" Raina asked.

"No, but I can tell. I'm just waiting for the roof to cave in."

"We will sit with you then," Raina said.

Stacia shot Raina a look of relief and Raina knew Stacia was about to crumble.

Walking around to stand next to the woman, Raina put her arm around her. "I've got this. You grieve with your husband."

Raina didn't leave their side as the firemen fought to save as much as they could, but the blaze put up a good fight. She watched with them when part of the roof caved in. She held Stacia's hand while her employee wept, and she patted Henry's back when he was trying to catch his breath from choking back sobs.

The fire eventually lost, and Jenks walked toward them with the fire chief on his heels. Raina realized that Violet and her friends had been taken away. A larger crowd had developed, and they all stood staring forlornly at the loss of the iconic building.

"There will be a thorough investigation," Jenks said while the fire chief nodded.

"We don't believe it was intentional, but we are going to do the investigation anyway. Once that's completed, I'll get the report sent your way, Henry, so you can send it on to your insurance company," the fire chief said.

"Take your time. I'm just thankful I can rebuild, and no one was hurt as a result," Henry said.

"That's awfully generous, Henry," Stacia said.

"Believe me, I'm feeling the sting of losing this building. It was passed on to me for safekeeping and it went down on my watch."

"You can't take that notion on," Stacia said.

"Maybe, but I feel like I let the Nilsson family down."

"Nonsense." Raina said. "As representative of the Nilsson family, I say you've served the history of this building well."

Henry smiled, and they talked for a while longer. The crowd eventually dispersed when Henry and Stacia left. Raina yawned and Conie offered to take her home. She declined but said she would meet him in the morning to look closer at the damage.

It didn't take long for Raina to return home and shower before crawling into bed. She instantly fell into a deep sleep with dreams of fire and lovers on a beach. The following morning, she rushed through updating her aunt but didn't stop to eat breakfast so she could get back to the burn site as quickly as possible.

When she arrived, she crossed the police line and Conie—who was talking to Jenks—handed her a latte. Conie's sisters and Stu helped with the café so he could stay as long as he was needed. Henry and Stacia were already by the charred building peering in at the carnage. Raina sipped her creamy liquid as she walked with Conie and Jenks toward them.

No one spoke as they studied the damage. Standing at the door, Raina squinted into the shadows of the partially burned building. It was deemed a total loss so would have to come down.

"Can we walk in there or is it unsafe?" Raina asked.

"It's probably best we don't until the fire department has a chance to do what they need to do to investigate and secure the premises," Henry said.

Raina nodded as a beam of light slid across the *Vide Fjärd* and she gasped. "It survived."

"What?" Conie asked.

"The *Vide Fjärd* it looks like it might have a few burn marks on it but it's mostly intact."

"That's something," Henry said.

"And look, your desk and things look to be unharmed as well. Plus, I can make out a few other boats," Stacia said.

They continued to study the area when an idea flitted through Raina's mind. A grin spread across her face. "Henry, I think I might have an idea."

"I'm all ears."

"What would you think about building this even bigger and better than before?" Raina asked.

"I don't know if I have enough insurance money to cover it," Henry said.

"What if I signed on as a business partner as representative of the Nilsson family?" Raina asked.

Stacia tilted her head to the side. "Go on."

"What if we expanded the building this way?" Raina asked, motioning to the left with her arms. "We could build a bigger section where the current building stands to get all the boats big and small in here. We could create a larger opening in the back to allow them to come off the water or move them back into it a little more easily. We could add an additional two-story space over here to the left, as office space for you, and the rest could be a museum of the nautical history of the town, featuring the

Vide Fjärd. We could take your small office building and double or triple its size into the field behind it and create a second museum dedicated to the overall history of the town. The boatwerks would be owned and operated solely by you and the rest of it would be run by the Nilsson Historical Foundation I'm going to create for museums and historical sites in the Willow Bay area."

The group fell silent as Raina looked from one face to the other and panic crept in. She worried it was a stupid idea or she had overstepped.

"Well?" Raina asked. "No one is saying anything."

Stacia hugged Raina. "Your aunt will be so proud. I think it's a splendid idea."

"I do too, for what it's worth," Jenks said.

"I couldn't have come up with a better idea if I wanted to," Conie said, beaming with pride.

Henry patted Raina on the shoulder before engulfing her in a bear hug. "Spoken like a true Nilsson."

Chapter Twenty-Five

Fumbling with her napkin, Raina stared at her aunt, trying to find the words to talk to her about the conversation she'd had with Violet. It had been several days since the fire, and she had been avoiding the topic.

"Raina, you're making me nervous," Aunt Kat said.

"I'm sorry. I'm trying to figure out how to say this," Raina said.

"Is it more about the idea for the history foundation and helping Henry rebuild? I hope you know I love the idea and I love the initiative you have in coming up with new ideas and taking them on. Which reminds me, I've been meaning to talk with you about something. But let's talk about this first."

Growing concerned, Raina said, "No it can wait. Is everything okay with you?"

"Well about that," Aunt Kat said, fumbling with her own napkin. She took a sip of wine and set it down on the table. She smoothed the tablecloth and looked out the window.

"Okay, now you're scaring me."

Aunt Kat reached across the table and patted Raina's hand. "I don't mean to. I'm not dying, at least not yet anyway. My heart isn't as strong as it used to be, and my doctor has encouraged me to slow down. She believes retirement would be the best."

"What's wrong with your heart?" Raina asked.

"Before I went to find you, I had a small heart attack and had to have surgery. They have done all they can do to keep it going for now, but it's much weaker and I have to control my stress level."

"A heart attack. Oh, Aunt Kat. Why didn't you tell me sooner? How can I help?"

"I would like to pass all my responsibilities on to you," Aunt Kat said.

"Oh my. Um. I don't know if I'm ready for that."

"I believe you are. But I understand the hesitation, so I was thinking we could do it in stages. You have already taken on some of the responsibilities, so we can just make it official. As you feel more confident in these other areas, you can start managing them as well."

"That sounds like a doable plan. But, Aunt Kat, are you sure this is best for you? While I admit I'm hesitant to take over, I don't want things to be too much for you either."

"Spending time with you while you learn this is not stressful for me. It's actually helping me. It's exciting to know I'm not going to let the legacy die with me."

"Okay, but when it becomes too much, please don't keep me in the dark. You must tell me, and I'll do my absolute best to take over and make you proud."

"You already make me proud," Aunt Kat said. "Now, wasn't there something else you needed to talk with me about?"

Raina paused. "Um. It can wait for another day."

"If you're sure. You seemed to be concerned about it."

"No, it's nothing. It can wait."

"Are you sure?"

"I am," Raina said.

"If there isn't anything more, I think I'll retire to my room to do some light reading until I go to sleep," Aunt Kat said.

"That sounds like a lovely plan. I might just do the same," Raina said, thinking of the journals.

Raina said goodnight and went to her room. She changed into pajama pants and a t-shirt and curled up by the fireplace. She picked up the latest journal she was reading and found where she left off. Would the journals hit different since she now knew who the mystery man was? Would all the information she was gathering hurt her aunt? As she deliberated, she realized the answers would not sway her from her task.

October 15, 1947

It's been weeks since I've seen *him*. I blame it on Stefan. He's been home recently and surprisingly attentive. Melia tells me he is trying because he knows he needs to do better. But all I want now is for him to leave me alone. I can't believe I feel this way, but it's true.

He was gone fighting in the war, and when he returned, we tried to get to know each other again. But having a family business and little girls takes its toll, I think. At least Mother always said as much to me. I suppose that's why she always tells me to find my own projects and focus on them. But what project could I possibly find here in the middle of nowhere?

Okay, I'll admit part of it is I don't feel like I belong here. I loved Stefan and I loved the idea of living in such a wild place, and I loved the idea of being a part of the top family in the community. But fantasy and reality are two different things. I've realized how silly and selfish I used to be. And now I'm in love with a man who is poorer than I could ever imagine. Which no longer matters.

Maybe I should find a project. Maybe it could be something to do with gardening. It would only be a natural and normal thing to have him help me with things on occasion. Does Mother have any flirtations with other men? I know Father does. But does she? I suppose I'm looking for a way to feel less guilty.

October 16, 1947

I saw *him* today. He smiled at me across the yard. I smiled at *him,* then Stefan came around the corner and my smile froze. Stefan thought I was smiling at him and crossed to me. He asked me if I wanted to go for a walk. I couldn't possibly—not in front of *him*—so I declined and suggested maybe later.

The girls came running out of the house and asked us to go for a walk as a family. How could I deny my girls? So, we went for a walk. And it ended up being a glorious day. Stefan was kind. The girls were brilliant and funny.

What am I supposed to do now? I am so torn between the potential of having my little family back and having this other man as my own. Or is it silly of me to think this other man could ever be my own, especially since he is much younger than I am.

October 17, 1947

Stefen left today, abruptly. He said he had to go to Duluth, then St. Paul, and possibly out to New York, and he had no idea how long he would be gone. No hug, no kiss goodbye. He barely even came into my room to tell me.

He hesitated when he left, and I considered telling him I loved him, but I couldn't quite say it, and neither could he. You would think it would make me feel better since I'm falling for someone else, but it hurts, and it makes me realize how much I still love my husband.

I need to end this.

October 18, 1947

I went to *him* in the greenhouse today. I knew he would be alone. I told him we needed to talk. He asked if this was it.

If I was ending it, and I told him I think it's best. He said he would meet me at our place tomorrow evening.

I dread that time. I dread it because I think I love him. I dread it because I don't want to hurt him. I dread it because this will be one of the hardest things I've ever had to do.

October 19, 1947

I met *him* at what has become our place—the old boathouse. I tried to break it off, but he wouldn't let me. He told me how much he loved me, and he knew how hard it was to keep going like this. I tried to leave but he stopped me. He grabbed my arms and shook me. When I told him he was hurting me, he let go and jumped back. He told me it was because he loved me so much.

I told him this was becoming too big. We couldn't keep doing this because it was only going to end up hurting everyone involved. He told me we needed to come up with a plan to escape Willow Bay and our families.

I told him I couldn't leave my girls. He told me it would only be temporary, and for a moment I believed him. In the end, I told him that we had to be done. I left him standing in the doorway of the old boathouse calling my name.

I didn't look back. I couldn't look back because if I did, I would have run into his arms.

October 29, 1947

I haven't written since that night because the words wouldn't come. I've been in a daze. My girls and Melia have worried about me, but I had to do it. I just had to. But why am I in so much pain?

October 30, 1947

I decided to start a new project. Gardening. I asked *him* to teach me. He looked straight through me and said it wasn't a good idea. I asked him why. He grabbed my hand and squeezed it hard. It hurt. When I yanked back, he said I knew why and left.

I wanted to call to him. I wanted to run after him. I wanted to tell him that although we could no longer be lovers, I still needed him, and this was the best solution I could think of to ease my pain.

But I said nothing and let him walk away.

October 31, 1947

Melia agreed to take the girls into town for the trick or treating and bobbing for apples downtown because I wasn't feeling well. I decided to go for a walk and found myself at our place. I cried. I cried out for *him* and then he was there.

I asked him why he came to the boathouse, and he said he just couldn't go home after work so decided to come here. He explained that most nights he struggled and would come here until he could trust himself not to think of me once he went home.

How did we get here? How did I let this happen? I told him I would leave to give him space, but he asked me to stay. He wondered if I really wanted to take up gardening and I shared that I did, that I needed to do something productive with my time or I was going to go crazy. He told me he would help me on one condition. I whispered that I would do anything for him.

He told me I could never leave him again. Was it his words that scared me or the wild look in his eyes as he caressed my cheek that caused me to pause. But his lips on my mouth and his hands in my hair made me forget he'd made me afraid, and I let him take me to the depths of our desire.

Chapter
Twenty-Six

The water slid down Raina's face and she sighed. She swiped at the droplets, opened her eyes, and shut off the shower. She grabbed her towel and dried off. She couldn't get what she read in the journals the night before out of her mind. The affair her great-grandmother was involved in was turning abusive.

She stopped reading in the middle of November, and she was sure he was becoming more possessive of her. They began working together on her gardening hobby, but the more they spent time together in the greenhouse, the more jealous he had become, especially if she mentioned Stefan being home or the girls. Raina had stopped reading, because her eyes had grown heavy, but she was worried about what she would find next.

Raina decided to wait to tell her aunt any of what she was discovering until she had read all the journals. She didn't want to speculate or share her findings prematurely, and in the end be wrong. Especially if her great-grand-mother's lover had been Donny Strand. But she decided she would talk to Conie.

When she had told him she needed to talk to him in private, he invited her over for a late dinner. It was Sunday so the pub would be closing at its usual earlier time. They would be eating with his sisters, but he promised they would also have time to talk. Raina was excited but was also nervous, realizing she had never actually been to his house.

Dressing in comfortable jeans and her favorite long sleeve shirt, Raina finished getting ready, but stopped in to see Aunt Kat on the way out. Her aunt had already eaten and was reading quietly in the living room.

"Have a lovely time, Raina," Aunt Kat said.

"I will. I'm not sure how long I'll be, so please don't feel like you need to wait up for me."

"If you decide to stay the night, just give the house a call and let someone know so I won't worry."

"Aunt Kat! Like I would stay the night," Raina said.

"One never knows how these things will go."

"Did these things go this way for you?" Raina asked with a teasing grin.

"A lady never tells," Aunt Kat said with a twinkle in her eye.

Raina laughed, kissed her aunt on the cheek, and promised to send any important updates on her whereabouts. She slung her purse over her shoulder and picked up the sweater she knew she would need later. Waving goodbye, she tossed Aunt Kat one more smile and was out the door.

It didn't take long for Raina to find her way to Conie's, and she admired the beauty of the two-story Victorian house set against the backdrop of the forest trees behind it. They had a large, treed lot with a stone fence running along the front of it. It looked like there used to be a gate blocking the driveway, but it now stood empty. Raina drove through the opening and parked in front of the house.

Annie opened the front door and waved just as Raina climbed out of the driver's seat. Raina returned the greeting and reached back into the car to grab the bottle of cabernet she'd stopped to get on the way. With sweater, purse, and wine in tow, she made her way onto the porch.

"This place is beautiful," Raina said.

"Thank you. It's been in our family for almost a hundred years."

"That's wonderful. It's good to see you. Hope you like Cab?" Raina asked, lifting the bottle of wine.

"I'll never say no to a glass of wine even if it isn't my favorite," Annia said, giggling.

Holding the door open, Annie motioned for Raina to enter. Noticing the shoes and jackets along the hooks and cubbies to the left of the door, Raina slid her flats off her feet. She was thankful she had painted her toes for the evening.

"Nice color," Annie said, pointing to Raina's feet.

"Thanks, Celia helped Aunt Kat and I with a spa day in the living room earlier this morning while we went over a new idea I had on providing more options for tourists to stay when they come to Willow Bay."

"Always coming up with new ways to improve."

"Just trying to do my part."

"Are you hogging our guest, Annie?" Murie said, walking down the hallway.

"We just walked in," Annie said.

Raina looked around the space for the first time and instantly loved the layout of the home. "It's my fault. I was taking in the grandeur of your place," Raina said.

Murie caught her glancing around and explained that the stairs to the right of the entrance went up to the second-floor bedrooms and bathrooms. She motioned for Raina to take a peek at the large living room just off the entryway to the left. Raina could picture herself curled up with a book in front of the bay windows. It was connected to a dining room through an archway, and Murie explained the kitchen was just beyond there. Back out into the entryway, Raina noticed the kitchen at the end of the hallway and Murie said there was a bathroom and office on the main floor as well.

"It's not Willow Bay Manor, but it's home," Murie said.

"Yes, well you seem to forget I've only lived at the manor for a short time. I grew up in a three-bedroom apartment above my Gramma D's Sip and Shop."

"Sip and shop?" Annie asked.

"Yes, it was a coffee shop, bookstore, and gift shop all in one. It was the only coffee shop and bookstore in a three-town radius, so she did pretty well."

"Raina," Annie said. "I didn't realize you were so familiar with running businesses like ours."

"That's okay. I haven't really talked about my past much."

"Okay, I keep hearing voices, but no one bothered to tell me she was here yet," Conie said, crossing the living room.

Raina giggled, but her eyes grew wide when Conie kissed her in front of his sisters. Her cheeks burned, and she tried to hide her face.

"You shouldn't feel embarrassed," Murie said, grinning widely. "It's fun watching you two become closer."

"Is it just us?" Raina asked.

"Stu had to run into Grand Marais and get some things for the pub for Tuesday," Annie said.

"Are you guys dating?" Raina asked.

"We've been seeing each other on and off for about five years." Annie said. "We're on again, I guess."

"Is there a reason for on again, off again?" Raina asked. "Or am I being too nosey?"

"You're fine," Annie said.

"Stu wants to marry her." Conie said. "Annie wants to wait. Stu gets impatient, but then realizes Annie is worth waiting for."

"I agree, Annie is worth the wait," Raina said.

"I knew I liked you," Annie said.

"Are we going to eat dinner here in the foyer too?" Murie asked with sarcasm.

"Oh, stop being so fussy," Annie said. "Come on, Raina, let's go open your wine."

Raina followed Annie into the kitchen. She wasn't sure what she was expecting, but she should have known it would be a true gourmet kitchen since Conie was a chef running his own restaurant and café. There was a cute eat-in kitchen nook connecting to the dining room.

But what she really loved was what was in between the nook and cooking area. A sliding glass door opened to a large back patio. Part of it was screened in for those buggy nights, but the rest of the space was an outdoor kitchen complete with small fridge, pizza oven, grill, smoker, bar, and counter space for prep. Beyond the patio was a steppingstone path leading to a large fire pit, with Adirondack chairs scattered around it and fancy tiki torches already lit for the evening. The whole setup beckoned Raina and she stepped forward.

"Conie put in a lot of work on the patio and fire pit. We spend a lot of time out there," Murie said.

"I love it," Raina said.

"Perfect, let's go outside then," Conie said. "We're going to grill anyway."

"You haven't started dinner yet?" Raina asked, checking her watch.

"You're not early," Conie said. "Sunday nights are just a pitch in, family bonding, cooking time for our family."

"And we were waiting for you to join us," Annie said.

"Oh, I see," Raina said.

"We started doing it after we all moved back after college," Murie said. "It's a way for us to stay connected with our busy lives."

"How many other people have joined family night?" Raina asked.

"Um, I believe you're the first," Conie said, pulling a container of food out of the fridge.

"He's right," Annie said, grabbing a basket and handing it to Raina.

Raina shifted the bottle of wine and sweater she still carried so she could grab the basket and watched the siblings gather the rest of the food. She had placed her purse on the bench by the door and was glad she had left it there when she was handed an empty bowl as well.

Murie opened the sliding door. "Come on, Raina, let's start our dishes and pour that wine."

"Sounds good," Raina said, following Murie outside.

Murie put her food on the outdoor counter and rummaged in a drawer selecting a bottle opener. She grabbed the cabernet from Raina while Raina studied the food items in her basket. It looked like she would be making potato salad.

"Do you like to cook?" Annie asked.

"Yes, I suppose I do," Raina said.

"Can you make potato salad?" Conie asked.

"I make a killer potato salad actually. It was a recipe from my Gramma D."

"Excellent," Annie said.

The wine was passed around while everyone focused on their own food. Raina was thankful the potatoes were already cooked and prepped for her. Murie kneaded dough she'd obviously started earlier in the day. Annie focused on cutting up root vegetables to roast, and Conie prepped the chicken.

There wasn't a lot of talking initially while everyone worked, and Raina enjoyed watching the siblings interact while she mixed up her dish. She would occasionally ask where she could find an ingredient, but mostly rummaged in the outdoor kitchen or inside until she found it. It was strange looking through a drawer the first time, but by the time she finished putting together the salad, she felt more at home.

As Murie finished putting together her bread, Raina realized she was making Swedish cardamom rolls. She hadn't eaten them since her mother died, and her mouth watered at the memory of Gramma D making them.

"Do you sell those at the café, and I just missed it?" Raina asked.

"No, we don't. This is a Tuva Nilsson recipe. Tuva gave it to someone in our family and we only make it for us."

"Can I see the recipe?" Raina asked.

"Sure," Conie said. "Let me go see if I can find it. We all do it from memory now, but we still have the recipe somewhere."

Raina offered to go with him so she could put the potato salad in the fridge until it was time for dinner. She found a spot for the bowl while Conie looked through a recipe box. Finding what he was looking for, Conie handed it to Raina, who studied the worn-out recipe card.

"It looks exactly like Gramma D's. That's if I'm remembering correctly," Raina said.

"I would imagine it's the same one since it came from Tuva," Conie said.

"To have such pieces of my past intermingled with this town and Aunt Kat and now you is such a strange feeling."

"I can't imagine," Conie said.

Handing the recipe card back to him, Raina moved to go back outside. Conie caught her hand and asked her to wait a second while he put the card away. When done, he tugged on Raina's hand while stepping closer to her. Raina waited for what she knew was going to be a deeper kiss than the one they had when she first arrived.

When they came up for air, Raina straightened her clothes. Conie ran his fingers through his hair and smiled sheepishly at her.

"You take my breath away, Raina."

"I could say the same."

"We should head back outside, or I will have to take you upstairs."

Raina's heart skipped a beat, but she didn't say anything more as she followed Conie back outside. Annie and Murie teased the couple, and Conie said something to relieve the tension. The rest of the dinner prep was filled with laughter and rambunctious talking between the siblings, and Raina soaked it all in.

When dinner was ready, everyone grabbed a plate and made their way to the fire pit Annie had lit right before the chicken finished cooking. Annie retrieved another bottle of wine, opened it, and refilled everyone's glasses. The conversation died down while everyone ate, minus a few murmurs of how delicious the food was.

After everyone finished eating, Murie and Annie offered to tidy up, but Raina wouldn't have it. The four worked together to clean up the mess and as the final bowl was being put into the dishwasher, Murie popped open another bottle of wine.

"Goodness, keep this up and I'm going to have to find someone to drive me home," Raina said.

"Or you could stay here," Annie said with a wink. "It's getting pretty late anyway."

"What would people say?" Raina asked.

"I hope someday you can stop worrying about that," Conie said.

"What do you mean?" Raina asked.

"You struggle with worrying about what people say about you," Annie said. "My hope is you can learn to let that go. Because you're amazing."

"Conie understands why I struggle," Raina said, "but I'm sure it gets annoying."

"No, we just love you. Was it bad growing up?" Murie asked.

Raina took a sip of wine and looked out the window before sharing the story of her childhood while everyone listened intently. She explained what it was like growing up as a child out of wedlock and being judged constantly. They made their way back out to the fire pit as she finished.

"So, you see, not all bad. Yes, some stuff was difficult. But Mom and Gramma D worked hard to make sure I still felt loved and accepted for who I was. I still often feel like I am being watched all the time and people are waiting for me to mess up."

"I hope you feel loved and accepted by Willow Bay," Annie said.

"And more importantly by us," Murie said.

"I'm beginning to. Years of habit are hard to overcome," Raina said.

"Understandably so," Conie said.

The conversation deviated to lighter subjects with more teasing amongst the siblings. When another bottle of wine was selected, Raina decided she would just have to stay the night. She excused herself to go call the manor to give the update and to stop at the restroom. When she returned, more laughter ensued as the fire was stoked.

They talked for another hour until Annie yawned. When Raina glanced at her watch, she was surprised it was almost midnight. Even though the pub was closed on Mondays, the rest of the shops were open, including the café, and Raina knew it would be an early morning. The siblings put out the fire and extinguished the tiki torches while Raina gathered the wine glasses.

"Just put the glasses in the sink," Annie said. "I'll wash them in the morning."

Raina followed her instructions but still rinsed them out. As she was finishing, Annie and Murie said good night and left her alone with Conie. He sidled up to her, kissing her gently. As he moved away, he stifled a yawn.

"Let's go to bed," Raina said.

Conie took her hand and led her up to his room. A set of women's pajamas lay on the bed and Raina was thankful Conie's sisters thought of her. She changed her clothes and crawled under the covers.

Moving closer to Raina, Conie put his arm around her and kissed her on the side of her head. "Goodnight, my beautiful Raina. This was a fun evening."

"It *was* a fun evening. Thank you for letting me be a part of it," Raina said, and drifted off to sleep.

Chapter Twenty-Seven

Opening her eyes slowly, Raina looked around the room. It took her mere seconds to remember where she was, especially when she caught sight of a smiling Conie holding a mug of steaming coffee. She sat up as he put the cup on the nightstand and kissed her cheek.

"Seeing you sleeping in my bed does something funny to my insides," Conie said with a devilish grin.

"Oh yeah?" Raina said, pushing the covers aside and stretching. She picked up the warm mug and breathed in the nutty aroma. Sighing, she took a sip and closed her eyes.

"Breakfast is almost ready, but no rush. Just come down when you're ready."

"Your sisters?"

"They have already eaten and left about a half an hour ago. We didn't get a chance to talk last night, so they are helping Stu open the café for me. We can take as long as we need to."

"You guys are the absolute coolest people I know."

"What do you mean?"

"You're just. I don't know. I guess I never had any siblings, so it's fun to watch you tease each other, help each other, and show your love to one another. I never had that, so it's awesome to see."

"Trust me, we have our fights and disagreements just like everyone else. One time, Annie didn't speak to me for a whole week. She would talk to Stu or Murie and have them pass on the message, even when I was standing right there."

Raina laughed, causing some of the dark liquid to slide over the rim of her mug. She caught the drip before it spilled and motioned to Conie to head back to the kitchen.

"I'll be down in a minute," Raina said.

"Bathroom, as you remember, is over there. If you want to shower, please feel free to do so. I set out a towel and washcloth just in case. And I will see you in a few minutes."

Deciding a shower might be a good way to clear her head after having so much to drink the night before, Raina turned on the water. She tried to hurry though as she didn't want to ruin the breakfast Conie was making. She slipped back into the same jeans and T-shirt, but it was a chilly morning, and her sweater was somewhere downstairs. She rummaged through Conie's closet, and finding a cozy flannel shirt, she put it on. She grabbed her coffee mug and went downstairs.

As she neared the kitchen, the latest hits played on the radio while Conie hummed along. She stood in the doorway watching him dance to the music while he filled their plates. He flashed her a grin and motioned for her to go sit at the table in the corner.

Raina obliged and scooted across the bench. The sun was bright, shining through the window, and it twinkled off her glass filled with orange juice. Conie plopped a fresh mug of coffee in front of her and went back to grab their plates filled with quiche, breakfast potatoes, leftover cardamom rolls, and fruit.

The smells engulfed her, and Raina's mouth watered in anticipation. Her stomach growled as Conie positioned her plate in front of her and they both laughed. He sat down next to her and took a sip of his orange juice.

"You have out done yourself," Raina said.

"It's not every day I get to cook for someone special," Conie said.

Raina took her first couple of bites but watched Conie enjoy the meal. She knew with every passing day this man was becoming more important to her. She tried not to let fear grip her, but it was hard to fight against it. Every man in her mother and grandmother's lives had disappeared on them. She tried to believe Conie wouldn't disappear on her, but it was difficult to trust he wouldn't.

"You look upset," Conie said.

"Oh, it's nothing," Raina said.

"It wasn't nothing, but if you don't want to talk about it, that's okay.

"I was thinking about us."

"And that upsets you?"

"How do I explain? My father chose to not be a part of my life. He literally left me behind to go live in another state. He left my mom and she never recovered from his betrayal. My grandmother was also a single mom—my grandfather chose not to be in the picture either."

"So, you're wondering if you can trust me not to leave. You're wondering if you can trust me with your heart," Conie said.

"Yes. I hate that I have these fears and doubts, but I can't help it."

Conie put his fork down and grabbed Raina's hand in both of his. He kissed it. "I can't promise you I will never hurt you. And I can't tell you I see our entire future. But I do know what I feel for you is real. And I will do everything in my power to never hurt you in a way that destroys our relationship. I'm not going anywhere, Raina. I want to see this through."

"I want to see this through too," Raina said.

"Okay, now that's settled. Tell me what you wanted to talk about," Conie said, letting go of her hand to return to eating his food.

Raina took a couple of bites trying to figure out where to begin. Taking a deep breath she said, "Shortly after the *Vide Fjärd* washed up on shore, I learned more about the scandal surrounding my great-grandmother and my great-grandfather. My aunt took me up to a room in the attic, which was filled with boxes and trunks of our family history. The purpose was to help me find clues about the boat wreckage, but I discovered stacks of journals my great-grandmother wrote in."

"I bet that's been exciting to read," Conie said.

"Yes, and no."

"Is this what you have been wanting to talk with me about?"

"I think something else happened that may have led to the murder suicide."

"What do you mean?"

"Every journal is a different month, and right now, I'm in the month of November before their death. Things with her lover are looking a bit, I don't know, abusive maybe."

"Have you told Kat?"

"No, I don't want to. Unless you think I should. I just feel like I'm missing something. That we are missing something. I thought about asking for a copy of the police report from that day but worried it might get back to Aunt Kat. And I don't want to alarm her."

"I think waiting to say anything until you find out more is a good idea," Conie said and took a sip of his coffee.

"Okay, that makes me feel better. I don't want her to think I'm deliberately keeping it from her to hurt her," Raina said and took another bite of quiche.

"No, that time was hard on her and her family. Your family. I think getting more information is a good idea. Jenks usually comes in the café a couple times a week to get coffee. The next time he comes in I'll ask him to get me a copy of the police report."

"But wouldn't it still get back to Aunt Kat?"

"Not if I ask him to keep it between us. Trust me. It will be okay."

"Okay. I trust you."

Changing the subject, they talked about lighter things and focused on finishing their breakfast. Raina cleared the dishes while Conie ran to get in the shower. Before diving into washing the dishes, she noticed the wine glasses were already cleaned and put away.

Raina was finishing the last pan when Conie walked in, ready to take on another day at the café. Her heart skipped a beat, and she focused on drying.

"It's really nice seeing you in my kitchen," Conie said, coming to stand close to her. "It's like you were meant to be here."

Putting the pan on the counter, Raina wrapped her arms around Conie's neck and pulled him into a heated kiss. His hands cupped her bottom as he lifted her to sit on the counter. Raina wrapped her legs around him and deepened the kiss while Conie's hand slid up the back of her shirt.

Moaning, Conie backed away. "I really hate that I have to go to work."

"Me too," Raina said, trying to catch her breath.

They stared into each other's eyes before Conie gently pecked Raina on the lips. "You will have to come back."

"I'll be back."

"How about Sunday."

"You mean this Sunday coming up?"

"Yes. And I think I need to start seeing you every day. I can't quite get enough of you," Conie said with a chuckle.

"I have no problem showing up at your work every day, especially if it will lead to hot kisses and delicious meals."

Conie threw back his head and laughed. "Hot kisses and delicious meals will always be on the menu if I'm there."

"Come to dinner at my house this week. Stay the night. Aunt Kat won't care. And it will be a bit more private than having your sisters in the next room."

"Which night?"

Kissing him again, Raina drove them to the edge but held back just before going over it.

"How about tonight?" they said in unison.

Conie chuckled while helping Raina off the counter. He commented on how lovely she looked in his shirt. He suggested she keep it until they saw each other again because he was going to enjoy taking it off of her later. She giggled while she gathered her sweater and went to find her purse.

Sliding her feet into her flats, Raina put her purse over her shoulder. "I had a really good time."

"Me too," Conie said, giving her a quick peck on the lips.

Raina opened the front door. "So, are we on for tonight?"

"You betcha."

They kissed once more, and Raina left for home. She watched Conie in her rearview mirror until he was out of sight. She rounded a corner and gasped at the view of the lake below her.

Her beauty continues to surprise me every day. No wonder our families settled here.

Chapter Twenty-Eight

The leaves were changing on the trees, and the winds of fall were starting to blow across the water. Raina squinted to block the sun as she rode her bike into town. She shivered and regretted not taking her car, especially with the large bag slung over her shoulder.

The investigation had been completed on the fire at the marina, and Henry was waiting for the insurance check. He knew roughly how much it was going to be, though, and they wanted to go ahead and start putting together a plan for the rebuild. They could have met at the manor, but Raina wanted to see Conie, so she suggested they meet for lunch at the pub—her treat.

When she walked into the restaurant, Conie crossed to greet her, kissing her on the cheek. "Gracious, you're frozen."

"The wind off the water is a bit brisk today, and I made the wrong decision in riding my bike," Raina said.

"Let me get you a warm cup of coffee while you wait for your lunch, and then I'll bring you a tall stout to go with your meal. You will be warmed up in no time."

"That sounds lovely," Raina said, kissing him squarely on the lips.

Conie shivered, put his arm around her and ran his hand up and down her arm. "You're going to make me cold."

"Henry here yet?" Raina asked.

"Not yet, but I have you at a booth close to the counter," Conie said.

"I see, so you can watch me."

"No. So I can stare at your beauty."

"Oh my god, you two," Annie said, giving Raina a hug.

"She doesn't like it when I sweet-talk you."

"Um, that wasn't sweet talk. That was puppy love crap," Annie said.

"Should I start talking that way to you?" Stu asked. He was behind the counter making a mixed drink, but the look he shot Annie sizzled.

"Enough now, you guys are going to make your customers in here uncomfortable," Raina said.

"Nothing we haven't heard before," a lady sitting at a table close by said.

The door to the pub banged open and the wind ushered Henry in with his arms full of papers and a notebook. He struggled to close the door but once secured, he caught sight of Raina and crossed to her.

"Conie, Raina, Annie, Stu," Henry said, nodding to each of them.

"I'm excited to get started," Raina said, rubbing her hands together.

"Me too."

"I've got you over there," Conie said, pointing at the booth. "Go sit. I'll bring you some menus and coffee."

Raina and Henry settled, and both laid out what they wanted to show the other.

"You go first since this was your idea," Henry said and took a sip of the hot coffee Conie had placed in front of him.

Raina smoothed out a large piece of paper and showed him a generic drawing of the building. "Obviously, this isn't to scale, but I was thinking we could have the *Vide Fjärd* in the lobby area. I want it to be the first thing people see when they walk in. I figured a nice plaque or write-up on the wall would be good so people could learn its history. It could be a way to honor my late uncle."

"What if we blew up the picture of the twins and hung it somewhere nearby?" Henry said.

"Oh, I like that idea. Okay, so here is where the front desk could be," Raina said, pointing with a pencil. "People can pay a nominal fee to get in, get brochures and even maps of the different historical sites throughout the area. A gift shop could go there, where we could sell locally made items. Your offices could be off of here."

"Do you want an office?" Henry asked. "You should probably have an office here too."

"You think I need one?"

"It might be nice for you to have one."

"What if we had several offices and decide later who needs them, plus an employee lounge-like area?"

"Good idea," Henry said.

"I was thinking we could have an entrance off the offices into the boatwerks area, but you could have a door off your office too," Raina said.

"I like that," Henry said.

Raina continued to point out different features and ideas as she went over the plans. Henry offered suggestions or nodded his agreement as she went on. At one point Conie interrupted them to get their lunch orders and stopped them again when he brought out their food.

Taking a swig of her stout, Raina sat back in her seat and noticed the bustling in the pub. She hadn't noticed how full it had become. As she glanced around, she caught sight of Violet and Donna standing close to the counter. Violet must not have noticed her because she was talking cheerfully to Conie who was making selections on the register.

"Everything okay?" Henry asked, looking around. "Oh, never mind."

"I don't think she has seen us yet," Raina said.

"Perhaps she won't notice."

"One can hope."

"She is sure sending your Conie some steamy looks."

"I don't think he is noticing it, or he is pretending not to."

When Conie walked to the back, Donna shot Violet a look that said stop it. Violet rolled her eyes and looked around the room. Her annoyed expression turned hostile as soon as she saw Raina.

"Well so much for that," Raina said, turning to Henry.

"Let's just focus on eating."

"Good idea," Raina said and smiled, taking a bite of her sandwich.

"Don't go over there, Violet. Just leave her alone," Donna said.

Violet yanked her arm away from her mother, said something Raina couldn't hear, and stormed out of the pub.

Donna sauntered over to the booth and nodded at Henry. "Look I'm sorry for all the trouble my daughter has caused you both lately."

"Flames of hatred have been fueled on this one," Henry said.

"I know what you're saying, Henry, but it's different now."

"Why is it different?" Raina asked.

Donna paled and stared at Raina. "It's just different now."

"Is it because your daughter has caused damage to people's property in this town, and you can't blame the Nilssons for that too?" Henry asked.

"That was harsh, Henry," Donna said.

"Your lot tends to stir things up against the Nilssons and for what reason?" Henry asked.

"My father—"

"We have heard it all before," Henry said. "Your father was slighted. But are you sure that's the way it was, Donna. Seems to me not giving him a job goes against everything they stand for. And everyone here also knows what a lousy drunk and worker he was."

"That wasn't until the end, and you know it."

"Do we though? Do we all really know what happened?"

The blood drained from Raina's face, and she looked down at her food.

"You know something, don't you?" Donna said.

Raina looked up at the woman and locked eyes with her. "I know probably about as much as you do. And something tells me neither of us is sharing secrets. Sometimes the truth isn't something you want stirred up."

"Maybe your family wants to hide behind secrets and lies, but my family doesn't," Donna said.

"Everything okay here?" Conie asked, handing Donna a bag of food.

"Yes," Donna said, snatching the sack away from him.

"Have a pleasant day," Conie said.

Donna didn't say another word as she huffed past him. She whirled around at the door sending another glare at Raina and left.

"What was that about?" Conie asked.

"Secrets about the past," Raina said.

"Is she sure she wants to go there?" Conie asked.

"My guess is she doesn't know all the facts," Raina said.

"Have you discovered anything else?" Conie asked.

"Discovered anything else of what?" Henry asked.

Raina shot Conie a look. "Nothing, just some old journals I'm reading. Please make sure this doesn't get back to Aunt Kat."

"If it's to protect her, you have my word."

"It is, and I hope you trust me," Raina said.

"Is there anything I can do to help?" Henry asked.

"Not really, unless you can tell me anything about that time."

"Donna was in beauty school when her dad took his life. The only thing I remember is the old rumors about the manor not giving his job back kept circling around. Donna's mother blamed the Nilssons because of it. Donna left for a while but came back pregnant and with a new husband. She lost the baby, and it took a while for her to get pregnant with Violet. She told everyone it was due to stress and said it was stress caused by the death of her father and how hard things were on her mother. And the blame fell at the Nilsson family door again."

"Such a hard story. Not unlike ours, only we aren't blaming anyone," Raina said. "Sorry, that must have sounded a bit snooty."

"No, it didn't," Conie said.

"It's true though, isn't it?" Henry said.

"I'm sorry things have been hard for them. I really am," Raina said.

Conie was called away and he said he would return in a bit. Raina changed the subject and dove back in to showing Henry her ideas. The two talked for another hour, going over details before they wrapped up the conversation. Henry said he had the perfect builders in mind and Raina agreed he should contact them to see if they could take on the job. They confirmed their next meeting, and Henry left.

Promising another stout and a drive home, Conie suggested Raina hang out at the bar for a bit. She obliged and sipped her beer while they talked about various aspects of the Nilsson business they were both working on.

"Oh, I almost forgot. I got the report from Jenks," Conie said.

"That should have been the first thing you told me today."

"What can I say? I was knocked off my feet by your beauty, and everything flew out of my mind," Conie said with a smile.

"Ugh, again," Annie said. "I swear every time I walk in here you two are ogling each other."

"Maybe you should stay in the bookstore," Conie said.

"I would love to, but I came to give your dishes back and to give Stu a kiss," Annie said.

"Now who is being sappy," Conie said.

"Whatever," Annie said and disappeared into the back.

"Have you read the report?" Raina asked.

"No, I felt like you should be the one to read it first."

"Is it here?" Raina asked.

"It's at home. He gave it to me yesterday, but I didn't want to leave it here. I meant to bring it with me this morning but was in a rush and forgot it."

"How about you run it by my place later this evening when you get off work?"

"It will be a little later since we close at eight tonight."

"I don't care. I'll wait up for you. I'll leave the side entrance unlocked, so let yourself in. I'll notify the staff."

"Okay, deal," Conie said.

"Bring a change of clothes and you can just stay the night," Raina said.

"It just keeps getting better and better."

Giggling, Raina said, "I'll read some, on the journals until you get there. Maybe I'll find out more information before you arrive."

"Sounds like a plan," Conie said.

"Looks like you're getting busy again. I can ride my bike home," Raina said.

"No, give me about ten minutes and I should be able to take you," Conie said.

The ten minutes changed into thirty before Conie could take a break, but he kept his word and delivered Raina home as promised. Raina put her bike away and went upstairs to shower. She was chilled to the core from her ride to town earlier and was looking forward to the hot water warming her bones.

As she was getting dressed, she slid on Conie's flannel again. It was fun helping him find new ways to take it off of her.

Chapter Twenty-Nine

November 22, 1947

I'm not sure about this man I've fallen for. He can be so gentle and sweet one minute and the next so possessive and almost mean. He doesn't like it when I talk about the girls, so I only share if what I'm doing with them affects the time I can spend with him. But even then, I have to be careful how I word it.

The girls bounded into the greenhouse today and his face turned so red. I couldn't tell if he was trying to hide his feelings of adoration for me or if he was mad my attention was elsewhere. When they left, he kissed me passionately, but there was a possessiveness there that hadn't been there before. If I hadn't pulled away when I did, who knows what would have happened? We have to be more careful. I have to be more careful.

November 23, 1947

He demanded I meet him later this evening in our spot. But I couldn't get away. He is going to be spitting mad and hurt I didn't get there. I worry what the consequences will be. Maybe he will break things off with me. Perhaps that would be better. It isn't as fun as it was when things first started, nor as exciting.

What have I gotten myself into?

November 24, 1947

He was so angry at me. I've never seen anyone so angry. He bruised my arms with his grasp. I was sure he was going to yell but he didn't. How anyone could sound so mean and hateful while whispering is beyond my comprehension. I was actually afraid he was going to hurt me besides my bruised arms.

This needs to stop, but I think I might be in over my head.

November 25, 1947

I met *him* at our place tonight. All anger, all meanness was gone. He was so tender. So, loving. He kissed my bruises and apologized and explained that he was scared I had finally broken things off with him. Usually, our lovemaking is frantic and full of unstoppable passion. But this time it was slow and gentle, and I could tell he was apologizing with his body and not just his words. Perhaps I was wrong about being afraid. Perhaps I'm causing his anger and I need to do better.

We won't have a moment alone together until after the Thanksgiving Holiday because we have out of town guests. He was a bit upset about that, but he understood. I will miss his touch. His hands. His body against mine.

November 26, 1947

Our guests arrived on time. *He* hovered and watched, pretending to be working on the fall foliage I chose to decorate the outside of the house. When one of the guest's brothers shook my hand with both of his, I was sure *he* was going to ruin everything. Thankfully he pretended to have dropped something and went back to work. Hopefully he doesn't see the dance we plan to have this Saturday. I'm not sure how he will handle me dancing with other men, even if it is Stefan.

November 27, 1947

This day was almost ruined. Our guests were inquiring about my new hobby. Stefan kept bragging about my gardening work and my flowers in the greenhouse. He insisted I show them around. When we walked in, I was surprised to see *him* there. We had given most of the staff—minus the few we would need for meals and small tasks—time off for the day to celebrate with their own families.

As we walked around, he trailed behind, almost hovering. I was surprised no one made a comment. But they didn't, either out of politeness or feigned ignorance. I let them all leave, pretending I needed to check on something. Once they were in the house, he grabbed my arms hard and kissed me. He reinjured my bruises, and I winced. Doesn't he realize he could have ruined us both? What was he thinking?

He must stop this. He must. Or we can't go on.

November 28, 1947

It was a lovely day. *He* was nowhere to be seen. He kept to himself, and I avoided any possibility of running into him. I had a lovely visit with our guests and the girls were positively delightful. Even Stefan was attentive. It reminded me of the life I could have without *him* and if things were like this all the time with Stefan. Especially if I were to focus more on my marriage and the girls.

November 29, 1947

The party was brilliant. The dancing was lovely. Stefan danced with me several times and we laughed and talked like we had in our younger years. Why couldn't our lives be like this? It reminded me of my love for my husband, and I think it reminded him of his love for me too.

Stefan came to my room tonight, drunk on fun and cocktails. It has been so long since my husband has made love to me. I felt out of practice, but my heart and body could not deny him. It was a gift for both of us. Perhaps this could be a new beginning. He is still lying in my bed snoring softly and as I look at his handsome face, I'm reminded of why I married him.

What have I done?

November 30, 1947

Our guests slept in and kept to themselves today until dinner. It was a lovely evening, but it will be nice to say farewell to them tomorrow. Stefan stayed by my side all day. He helped me with the girls, and we went for a walk around the grounds as a family. It was then he told me he was going to be gone until Christmas.

He must have registered the hurt on my face because he put his arms around me. He suggested I come with him but we both knew that was out of the question. He said he promised he would call and write, but I know better. The past few days were only a fairytale, and now it's time to get back to reality. Perhaps this time he will write. Perhaps he will actually call. One can hope.

December 1, 1947

Stefan left. The girls went back to their studies. All our guests are gone. And I avoided *him* all day.

December 2, 1947

I avoided *him* again today. What do I say? It's over. I want to try and work it out with my husband. Yes, the same husband who is gone until Christmas. I don't know what to do.

December 3, 1947

I still haven't heard from Stefan. I did receive word from his assistant—they arrived at their destination. I stayed in my rooms most of the day.

December 4, 1947

I know I can't keep avoiding *him*, but I don't know what to say. To add to my confusion, I still haven't heard from Stefan.

December 5, 1947

I saw *him* in the greenhouse. He came to me, but I rushed past him into the house. I'm not ready to face him.

I still haven't heard from Stefan.

December 6, 1947

Stefan's assistant sent word they may not even return for Christmas. What business for Willow Bay is out of town that would keep him from coming home? Perhaps he's having an affair too. Perhaps our marriage is just for show. A sham. Perhaps I just made a mess of things with *him* for no reason.

December 7, 1947

Still no word from Stefan. It's been a week. My husband has broken his promises again. I stayed in bed, telling everyone I wasn't feeling well, but really my heart is aching.

December 8, 1947

I faced *him*. I finally faced him today. The look of fear on his face made my heart melt and I instantly felt bad for keeping my distance. Instead of rushing to him like I wanted to, I told him we would have to meet another time at our spot so we could talk. He said the path was too deep with snow so we would have to go somewhere else. I told him to meet me in the greenhouse after midnight.

He never showed. He's punishing me.

December 9, 1947

Still no word from Stefan. Thanksgiving was a sham. This is my true reality. And *he* is avoiding me, too. I have ruined my life.

December 10, 1947

I saw *him* today. We talked in the greenhouse briefly. He told me to meet him there at midnight. We sat on the bench in the corner, hidden from view, and he kissed me softly. We promised earlier in the day we would just talk, but the kiss deepened, and we brazenly made love. The idea we could be caught made it more exciting somehow.

When we were done, we settled back on the bench, he asked me what happened to keep me from him for so long. I told him I got scared. He asked if it was because of his behavior, and I told him that was part of the reason. He asked me if I pondered breaking things off with him. I told him I did.

He paced the floor, and I told him he was going to draw attention. He screamed he didn't care. He professed his love to me. He said he was more in love with me than any other person in the world. And the idea of being without me terrified him.

I rushed to him. I tried to reassure him. I kissed him. I hugged him.

He asked me if I had made love to Stefan. I had to be truthful, but I should have lied. He struck me and I fell to the floor. While I lay there, he kicked me in the stomach and called me a whore. I curled in a ball and cried.

He grabbed my hair, yanked my head up, and held my face inches from his. He said I couldn't sleep with both men. I had to choose once and for all. I was so afraid to answer. How was I just now seeing that he was not the man I believed him to be. I also realized I had no escape, and I pledged my undying love to him while my heart shattered into thousands of pieces.

He said I no longer belonged to my husband. I was forever his. He brought his lips to mine and he took my body once more. He was branding me. It was urgent, he was demanding, and with no other choice, I gave in. It felt like I had sold my soul to the devil.

Chapter Thirty

The fire blazed and Raina sat curled in a ball on the chair next to it. The journal slid to the floor and her hand flew to her chest when she saw Conie in the doorway. "Where did you come from?"

Conie crossed the living room and kissed her before settling in the chair opposite her. "I'm sorry. I tried to make a noise, but you were so focused on what you were reading."

"I suppose I was," Raina said, biting her lower lip.

"You look concerned."

"My great-grandmother was in over her head. This Donny Strand, if this man really was him, was not kind to her toward the end. I worry he was somehow involved with their deaths."

Conie pulled a folder out of his bag and handed it to Raina. "Jenks said he skimmed over it. He said there weren't a lot of details pointing to anything other than what it was."

Raina read through the documents carefully. Her eyebrows raised a couple of times at the description but didn't say anything until she was done.

"So, as you see, there isn't anything saying there are holes in the investigation," Conie said.

"True, but if someone else had been there, it could have been someone they both knew. Someone who was having an affair with her."

"But wasn't he gone?"

"They say he left about the same time. But when exactly did he leave? Was it before or after the incident?"

"Why, Conie, it's a pleasure to see you, albeit a little late," Aunt Kat said, walking into the room. She wore a beautiful navy-blue nightgown with matching robe and looked every bit as elegant as ever. Raina beamed at her aunt and hoped she had the same refinement when she was her age.

"Conie was just dropping something off for me. I thought if it got to be too late, he could just stay the night," Raina said.

"And what was so urgent that couldn't wait?" Aunt Kat asked, winking at Raina.

"Well. Um. I," Conie said.

"He was bringing me the police report from that day, Aunt Kat," Raina said.

"The fire?"

"No, not the fire."

Aunt Kat's face grew pale. "Ah, I see. *That* day."

"I'm sorry. I just didn't want to lie to you," Raina said.

"Are you going to share with me what is going on?"

Raina glanced at Conie, worried he might be upset with her if she proceeded, but she hated the idea of keeping things from her aunt.

"I think the relationship your mother was involved in was not a very kind one."

Conie sent Raina a look telling her to stop sharing, but she ignored him. Aunt Kat sat on the closest couch cushion and looked at the folder in Raina's lap.

"Is that the police report?" Aunt Kat asked.

"Yes, but it's telling us the same story we've all been told," Conie said.

"I'm sorry I don't mean to upset you." Raina said.

"I told you to read those journals. I knew it meant we were digging up the past. And I've been preparing myself for it," Aunt Kat said.

"Why now?" Raina asked.

"Why am I okay with it now? Why am I encouraging you to read her journals?"

"Yes. Gramma D couldn't face it, and when I first arrived at Willow Bay, this subject was all but taboo around you."

"Perhaps I want to finally have some questions answered. My Gramma Melia had to step in and take over the running of the family business, and she worked very hard. She had to raise two girls who were devastated by the horrific loss of their parents. My sister was never the same. And for years, I've had these nagging questions. They won't go away no matter how hard I try to ignore them. Why did this happen? How could my mother, who I loved, who I believed was beautiful and good and kind? How could she kill my father and then take her own life? Perhaps in my old age, I'm ready to face those questions and find out the answers."

"Aunt Kat, I think your mother had an affair with an abusive man. I believe she was conflicted. I also believe she wanted to leave him multiple times. She loved your father. She was also very lonely. Perhaps she believed death was her only way out."

"People make terrible decisions sometimes when they are lonely and afraid," Conie said.

"Does she ever mention his name?" Aunt Kat asked.

"She hasn't yet that I've read." Raina said. "But, Aunt Kat, I think it was Donny Strand."

"What? That can't be. Wait, how do you know?" Aunt Kat asked.

"Violet said as much," Raina said.

"What exactly does the police report say?" Aunt Kat asked.

"It says there was no forced entry. It says there appeared to have been a struggle, but they ruled it as a struggle between the two of them. The knife was found next to him. The gun was on the floor right next to her hand. The bullet entry was consistent with self-inflicted wounds. The only possible motive they listed is due to the financial struggles of the Nilsson Family Enterprises at the time or a possible affair. I'm assuming Gramma Melia told the police what she read in the journal. "

Aunt Kat's eyes filled with tears, and she crossed the room to stoke the fire. She stared at the blaze for a few minutes before returning to the couch. Instead of sitting, she whirled toward Raina and frowned.

"Should I not have said anything," Raina asked.

"No. I'm glad you did. I'm just surprised Donny is the one she had the affair with. I assume the loss would be the reason he didn't want to come back to work for us. But why the lies about us? I don't understand it."

"Something doesn't add up where he is concerned. I plan to keep reading. And maybe one day we can get the opportunity to ask Donna some questions. Maybe she has some old documents or letters that could shed light on some of this," Raina said.

"Good luck with that," Conie said.

Aunt Kat chuckled and crossed to Raina. She caressed her cheek. "I'm so thankful you're here. Now I must fetch my glass of water and head to bed."

"Good night, Aunt Kat. I love you."

"I love you too, dear. Conie, should I expect you at breakfast then?"

"Um, probably not, I have to be at the café early. But it was a joy to see you as always. Oh, and I have those numbers for you when you're ready."

"Oh yes. Just get with Raina on that. She is taking over the work more and more these days at my request."

"Okay, I'll follow up with her."

"Good night, children."

Conie yawned after Aunt Kat was out of sight and Raina asked if he wanted to head to bed too. He shook his head and said it would be nice to have a glass of wine by the fire and just spend time with her without discussing work or the mystery of the tragedy.

Raina obliged and went to get two glasses of wine. When she returned, he was sitting on the couch looking through the journal she had been reading. Her smile faded as she waited for him to finish. *What must he be thinking as he reads such intimate words from her great-grandmother?*

Sitting next to Conie, she handed him a glass while he placed the journal on the side table next to him. Raina rested her head on his shoulder, and he put his arm around her. They sat like this for several minutes sipping and staring at the fire.

"Do you think killing her husband was an accident, and with everything else going on, she knew things would end badly for her, so she decided to end her life, too?" Conie asked. "Sorry, I know I said we wouldn't talk about work and your family, but I can't get it out of my mind."

"It's okay. I think about it a lot too. I've often wondered the same as what you're suggesting, especially the more I read."

"It would make sense," Conie said, lifting his glass to his lips.

"Are you sure you want to get tangled up with a woman who has such a sordid family history?"

"Are you sure you want to get tangled up with a bossy, pushy man?"

"You're not bossy or pushy," Raina said.

"Ha, that's not what my sisters say."

Raina giggled, took a drink, and changed the subject. "I had a thought about the White Hurricane Festival."

"Oh?"

"What if we broke ground for the new boatwerks and announced our plans for the museum and the Nilsson Historical Foundation as a part of the weekend?"

"That's not a bad idea. Have you discussed this with Henry."

"No, but I'm sure he would go for it. And I know they can't do much building this time of year, but we could have a breaking ground ceremony at least. It could be a highlighted part of the festival. We are already honoring those who lost their lives on the *Vide Fjärd* and making it an important part of the festival, so it feels like this would tie in well with our plans."

"I think it's a good idea, but definitely talk with Henry."

"I'll go see him tomorrow."

Conie yawned and Raina grabbed their glasses. She put them in the kitchen and when she returned, Conie was standing by the fire. She snaked her hands around his waist, and he rotated toward her. He leaned down and kissed her gently.

When they parted, Raina glanced at the fire to make sure it was good for the night, and grabbed Conie's hand. She led him upstairs to her bedroom band went to change. When she returned, he was lying on the bed with the journal in his lap, reading.

"I'm not sure how I feel about you reading those."

"Why, because she doesn't hold back?" Conie asked.

"Yes."

"If it makes you feel uncomfortable, I won't read them. I just thought maybe I could help."

"Actually, I like that idea. Keep December and I'll also give you January and February. I'll take on the rest. They end in May anyway."

"I suppose they would."

"Yes, that's when they died isn't it?"

"No more talk of the past. Come to bed, Raina."

Raina complied and crawled into bed next to him. They curled up in each other's arms and talked about their schedule for the next couple of weeks. They eventually shifted the conversation back to Raina's great-grandmother and what she could have been thinking the day she died, until they both fell asleep.

Chapter Thirty-One

The White Hurricane Festival was fast approaching, and Raina was spending most of her energy during the day focusing on planning, while also handling any urgent matters for the family business. At night she was learning more from Aunt Kat, which kept her from seeing Conie other than when she would get the occasional coffee at the café.

Henry had approved of her plan for including a ceremony for breaking ground on the new boatwerks as part of the festival. He volunteered to manage it and work with the contractors, which relieved Raina. She wasn't sure if she could take on one more thing.

Raina rushed into the café to get a latte and was disappointed when she didn't see Conie behind the counter. She peeked in at the bookstore to ask Annie where he might be, but she was with a customer, so she got her coffee to go.

While she waited, she thumbed through some papers Henry wanted her to sign. Violet wandered in, looking haggard and pale as she stumbled over to the counter.

"Violet, are you okay?" Raina asked.

"Leave me alone," Violet said, slurring her words.

"Maybe you should sit down. Let me know what you want to order, and I'll get it for you."

"Why can't you just leave me alone? You're everywhere and I hate it. I hate you."

"Okay," Raina said, taking her beverage while thanking the server.

As she turned to leave, Violet weaved and stumbled into her. The lid of Raina's latte popped open and spilled down her front.

Violet grabbed some napkins and tried to sponge the mess off of Raina's shirt. Raina clasped Violet's wrist gently, thanked her, and explained she would take care of it. Violet stumbled back, laughing hysterically.

"Go get Annie next door please," Raina said to the server, who had a horrified expression on her face.

Raina guided Violet to the closest chair and helped her sit as Annie appeared. Raina explained the situation and Annie offered to call Donna.

"Yes, I think that's best," Raina said.

It didn't take long for Donna to arrive, and Raina stepped back, allowing Annie to explain the situation beyond what she had already shared on the phone. Donna helped Violet stand, and as they moved toward the door, Donna stopped in front of Raina. She started to say something, but must have changed her mind, for she closed her mouth and continued to help her daughter out the door.

When they were gone, Raina thanked Annie and started to leave but Annie stopped her by asking, "Are you okay?"

Raina moved closer to Annie. "I will be. I don't know. This whole thing stems from something that took place between people who are no longer alive. And yet I feel guilty. I feel sad. I feel like it's my responsibility to get to the heart of the matter, to find out the truth, and make things right. No matter what that might look like."

"It isn't your mess to clean up," Annie said.

"Maybe. But it's one I've inherited along with everything else. For Aunt Kat's sake, I would love to find a peaceful resolution."

"You're a good niece," Annie said.

"I try to be."

"I'll let Conie know you stopped by and what happened. I know he will be sad he missed you. He always looks forward to seeing you."

"Where is he, anyway?" Raina asked.

"He had to run to Grand Marais for a few things," Annie said.

"Oh, that's right. He mentioned he had to go there today. I just forgot."

"You guys haven't seen each other much the last couple of weeks."

"I've been busy with the festival and the family business."

"You should come over for family dinner on Sunday, after the festival," Annie said.

"Only if you invite Stu," Raina said with a wink.

"I've been meaning to. He would love that actually," Annie said, giggling.

"Should we see if Murie wants to invite Oliver? I heard he is moving back to Willow Bay soon, since his last assignment is almost over."

"I'll talk with her. I know things are getting serious between the two of them, but I'm not sure if he would be able to come. Either way, though, I'll talk with her."

"No matter what, I'm excited. It should be fun."

"Hey, can I ask you something?" Annie asked.

"Sure. What's up?"

"Come with me to the bookstore," Annie said.

Raina followed her until she paused in the corner by the register. Annie frowned while biting her lip.

"Annie, what is it?" Raina asked.

"Um. I just. Well. Do you think it's inappropriate for a woman to ask a man to marry her?"

Raina burst out laughing. "No, of course not, Annie. Is this for real? If it is, I think this is a lovely idea. When do you plan to propose?"

"How about I do it at family dinner?"

Raina's smile faded. "So soon?"

"So soon? Stu and I have been together on and off for so long I've forgotten when he wasn't a part of my life."

"No. I mean. Sorry. I didn't mean to sound like I disapproved of when you were proposing. Sorry, it came out wrong, and it's still coming out wrong," Raina said, taking a deep breath. She smiled and squeezed her friend's hand. "Look I think it's a great idea. I was just surprised you made the decision for Sunday that's all."

"To be fair, I hadn't decided until this conversation just now, but it feels right."

"Then I say go for it," Raina said.

"I think I will," Annie said, engulfing Raina in a hug. "Thank you for letting me talk this through."

"Anytime. That's what friends are for," Raina said.

"Yes, friends, and maybe even sisters someday," Annie said with a teasing tone.

"Let's not get ahead of ourselves. I love your brother, but I'm not sure I'm ready to marry him." Raina's mouth dropped open and closed again. Her face grew warm as she mentally went back over her declaration of love for Conie.

"I think he loves you too, you know. But by the look on your face, I would say you guys haven't talked about this. I mean of course you care about each other. That much is obvious, but have you talked to each other about how serious things are becoming?"

"No, and I would so appreciate it if you wouldn't say anything," Raina said.

"Your secret is safe with me," Annie said.

"Thank you."

"Raina, I'll share this with you though. Conie has never let anyone in. He has had dates here and there. He has even had girlfriends. But none of them lasted. None of them came to family dinners. And none of them stole his heart the way you have managed to steal his. Careful with him if you ever realize what you feel isn't what you feel," Annie said.

"Is this your way of being his sister and warning the girlfriend not to hurt her brother?"

"Something like that. I care about you as my friend. But he is my brother."

"I understand. And it's okay. I have no intentions of ever breaking his heart," Raina said.

"I knew you would understand."

Raina looked at her watch and realized she was late for a meeting with Henry. She hugged Annie once more and left. She met with Henry but couldn't get the incident with Violet out of her mind, and the journals called to her because of their exchange.

It had been several weeks since she had last picked up a journal, but she had at least gotten through the month of March and was halfway through April. The more she read, she realized the situation was as she had feared. Adding the information Conie had shared based on what he read, they had agreed the man her great-grandmother was involved with had become controlling and abusive.

Raina was sad for her since she was in an unhappy marriage and her lover was cruel. She may not have agreed with everything her great-grandmother had done, but she could empathize with her situation.

Henry asked if she was okay while he studied her intently. When she said she was just distracted with her list of things she still needed to do for the festival, he suggested she move on to finishing the list. She thanked him for understanding, set a time to meet again soon, and went home.

Raina made several phone calls and crossed items off her list, but she had to force herself to focus on her tasks the rest of the day. She couldn't stop thinking about her great-grandmother's writing. She decided as soon as dinner was over, she would curl up in front of the fire and dive back into her great-grandmother's world.

Chapter Thirty-Two

April 20, 1948

Stefen returned home. He was distant at first but asked to talk with me. He said it was important. Has he discovered my secret? Has he found me out? We agreed to have a quiet lunch together tomorrow. I'm so nervous. What should I tell *him*? Should I even tell *him* Stefan is suspecting? Maybe it's best I wait.

April 21, 1948

I worried over nothing. When I arrived at lunch, Melia was there too. Stefan shared some struggles he was having with work, and we would have to be careful about our spending for the spring clothes shopping trip I was taking the girls on in a few weeks. I will admit the struggles he mentioned went over my head, but Melia seemed to understand. She looked worried, but didn't say anything. She just agreed she would be careful with her spending for a couple of months. Melia looked at me strangely when I looked relieved though. I need to be more careful.

April 22, 1948

I went for my weekly flower and gardening lesson with *him* today and he was waiting impatiently for me. He didn't look pleased. I worried I might have been late and apologized. He said not everything was about me, and we dove into my lesson. He was teaching me about the latest seeds he had planted and how long it would take for us to see anything pop above the dirt.

Our faces were so close, and I knew he was about to kiss me when the girls ran in. The anger that flashed in his eyes made me nervous, and I was sure he was going to yell at the girls. I answered their questions and showed them a few things. Thankfully, they quickly got bored and ran off to find something else to do. I turned to admonish him for not hiding his feelings and he kissed me.

I was stunned he would be so bold, and I just stood there while his hands ran up and down my back and into my hair. I moaned and wrapped my arms around his neck. When we heard the sound of footsteps outside, we sprang apart. He stared at me wildly, and my face burned with embarrassment. When will I learn? When will I realize this fire we are playing with will, at some point, burn us both?

April 23, 1948

He said we had to meet again soon. He said he was longing to have me. He said his body ached for mine. It's been too long he said. But where? Stefan is home. Doesn't he know this is not a good time to plan to meet and make love? Or perhaps he doesn't care if we get caught. I told him to meet me in the greenhouse at midnight tomorrow.

April 24, 1948

Stefan asked me to go to Duluth with him today. I had to send word to *him* so he wouldn't try to meet me. But how, without getting caught? So, I had to track him down my-self. It was hard, but I eventually found him and handed my note to him. He was surprised but didn't cause a scene and hid it quickly before anyone saw anything.

When we got to Duluth, we met with a few of Stefan's associates before we had dinner. He said we would be staying for a couple of nights. What was this game he was playing? Maybe he did find out and is just trying to find a way to tell me he knows my secret.

April 25, 1948

As I write this, I feel like such a horrible woman. One who has betrayed my vows because I was sure my husband no longer loved me. He shared with me at dinner that he was sorry he had not talked with me until now. We had been on the brink of financial ruin for quite some time. He was embarrassed. He felt like a failure.

He believed he was letting me down. He was filled with so much shame so he couldn't face me. He said the time with me at Thanksgiving was wonderful, but when he left, he was even more ashamed and couldn't come home. He apologized for how things had been between us, and he promised he would try to make things right.

He tried to make love to me, but I told him I wasn't ready because I was so hurt, but really how could I? He kept away from me because of his shame, and now I'm keeping away from him because of mine. Perhaps I should tell him. No. That would devastate him. I can't.

April 26, 1948

I made love to my husband tonight. We had a glorious day together. He courted me all day. He bought me a few small gifts and a few things for the girls. We went to lunch and dinner, and we went for walks and talked like we hadn't in years. When I asked him about our overindulgence and how it would affect our finances, he said we still had a ways to go to get things right, but he was optimistic for the future. How could I not end the day by making love to my husband?

But now, the shame and guilt are eating me alive. I have to end things with Donny Strand before this destroys everything important in my life.

Raina stopped reading at the mention of Donny's name. It was the first time her great-grandmother had written it. Here was proof that the Strands and Nilssons were for better or worse connected by the affair and the tragic consequences it had on both families. She knew in her heart it had been true, she was just looking for evidence of it, and here it was in her own great-grandmother's words.

Chapter Thirty-Three

The chilly evening didn't stop the town and the tourists from coming out in droves. The first night of the festival was well underway with music and an ice sculpture contest. Lights were strung across the road in a crisscross pattern all the way up the street in front of the pub. People strolled along, stopping at food and drink vendors, while others gathered around bonfires, benches, or picnic tables to socialize.

Raina looked through the crowd for Conie to return with her stout. She was helping Aunt Kat find a warm place to sit and visit with her friends while Conie had offered to get drinks for everyone. He had taken longer than usual, and she worried what could be keeping him. She finally caught sight of his head before he poked out of the crowd with Annie and Stu trailing behind.

"Who is minding the pub?" Raina asked as she grabbed her beer from Conie.

"We have a few extra staff for tonight, but we are slow," Annie said.

"Yep, everyone is out here. Annie and I thought we would come hang out with you guys for a little bit, then we'll head back in to relieve the extra staff and stay until we close," Stu said.

"Sorry, Raina, Conie will have to go too. Even you can't keep him away," Annie said with a laugh.

"Once I get Aunt Kat settled at home, I'll come help," Raina said.

"You don't need to get me settled at home," Aunt Kat said. "Just get Johnston for me when I'm ready and he will take me home. I can manage on my own. You have fun with your friends."

"Are you sure? I don't want to miss out on spending time with you."

"You spend time with me every day. This is a fun occasion you helped make happen and you should be spending your time celebrating your success and enjoying time with your friends. I'll be fine."

"If you insist."

"I do."

Conie put his arm around Raina, kissed her cheek, and asked if she wanted to go check out the ice sculptures with Stu and Annie.

"That sounds lovely." Turning to Aunt Kat, Raina said, "I'll see you later then. Love you."

"Love you too, Raina."

Hugging her aunt, Raina kissed her cheek before she straightened. She grabbed Conie's hand and left. They meandered along, talking about the success of the evening and how people were having a good time. Raina asked where Murie was, and Annie explained she went to Grand Marais to be with Oliver, but she would be back tomorrow.

As they neared, the ice sculptures glistened in the moonlight and Raina studied them intently. Their beauty was overwhelming, and Raina pressed a hand to her chest, examining each one. When they happened on the last one, she paused with a slight gasp.

"What is it?" Conie asked.

"It's the *Vide Fjärd*."

"Wow, that's so impressive," Annie said.

"I think my buddy Jim did that one," Stu said. "He's really good at carving stuff out of anything."

"It's gorgeous," Raina said.

"He carved the name of the boat into it," Annie said. "But he also carved a plaque and a title."

"What's it say?" Raina asked, stepping closer.

"The Willow Bay Ghost of the White Hurricane," Conie said.

"I hope he gets first prize," Raina said.

"It would be quite an honor for your family if he did," Annie said.

"No, the honor shouldn't be about us Nilssons," Raina said. "But about the beauty of the sculpture and what it represents. This whole festival is meant to honor those who lost their lives and to honor those who had to keep on living. It's meant to honor what this town went through. It's a tragic story and one that should never be forgotten."

"So profound, Raina," Annie said.

"Thank you. I feel very strongly about this."

"Just as a Nilsson would," Stu said.

"Let's grab a bite to eat, then head back to work," Conie said.

"I'll catch up. I want to make sure Aunt Kat sees this, but I don't want to hold you up since I know you have to get to the pub soon," Raina said.

Conie agreed, but instead of walking away, he gazed at Raina. She giggled and looked down at her feet. When she met his eyes again, the look of adoration on his face took her breath away.

He stepped closer, careful not to spill their drinks and gathered her into his arms. "You're beautiful. You're just glowing. It's your face and body, but it's also your essence. Plus, your hair is shiny from the string lights and the moon. And the sparkle in your eyes. You're breathtaking. I'm just so..."

"So, what?" Raina asked, tilting her head.

Instead of responding with words, Conie kissed her gently on the lips. Raina eventually drew back slowly and grinned. She stared into Conie's eyes and didn't miss the shadow behind them.

"What is it?" Raina asked.

"Nothing," Conie said, giving her a quick peck before letting go.

"If you say so. I'll find you as soon as I get Aunt Kat settled again."

"See you in a little bit," Annie said.

Raina went in search of her aunt but couldn't stop thinking about Conie and his words. She hoped Aunt Kat wouldn't notice her musings and ask her about it.

"I thought I told you to run along," Aunt Kat said.

"Yes, but I want to show you this most amazing ice sculpture. I think you will really like it. Besides I want to help you find Johnston when we are done, because I know you were wanting to head home soon."

"Lead the way."

Raina linked arms with her aunt and took her through the ice sculptures one by one. Aunt Kat had kind things to say about every one of them, but when she saw the *Vide Fjärd* her hand flew over her mouth. Tears sprang to her eyes, and she ran a gloved hand over the smooth surface.

"This town sure knows how to show its love for our family," Aunt Kat said.

"Do you ever feel like it's undeserving?" Raina asked.

"What do you mean?"

"I guess sometimes I feel like people do this because we expect it of them or like its owed to us."

"I had those same thoughts once, and I asked Gramma Melia about it. She said the town doesn't owe us anything. We owe everything to this town. They are what has made Willow Bay what it is. Our debt or what we owe to them is our undying gratitude, love, and, if needed, assistance. And of course, our proper management of it. And perhaps because we give those things to Willow Bay, the town returns it to us in kind."

"Okay that makes me feel better."

"Maybe that makes *you* feel better, but it doesn't make *me* feel better," Violet said, stepping out of the shadows.

Raina looked past her aunt. "What do you want now, Violet?"

"Maybe some respect, or maybe you should assist me by giving me a job or housing that doesn't suck."

"Come on, Violet," Ginny said, tugging on her friend's arm. "Sorry, Miss Kat. Raina. She's a little sore since she lost her job last night."

"Yes, and it's your fault," Violet said.

"How is losing your job my fault?" Raina asked.

"Don't engage with her, honey. She's just looking for a fight and we don't have to give it to her," Aunt Kat said.

"That's right. Hide behind Old Kat there," Violet said.

"Enough, Violet," Donna said, appearing out of nowhere.

"Donna, hello. It's been a while," Aunt Kat said.

"Yes, well, your kind tries to avoid our kind," Donna said.

"I'm not sure I understand what you mean."

"You and your family have avoided us and ours for years. Even when things were hard."

"I think perhaps there is a misunderstanding on both sides," Raina said.

"What do you know about it?" Donna said. "You weren't here."

"You're right, but I know enough to understand there are things we all don't know about what happened back then, and perhaps we should just make peace."

"It sounds to me like your family is trying to hide something from mine," Violet said.

"Violet, why would I try to hide anything from you?" Raina asked.

"Because you Nilssons have to protect your image."

"You can believe what you want I guess," Raina said. "Come along, Aunt Kat. Let's go find Johnston."

"Can't you at least admit your mother was having an affair with my grandfather?" Violet asked Aunt Kat. "For my mother's sake. For my family's sake. Take ownership for what your family did to ours."

Raina paused and spun back toward Violet.

"It's not worth it," Aunt Kat said.

Ignoring her aunt, Raina said, "The only thing Aunt Kat's mother did was have an affair with your grandfather, Violet. And the Nilssons didn't turn their back on your family as a result of it. We didn't even know it was him until recently. *He* made the choice to stop working at Nilsson Manor, not my family. They were reeling from a tragedy, and then they had lost a worker. They were trying to keep things as normal as possible."

"That's not true. My grandfather told my mother he was fired for leaving town to help family," Violet said.

"It is true. We have journals kept by all the women in the Nilsson family that confirm this. Not to mention the word of Aunt Kat who lived it."

"Prove it," Violet said.

"I don't think you want me to drag out these journals and prove anything to you," Raina said.

"Why not?" Donna asked.

"They don't paint a very kind picture of your father."

Donna's face grew pale, and Aunt Kat placed a hand on Raina's arm. "Raina, that's enough. We don't need to talk further, especially in front of so many people."

Glancing around, Raina realized they were causing a scene. She noticed Conie moving through the crowd, trying to get to them. Raina's cheeks flamed and she mouthed an apology to her aunt.

"It's okay, my dear," Aunt Kat said, patting Raina's hand. "But we should probably call it night."

"But I want to know what the journals say," Donna said, stepping closer.

"Perhaps another time," Conie said.

"Stay out of this," Violet said.

"No, I don't think I will," Conie said.

"It's none of your business."

"Raina *is* my business. And so is Kat."

Anger flashed in Violet's eyes. "You would choose the richer one over me."

"Violet, there has never been any choosing one person over you. There was never a me and you. So there never was a choice for me to make. I'm just sorry you can't see that or let it go."

"Enough now, Violet," Donna said. "Let's just go."

"Have a pleasant evening," Aunt Kat said, nodding toward Donna.

Conie steered Raina and Aunt Kat away from the crowd and made sure they were settled on a bench before running to find Johnston. Raina stared at the moon reflecting on the water and focused on her breath gathering in puffs outside her mouth. It didn't take long for Conie to return with Johnston in tow, and Raina said goodnight to her aunt.

After she confirmed her aunt was okay and on her way home, Raina went with Conie to the pub. She settled behind the counter, making drink orders, and occasionally delivered plates of food. As the festivities outside died down for the night, more people came into the pub for a nightcap before heading home. The pub eventually emptied one by one until there were only a few stragglers. Raina was mixing a cocktail for one of them when Donna appeared at the counter.

"Was it bad?" she asked Raina.

"Was what bad?" Raina asked.

"Was the story in the journals bad?"

Raina studied the older woman. "I can tell you're worried, but it's almost like you don't plan to deny it. What do you think might be in them?"

"I just know my daddy wasn't always a very kind man to my mama. It's possible I may have been led to believe it wasn't always like that. And I saw what I wanted to see. I believed what I wanted to believe."

"Sometimes our family stories are not ones we like to hear. Especially when it can paint the ones we love in a bad light."

"Like your great-grandmother and my father."

"Exactly like them."

"Was he unkind to her at times?"

"Unkind is an understatement on how he was with her."

"Say no more," Donna said.

"Do you think it's possible we all got some things wrong?" Raina asked.

"I think it's possible I may have gotten some things wrong," Donna said, her shoulders drooping.

Raina grabbed a wine goblet. "White or Red? And it's on me. Consider it a peace offering."

"White. I like it a little sweeter though."

"Done. I have a delicious white out of Minneapolis you just might like."

"Thank you."

"You're welcome," Raina said, setting the goblet in front of Donna.

"You know, you remind me of them—Del and Kat. Delany was something. I always looked up to the Nilsson girls. I wanted to be like them. But while Kat was sweet and timid, Del, well, she was fierce, and nothing was going to stand in her way. She was always kind to me whenever we crossed paths, which wasn't often. I usually just admired them from afar. Reflecting on that time I see now there was a sadness about her...and a hard shell. Of course I didn't understand it then. But I understand it now. We were all hurt by the choices our parents made."

"Which doesn't make us really that much different," Raina said.

Donna drained her glass. "Maybe. Goodnight, Raina."

As Raina watched the older woman leave, Conie came up behind her. "What was that all about?"

"I don't know, but I feel like this may have been the beginning of a truce."

"Does she want to see the journals?" Conie asked.

"She didn't say, but I know I want to finish reading them."

"How far did you get last night?"

"I'm done with April, and just started May. How about you?"

"I finished reading them. I'm not sure how to share this—um, how do I say it? Um, he was forcing himself on her and she kept telling him no. There was also a hint at planning an escape from their reality."

"Escape from their reality?"

"Yes, that's how your great-grandmother put it," Conie said, waving at the last customer.

Annie went to lock the door and sweep the floor. Dropping the subject for now, Raina helped Conie wipe down the few remaining tables while Stu worked on washing the last of the dishes. As Raina moved to leave, Conie offered to drive her home. She accepted and said goodnight to Stu and Annie.

As they stopped under the carport, Raina kissed Conie goodnight. "I look forward to the fun day ahead of us tomorrow."

"It will be a fun day. I'll meet you at the boatworks tomorrow morning at ten."

"See you then."

Raina gave Conie one more quick peck on the lips, climbed out of his truck, and watched him drive out of sight. She went up to her room and threw on her favorite pajamas before crawling into bed. She turned off her lamp and closed her eyes, hoping sleep would come quickly.

Escape from their reality.

Turning the lamp back on, Raina flew across her room to her chair by the fireplace. She picked up the journal and flipped to the page she had left off with the night before. It was time to find out what her great-grandmother was thinking on *that* day.

Chapter Thirty-Four

May 5, 1948

Stefan is set to return tomorrow. We haven't seen each other much since our time in Duluth. I've also been keeping my distance from Donny. I know he will be furious, and I worry about what pain he will try to inflict on me, but things can't continue this way. They just can't. Especially now I know Stefan wants to make things work with me.

But will he still feel that way if I tell him my secret?

May 6, 1948

Stefan was delayed, which is probably for the best since Donny asked me to meet him in our place tomorrow night.

He said the path was nice and clear and we needed to talk. I'm nervous but I have to stay firm. I must end this.

And I must get up the courage to tell Stefan.

May 7, 1948

The girls were in a rambunctious mood this evening. I thought I would never get away, so I was late. *He* was so angry with me he grabbed my arms, shook me hard and kissed me roughly. It bruised my lips and arms. I told him if he was going to be cruel, I was leaving. He blocked the door and pleaded with me not to leave. He said he was going crazy with his desire for me, and the sneaking around had to stop. I told him we had to stop all together. The relationship had to end.

I was facing the window and staring out at the water when he grabbed my hair, yanked me toward him, and into his arms. He kissed me hard again and told me I was his. He reminded me of the promise I made to him months ago. I said I made promises to my husband too, just as he had made promises to his wife. He said none of it mattered to him anymore. I shared that I slept with my husband in April, and he pushed me away from him.

As he paced about, I pondered why I was drawn to him in the first place. He stomped over to me, jerked me into his arms, and burst into tears. He told me we couldn't be over, that he loved me too much. I'm not sure what came over me, but I put my arms around him and hugged him. I kissed him all over, hoping it would be enough, but he wanted more. And lord help me, I gave my body to him once more.

Upon my return to my room, I looked in the mirror and no longer recognized myself. I love my husband, but I'm entangled in a love affair with this other man. I no longer want *him*. I want my husband. But when I'm with *him*, I get so confused and fall into his trap. He is so cruel to me. He hurts me in so many ways, but I feel ensnared in his control over me. What will become of me when I finally tell Stefan? What will become of me if I don't?

May 8, 1948

Stefan returned this morning. We had a nice lunch together. Donny found out Stefan was home so when I stopped by the greenhouse this afternoon, he demanded I meet him in our spot again tonight. I told him Stefan would probably want to come to my room tonight. Donny became so angry I thought he was going to scream at me. Instead, he kissed me. I yanked away from him and asked if he wanted us to get caught. He said he didn't care anymore, and I needed to meet him tonight or he was going to march into Stefan's office and tell him everything. Stefan needs to know the truth, but he needs to hear it from me. So, I agreed.

When I arrived, I knew exactly what he wanted from me. I told him I couldn't, but he said I had to. He said I had to prove my love for him. He said he wouldn't take no for an answer. He grabbed my wrists and forced me to the floor. I told him I wanted to leave. He said it didn't matter what I wanted. I told him to stop. He ignored my request and took my body anyway. Fighting him was pointless. I knew trying to get away was impossible, so I let him ravage my body and when he was done, I clung to my clothes and cried.

He put his arms around me and held me to comfort me. He told me he loved me, and I could never leave him. He demanded I meet him again tomorrow night.

Dear god, what do I do?

May 9, 1948

Stefan asked me to go for a walk with him today. I told him I wasn't feeling well and stayed in my room. I eventually snuck down to the greenhouse to tell Donny I wasn't well, and I wouldn't meet him tonight. He wasn't there. When I was returning to my room I ran into Stefan. He studied me for so long I wondered if he read my thoughts. He eventually told me I looked pale and caressed my cheek. He kissed me gently and told me to return to bed and he would manage the girls that night.

It took so long before I knew it would be safe for me to sneak out. When I arrived, he was standing outside. I told him I was going to tell Stefan and it would all be over. I told him we had to be over and ran away.

May 10, 1948

I think I'm pregnant. There is no way it could be Stefans. It has to be Donny's. What do I do now?

May 11, 1948

I searched the grounds until I found Donny and told him to meet me at our spot again. The anger in his eyes went away and he smiled triumphantly, but I only felt sick to my stomach.

When I arrived later, he was so tender. He could tell I was worried about something beyond our current circumstances. I told him I was pregnant. Instead of being upset or worried along with me, he became excited. He held his hand to my stomach and kissed me. He said he wanted to take care of me. He said we could run away together. We had to start our own lives. I cried. He laughed. I told him I wanted to return home. He insisted we celebrate by making love. Any fight left in me was gone, so I let him celebrate.

May 12, 1948

The girls were rambunctious today, and I kept my distance from them by staying in my rooms. But I felt like I couldn't breathe, and with Stefan's worry over me, I just had to get away. I decided to take a walk in the woods alone. I ran into Donny, and he was so thrilled to see me. Since we were alone, he pulled me into his arms and held me. He kissed me. He wanted more. I told him I couldn't possibly give him more right now in the woods, especially since I was pregnant.

He told me we needed to make a plan. I told him I didn't want to, and I was going to tell Stefan everything. Donny said once I told Stefan I was pregnant, I would lose my husband forever, and when that happened, he would be waiting. He loved me that much, he wanted me that much, so he would wait for Stefan to cast me aside. And since this was my fate, I needed to help make a plan.

I told him my family was supposed to be going to Duluth in a couple of days, but I would send Melia with the girls with the excuse Stefan and I needed some time together. I will tell Stefan then. Since a woman in my position can't fend for herself when she no longer has her husband or his money to protect her, if Stefan no longer wants me, I won't have a choice but to go away with Donny.

May 13, 1948

I sent Stefan a note suggesting my plan to send the girls with Melia to Duluth so he and I could be by ourselves. He came to me and asked if I was okay. I wept, while he held me. He was so kind. He looked so worried about me. I must look like a mess. I told him we had a lot to talk about, but I wanted to wait until the girls were gone. He didn't leave my side that night. He didn't force himself on me either. He just held me until I fell asleep. When I woke with the moon so high and the stars shining bright, I stared at him, scared of what would become of us.

May 14, 1948

I found Donny and told him the girls were leaving tomorrow. He said he would pack his bags and get ready to go with me. He told me to meet him in our spot tonight because he had to make love to me one more time before the truth came out. I didn't go.

May 15. 1948

Donny found me in the greenhouse. The girls had been gone for several hours. Stefan was in town. Most of the staff had been given a few days off, minus the cook and one housekeeper. Donny was so angry. I told him I couldn't get away. He called me a liar and told me I'd better meet him tonight or else he was going to tell the whole town of our affair. I begged him to calm down, and I would find a way to meet him later. Thankfully, he finally left.

Stefan and I had a pleasant dinner, despite my bundle of nerves. I told him I was starting to feel better, but I had a terrible headache and asked to go to bed early. He asked to join me, but I told him I wanted to be alone. He didn't push.

I snuck out and met Donny. He showed me his packed bags. He said he told his wife he was leaving town for a few days to visit his sick mother. Once we were settled, he would write her a letter. He said he would stay here until I was ready to leave.

He told me he needed reassurance. He said he was scared he would lose me, and I needed to show him how much I loved him. He wrapped me in his arms and kissed me until I complied. I knew I would be telling Stefan tomorrow. But for now, I was numb while he took any remaining pieces of me.

May 16, 1948

I told my husband. I told Stefan I'd been having an affair with another man, and I was pregnant with this other man's baby. He didn't yell, he didn't scream. He left the room and told all the remaining staff to leave, because we needed our privacy.

I went to the greenhouse and Donny was there sitting on the hidden bench. I said he had to leave because I'd shared the truth with Stefan. Donny asked if Stefan knew it was him. I told him not yet but he had to leave. Donny kissed me long and hard and said he would be back tomorrow to check on me. I just stood there. How does he have so much power over me?

Stefan kept his distance from me for the rest of the day. After dinner I went to sit outside on the front porch because I needed some air. Stefan was sitting in the shadows. He had a drink in his hand and was crying. I begged him to talk to me. I begged him to yell at me. I begged him to make love to me. Anything.

Stefan threw his glass to the porch and kissed me. He kissed me until I couldn't breathe, and I took a step back. He asked me if I loved him, and I told him I did. He asked me who it was, so I confessed. He asked me if I had ended things. I explained I was trying to, but Donny wouldn't let me. And then it happened, the whole story came pouring out. How it started, how lonely and hurt I was by Stefan's treatment. I shared how Donny eventually began to hurt me, the times he insisted on the love making when I didn't want it. How I would beg him to stop, or pray he would stop. And something changed. Stefan asked me if I understood how Donny's treatment of me was unkind. He said he would fire Donny and send him away and that we could work on this. He explained it wasn't all my fault and the abusive relationship I had entangled myself in would be taken care of.

Abusive? How did I not see it before. How could I have allowed this to happen? I remembered all the times he wanted to make love to me, and I told him no, but he did it anyway. I contemplated all the times he demanded I see him, but I wanted to end it. Why did I keep going back to him over and over even though he was so cruel?

May 17, 1948

It was a weird day. We kept to ourselves. Stefan was attentive. He went into town to get some food from the diner. Donny appeared at the front door, bags in hand. I told him Stefan didn't turn away from me and that he knew everything. That Stefan still loved me and we were going to work it out. I thought I had finally convinced him we were over. Our affair was finished.

Donny denied it. He said Stefan was in shock and he would be back tomorrow. I explained to Stefan that Donny came by, and he might stop by again tomorrow. I spilled the last part of my secrets that Donny was waiting for

Stefan to cast me aside, and when he did, Donny was going to take me away from Willow Bay.

Stefan told me I wouldn't be going anywhere. He shared that although it may take a while for us to get past this, we would remain together. There is a part of me that can't wait until tomorrow because that means I will finally be free of *him*. As I watch Stefan sleep in my bed, I wonder what our future will be. I do love him so. I never stopped.

Raina turned the page and found it empty. There were no more entries from her great-grandmother. Reading the last two pages in the journal a second time, Raina knew there was another person in Willow Manor that day, and she believed he played a part in the deaths of both of her great-grandparents. But how could she ever find proof?

Chapter Thirty-Five

S nowflakes glided to the ground even though the sun tried to peak through the clouds. It was a cold day, but the small snowstorm was almost gone. The winds had died down, and despite the chill in the air, a large crowd of townspeople and tourists showed up for the groundbreaking ceremony of the boatwerks.

Glancing at the *Vide Fjärd* on display where the ceremony was to take place, Raina scanned the crowd for Conie, who was saving a seat for Aunt Kat. Raina helped her aunt to the chair and made sure Aunt Kat was warm enough before moving on to where she was supposed to be. Raina found Henry at the front talking to the owner and two representatives of their hired contractor and she moved in their direction.

A gust of wind blew across the water, taking her breath away as she approached. Raina loved the idea that it was really the spirits of her ancestors making their presence known and she hoped they would be proud of her.

Henry made a final comment to the construction workers and swayed toward Raina. "Ready?"

"As I'll ever be."

"Good, let's get started."

The crowd quieted as Henry and Raina took their places with the contractor team off to the side. Raina squeezed Henry's arm and nodded.

"Ladies and Gentleman, Katarina Nilsson, townspeople and guests, Raina Nilsson and I are honored you have joined us here today," Henry said.

Raina caught the slip of the name and looked over at Aunt Kat, who winked at her. She decided he must have said it that way on purpose, so people had no doubts in their minds about who she was. She forced herself to listen as Henry finished and passed the attention on to Raina. Looking out at the crowd, at her town, her people, a wave of emotions flooded through her body as she stepped to the microphone. Clearing her throat, Raina dove into her speech.

"Thank you all for coming out to celebrate with us today despite the slight chill in the air."

Raina paused while several people chuckled at her comment about the weather. As they quieted, she took a deep breath, and said, "I'm truly honored to be here today. When Aunt Kat came to me after Gramma Delany passed away, I didn't realize it at the time, but she was really inviting me to come home. I never knew such a place existed. I never knew I had roots so deep in a town as beautiful as our wonderful Willow Bay. As I learn more about my family's history, the history of the town, and the history of this land before it was our established community, the more I feel proud and excited to be a part of continuing its legacy. As we break ground on rebuilding Nilsson Boatwerks, I truly believe Henry will take the torch given to him and make it shine brighter than ever before."

Clearing her throat, she continued, "It's with this assurance and excitement for the future I'm happy to announce the beginning of a partnership with him. Some of you may already know I have a love and passion for history. And combining that with my love for this town and our heritage, I've decided to establish the Nilsson Historical Foundation in honor of our town's history, my family history, and the history of this beautiful land and the lake it sits on. I believe a large part of continuing the legacy passed on to me is honoring and remembering the past. So, with the rebuilding of the boatwerks, Henry and I have agreed to establish a Willow Bay Nautical Museum, which will be a part of this beautiful marina."

Pausing again, Raina turned toward the *Vide Fjärd* looming proudly behind her. As she gestured in her direction, she said, "This beautiful broken boat, whose captain was my ancestor, will be the first to greet you when you enter the museum doors. The white hurricane will tell its story many times to those who visit her. Many who are here today know the tragic tale of the storm. They remember it took so many lives, not just from Willow Bay, but all across the Great Lakes. It's in their memory we are gathered, not just today, but this entire weekend. Yes, we are enjoying our time with friends and family. Yes, we are celebrating the beauty of how life does go on even when it's difficult. But it's also important to remember the lives of those who were lost and honor them. I would like to take the opportunity to remember not just my ancestor but all the souls who perished. Please join me in a moment of silence as we reflect on why we are here today."

A hush fell over the crowd as men removed their hats and women wiped at tears in their eyes. Raina stared at the *Vide Fjärd* for a second until her focus was drawn to the bay beyond. Waves flowed gently toward land, and she let the cold breeze settle into her bones. The peacefulness of her ancestors' presence danced around her.

Raina inhaled, allowing the air to fill her lungs. As she let her breath out slowly, she smiled and wiped at the tears gathering in the corners of her eyes. The loud clang of a bell rung by Henry, jolted Raina back to her speech.

"Thank you all for honoring those who lost their lives. As I close, I would like to also thank those of you who have opened your arms to me and have helped me feel at home here in our beautiful bay. Your friendship, your love, and your patience when I ask a lot of questions fill me with gratitude. I would like to thank Mike Johnson, the owner of Johnson Construction, and his amazing crew who have joined us today to help us commemorate this new beginning for the boatwerks. And I must thank our amazing people of Willow Bay. This day would not be complete without showing the gratitude Aunt Kat and I have for you. Your dedication to our community, your steadfastness through difficult times, and your love for the town and my family does not go unnoticed. As Aunt Kat continues to transition the reins over to me, I know you will continue to show your patience as we grow and become stronger than ever. So, as we remember those lives who were lost, celebrate the boatwerks and the future, we honor you, Willow Bay. Thank you again for joining us today and my hope is you have a wonderful weekend of reflection and joy. Thank you."

Applause erupted as Raina stepped back so the microphone could be taken away. As the townspeople cheered,

Raina looked at her aunt, then Conie. They were both standing and clapping with the rest of the crowd with looks of pride on their faces. Love for both seeped through her body.

Someone handed Raina a shovel, and she took her place next to Henry, who was shoulder to shoulder with the contractors. Several photographers moved forward and stood ready for their shot. Henry glanced at Raina and bobbed his head, she smiled and nodded in return. In unison they all lifted their shovels and dug out the first pile of dirt, marking the beginning of a new era. Cheers, whistles, and applause echoed across the bay as Raina and Henry shook hands with the contractor.

When it was all over, Raina hugged Henry and said, "I look forward to many years of working with you."

Stacia rushed to hug them both, and as she took a step back, she said, "I love this partnership."

"I don't think I've ever seen a smile so big on your face, Stacia," Raina said.

"I'm not at work. One must have proper decorum at work, but I'm not there now."

Raina giggled and hugged the older woman. "I love you no matter what decorum you have."

Surprise registered on Stacia's face as Conie and Aunt Kat joined them.

"What a lovely event you put together," Aunt Kat said, hugging Raina. "I'm so proud of you. Delaney would have been proud of you as well. I hope you know that."

Swiping at her tears, Raina said, "Thank you, Aunt Kat. That means so much."

Conie put his arm around Raina. "You did us all proud."

"I saw Annie in the crowd. Did Murie make it back from Grand Marais in time?" Raina asked.

"I made it just in time to hear you speak," Murie said, coming up from behind.

Wrapping her arms around her friend, Raina said, "Oh I'm so glad. My thanks were for you and your sister too, my friend, and I wanted you both to hear that part."

"We heard it and understood your message," Annie said, giving Raina a hug too.

Aunt Kat squeezed Raina once more and said, "I'm starving, I'm going to head home to eat. You run along and enjoy the rest of the day's activities."

"Aunt Kat, I insist you join us at the pub. We're all going together to have lunch and celebrate. Henry and Stacia will be there of course and so will Celia," Raina said.

"Yes, Mrs. Nilsson, you should join us," Stacia said.

"Only if you call me Kat while we're eating lunch," Aunt Kat said.

"Deal."

Clapping her hands together, Raina said, "Yeah, let's head to the pub. I'm famished."

The group made their way to the pub, and it wasn't long before they were all settled at the table reserved for them. They ordered food and beverages while conversation jumped from the festival to the weather. Once the drinks arrived, Conie clanged his glass to get everyone's attention.

"The town, Henry and the boatwerks, the white hurricane, the history of the Nilsson family and Willow Bay were all honored and celebrated today. But there are two people who must not be forgotten in this. They are the ones who lose sleep at night and shed tears of sorrow and pain for this place. They are also the ones who celebrate with us and spread the joy we need. They are our fearless leaders"—raising his glass in the air—"To Kat and Raina."

"To Kat and Raina," everyone said, raising their own drinks.

As Conie settled back into his seat, Raina leaned over to kiss him on the cheek. "Thank you."

"You're welcome, my love." Surprise registered on Conie's face at his words, but he tried to hide it by taking another drink of his beer.

Raina pretended not to notice, but the warmth pulsing through her body made it hard to forget. She glanced across the table just as Annie winked at her. The food arrived shortly after, and everyone focused on eating with occasional comments about the meal and what they would be doing the rest of the day. Some would be going out on boat rides around the bay, which was a planned event to commemorate those who were on the water when the storm hit. It was the last big event planned, minus the concert at the bandstand tomorrow afternoon, where they would be playing songs written by various members of the Nilsson family.

As lunch wound down, and plates were cleared, Aunt Kat leaned over to Raina. "I would love to go with you and Conie out on the water, but I must get a nap."

"Are you feeling okay?" Raina asked.

"Don't fret about me. I'm just tired. It's been a full weekend already and I just need a little rest so I can head out on the town with you this evening."

"Okay. Let me take you home and get you settled."

"No, you stay and have fun."

"Aunt Kat, please, I'll feel better knowing you're okay."

"I can go with her, Raina," Stacia said.

"This is your day off."

"It's okay. Henry will come with me."

"Weren't you going to join us on the water?"

"We can go anytime," Henry said.

"You go have fun," Stacia said.

"Feel free to walk around the grounds or have a couple of drinks by the fireplace or whatever you want while she rests," Raina said.

"I can stay back as well," Celia said.

"Nonsense," Stacia said. "There is no need for all of us to stay back. You go have fun."

"You're all talking like I'm not here," Aunt Kat said. "I would be fine all on my own."

"Not with your health right now," Raina said.

"Is everything okay with her health?" Annie asked.

Aunt Kat gave Raina a look.

"It doesn't change how we view you, your strength, or your leadership when we talk about your health struggles, Aunt Kat."

Patting Raina's hand, Aunt Kat said, "Very well. I'll let you all take care of me."

Raina leaned over and kissed her aunt on the cheek.

Aunt Kat wrinkled her nose. "I love you, my girl."

"Love you too."

Stacia and Henry said goodbye and helped Aunt Kat out the door, while the rest ambled toward the Marina. The sky had cleared, and the sun was warm despite the cool breeze coming off the water. Several other small groups of people were already gathered by the docks waiting to board the boats.

Raina strolled along with Conie while his sisters and Stu brought up the rear. They laughed and talked about different things, which made the walk go by quickly. Once they got to the marina, Conie led them past the crowd and onto his new boat. It was the first time Raina had been on board and Conie told her to make herself at home. She kissed him before he left to go talk with the captain while she explored. Conie's sisters had already been on board a couple of times, so they made their way to the deck.

Raina admired the galley, and the two bedrooms before heading back up top to the deck. She wondered what it would be like to take it out on the lake for several days and decided she would use one of her own boats for such a trip.

Settling into a chair on the deck next to Annie, Raina looked out across the bay toward Willow Bay Manor and smiled. *How is this my life?*

"Penny for your thoughts," Conie said, sitting next to her.

"Just thinking about the beauty of the day and how wonderful it is to be part of this community," Raina said.

"Is anyone else coming aboard?" Annie asked.

"Yes, we'll have five more people who bought tickets to join our boat ride and one of our other boats will have about fifteen people. I know there are a couple of other people who sold tickets for rides on their boats. Of course, there are those who are going out before putting their boats up for the winter."

"Why the tickets?" Stu asked.

"The money will go into next year's festival fund," Conie said.

"Love that," Murie said.

"It was Raina's idea. I just took on the task to make sure it got done," Conie said.

It wasn't long before the rest of the party was on board, and they were gliding away from the dock. Raina walked over to the rail to get a closer look at the water and smiled at the sparkles on the waves from the sun.

Conie moved to stand beside her, but instead of looking out across the bay he studied Raina.

"You have that same frown," Raina said, glancing in his direction.

"What same frown?"

"The same one where I can't tell what you're thinking or feeling."

"What I'm feeling scares me."

"Which is why you're frowning?"

"Yes."

Raina shifted toward Conie, grabbing his hand. "Do you want to talk about it?"

"I love you, Raina."

Heat mixed with fear shot through Raina, and she wanted to take a step back.

"Did I scare you?" Conie asked.

"No. Yes. Maybe. But it's only because I love you too."

Conie gently gathered her in his arms. He kissed her forehead and held her. "I think I grow more in love with you with each passing moment."

"That makes two of us," Raina said, wrapping her arms around him. She tilted her head toward his and he leaned down to kiss her on the lips.

When they broke apart, Conie grabbed her hand and they returned to their seats. Raina nestled against Conie while he slid his arm around her. Annie handed them glasses of champagne.

"What's this for?" Raina asked, glancing around to make sure the other passengers were taken care of as well.

"This is to celebrate the new boat and all of your hard work to make the festival happen," Annie said.

"I'll drink to that," Raina said and took a sip.

Raina didn't say much for the rest of the boat ride. Occasionally she would glance in Conie's direction, and he would return her gaze with so much love and adoration Raina would force herself to look back out at the water. She reveled in watching Conie and his siblings tease each other, embraced the beauty of the day, and hoped her ancestors would be pleased with how they were honoring them.

Chapter
Thirty-Six

The waves lapped onto the pebbled beach as Raina meandered along its edge waiting for Conie. He had returned to work after the boat ride while Raina followed up on things to ensure everything was still running smoothly with the festivities. She looked out over the moonlit water and paused. It still called to her the same way it did the first time she saw it on another pebbled beach with the mother and son adoring the lake. Raina smiled at the memory and returned to her walk. She was enjoying her solitude when she happened upon Violet sitting with friends by the water.

"Violet, I hope you're well this evening," Raina said as she went past the group.

"I was until you walked by," Violet said.

"Okay, well, I hope it starts getting better for you," Raina said without looking back.

"What did you say to my mom last night?" Violet asked.

"What do mean?" Raina asked, stopping to turn toward Violet.

"She was pretty upset when she got home, and she told me she had been talking with you at the pub."

"You will have to ask her."

"I did, but she wouldn't talk to me about it. She locked herself in the attic most of the day digging through boxes and trunks."

"I don't know what you expect me to say," Raina said.

"Whatever you said to her made her upset. Why can't you people just leave us alone," Violet said, standing up.

"She came to me, Violet. She asked me questions. I just answered them."

"You could have been nicer with your answers," Violet said, moving to stand closer to Raina.

"My answers were honest. Sometimes the truth is difficult to hear, but it's still the truth."

"Your truth maybe."

"You know what. I'm not doing this with you," Raina said.

She veered toward the road just as Violet pushed her from behind, knocking her to the ground. Raina fell to her hands and knees and winced at the pain of rock cutting her skin. She slowly got up, careful not to injure herself further. She eyed the cuts and redness on her hands before attempting to walk away again.

Violet grabbed Raina's arm and spun her around to face her.

"Seriously, Violet, you have to stop this," Raina said, taking a step back toward the water.

"I can't stop. I hate you so much. I hate your family so much. I hate this town so much."

"Then leave," Raina said so softly she wasn't sure she said it.

This apparently caught Violet off guard, and she shut her mouth. Hoping this was her opportunity to get away, Raina took another step back.

"I can't leave," Violet said with a catch in her voice. "Where would I go?"

"Believe it or not, Violet, I understand what it's like to feel trapped in a place I hate. It makes me sad the place I love is that place for you. But part of me has learned that how we view our surroundings comes from ourselves and our own decisions. Yes, there were people there who were cruel to my family. But I also never allowed myself to give others a chance either, so I was more often than not, very lonely. Was it their fault or mine? Perhaps it was both. Or perhaps no one was at fault, and it just was."

"Stop trying to compare yourself to me."

"I'm trying to show you that I understand how you feel," Raina said.

"You couldn't possibly understand how I feel."

"Maybe you're right. But I can at least show you compassion and empathy."

"I don't need your pity."

Throwing up her hands, Raina said, "What do you want from me? I apologize and you throw my apology in my face. I try to be your friend or show kindness or try to make peace and that's not accepted. I try to show you compassion and you don't want that either. I try to leave you alone and you bother me. What do you want from me?"

"I don't know!"

"Can we at least agree that what happened in the past isn't anyone in the present's fault and try to move beyond it?"

"I can't!"

"Why?"

"Because if it weren't for your family, my family wouldn't be so lost or poor."

"This again. Come on, Violet. You can't really believe that."

"Of course I believe it. The impact my grandfather's death had on all of us was devastating. And he wouldn't have taken his life if he hadn't been so lost after having his affair and losing his job."

"Violet, there are things about that affair you don't understand. Things weren't as you believe they were."

"Like what?"

"You don't want to know," Raina said. "At least I don't think you're ready to hear them. So, let's do this some other time."

"No, you have to tell me," Violet said, inching closer to Raina.

Studying the woman in front of her, Raina considered sharing what the journals said, but decided against it. Violet had a wild look in her eyes as the wind whipped her hair around her face. Her hands clenched into fists at her side, and she stood ready to pounce.

"I think maybe this isn't the time," Raina said.

"Tell me!"

"It wasn't just a fling between them. Your grandfather raped and abused my great-grandmother. It was an abusive relationship. One which I think is what caused the deaths of my relatives. I think he took his life because he felt guilty for the part he played."

The words were out before Raina could stop them and Violet shrieked, charging Raina. "Liar!"

Falling backwards, cold-water rushed over Raina. Sputtering, she tried to gain her footing but was knocked about as another wave engulfed her. Fighting to get her head above water, warm hands snagged her arms, and pulled her to the surface.

Catching Conie's eye as he continued to move her away from the lake's edge, Raina dissolved into tears. Annie rushed forward with a warm blanket and placed it around her shoulders. Raina drew the blanket tighter as Donna held Violet with Ginny standing close by.

As Raina got her bearings, she realized a crowd had formed, capturing the scene as it had unfolded. Aunt Kat and Murie were peering down on her from the boardwalk.

"Damn it. I caused a scene again," Raina said through chattering teeth.

"Let's get you home," Annie said. "A warm shower and dry clothes will do you some good."

"I won't say no to warmth," Raina said.

Conie led Raina away but she spun toward Violet, and said, "I'm sorry it came to this. Truly I am."

Annie rubbed Raina's back and encouraged her to let it go for now. Conie slid his arm around Raina and helped her across the rocky beach until they were up by Aunt Kat and Murie.

"I'm sorry, Aunt Kat," Raina said and buried her face in her hands.

"You have nothing to be sorry for dear. What is done, is done. What my mother did can't be changed. What Donna's father did can't be changed."

Raina snapped her head up. "Oh no. I just told the whole world I believed he killed your mother, and I hadn't shared it with you yet. I'm so sorry."

"You need to stop apologizing. I know you were only trying to protect me, and what happened here wasn't your fault. Come along. Let's get you home and cleaned up."

Conie handed Raina over to Annie so he could run to get his truck. The crowd moved out of the way to let his truck through, and Annie helped Raina climb in. Annie agreed she and Murie would help get Aunt Kat home and Conie drove away. The short drive didn't last long and when Conie parked his truck under the carport, he ran around to help Raina inside and up to her room.

"I can't stop shaking," Raina said.

"It's shock and the cold from the water," Conie said as he helped her into her bathroom.

Raina leaned against the wall as she watched Conie get the water going in her bathtub. He studied her intently while he waited for the water to heat to the right temperature and rushed back over to her.

With teeth chattering, Raina asked if he could help her get undressed. He only nodded and slowly took off one item at a time, careful not to hurt her cuts and bruises. Once Raina was undressed, Conie wrapped a dry blanket around her until the bathtub was full enough. He would occasionally check the depth of the water but kept a close eye on Raina.

Just when Raina believed she would fall over from waiting, Conie took the blanket off and picked her up. Raina curled against the heat of his body as he carried her to the tub. He gently put her into the soapy water, and she sighed at its warmth. There were some tingles where the warmth fought against the cold, but she leaned back, closing her eyes, and eventually her body stopped shaking. Not opening her eyes, Raina lifted her hand out of the bubbles, searching for Conie's.

Wrapping both hands around hers, he said, "I'm here. I'm not going anywhere."

Raina sighed and let her mind wander until the memory of the cold lake taking her body flooded through her. She lifted her head, looking around.

"It's okay. I'm here," Annie said.

"Where's Conie?"

"I'm here," Conie said, tugging on a sweater. "I was just changing my clothes. You drifted off, so I took the opportunity to get out of my wet things. I got a little damp when I fished you out of the lake."

"Aunt Kat?" Raina asked, settling her head against the tub.

"Murie, Celia, Henry, and Stacia are with her downstairs," Conie said.

"Is Violet okay?" Raina asked, closing her eyes again.

"I think so." Annie said. "Donna took her home."

"How did you happen to reach me so fast? One minute she and I were arguing, and then she pushed me so hard. I can't believe how quickly I was under water."

"I had sent Annie out to tell you I was going to be a few minutes late meeting up with you," Conie said.

"And when I went outside, there was a small gathering at the rocks and I noticed the commotion down by the lake," Annie said. "She had just pushed you to the ground and you were trying to get back up."

"Annie ran back inside and told Stu to call Donna and told me to head to the beach as fast as possible," Conie said. "Murie was at the bar, and she followed behind me. Kat had just arrived with Henry and Stacia and when she realized what was going on, Henry had to stop her from going down the stairs. I told her I would go. I was just running down there when Violet shoved you into the water. She almost fell in herself, but only got her shoes and lower part of her jeans wet."

"I had just come out when you were shoved into the water, so I ran to Murie's store and got you a blanket. You owe her fifteen dollars by the way," Annie said.

Raina's eyes flung open, caught the mischievous grin on her friend's face, and giggled. Her laughter built until she was holding her sides and tears were streaming down her face.

Conie kneeled by the tub, kissed Raina on the lips, and wiped the tears from her face. "Feel better?"

Nodding, Raina said, "Yes, but I don't know why that was so funny."

"It's been a long day," Annie said.

"I think I'm ready to get out," Raina said.

"Want some help?" Conie asked.

"Actually, I think I can do it myself, and as much as I love both of you, I kind of want to be alone for a few minutes while I get dressed."

"Okay, we'll wait for you downstairs," Annie said.

"Are you sure?" Conie asked.

"She's sure," Annie said, tugging on Conie's arm. "Come on, brother."

Once she was alone, Raina climbed out of the bathtub and wrapped a towel around her body. She sank into its warmth and closed her eyes for a second. She went about the task of drying off, careful not to bump her bruises and scrapes. She pulled medicine and bandages out of a cabinet and doctored the cuts on her knees. After getting dressed, she started toward the door, but changed her mind and went to sit by her fire instead.

Staring at the blaze, Raina pondered her exchange with Violet. She regretted what she'd said, but she was also relieved it was out in the open. Maybe now things could be different, and Violet could stop blaming Raina and her family for all of the Strand family problems.

Raina yawned and contemplated crawling into bed, but the need to be held by people she loved won out. She made her way down to the living room just as Donna was being let into the house. Raina curled up beside Conie on the couch as he tugged a blanket around her.

Standing in the doorway, Donna hesitated until Aunt Kat told her to come sit across from her by the fire. Aunt Kat offered her a drink, but she declined. She kept ringing her hands in her lap until Aunt Kat asked how she could help.

Donna glanced at Aunt Kat but focused on Raina. "I'm sorry for what Violet did to you. I see now I should have done things a little differently with her. Nurtured forgiveness instead of hate. I was just so indifferent to it all. Holding a grudge was something that settled into her bones. And I didn't have the strength to even face it. I was weary with it all, so I let it be what it was."

"What's changed?" Raina asked.

Donna looked at her hands before removing an envelope from her pocket. "This is a letter my father wrote to my mother right before..." Her voice broke, so she paused. Swallowing, she continued. "He left it for her when he died. I didn't know about the letter but after our conversation, Raina, I was desperate to find something, anything, to prove you wrong."

Raina studied the woman as she spoke and admired the strength it must have taken to even come here tonight.

"I can't read it to you" Donna said. "I'm too ashamed, but I'll leave it here for you. I've already shared this with Violet, and we've agreed we need some space from this place for a while."

"Do you think you'll be back?" Aunt Kat asked.

"Yes, but we plan to be gone for several weeks, if not longer."

"What about your business?" Raina asked.

"I'm going to close its doors. I may even have to sell the house, but we have to get some time away to heal our own wounds, and let go of bitterness toward a family who never deserved it."

"Where are you planning to go?" Aunt Kat asked.

"I'd like to take her to a beach somewhere so we will do that for a couple of days. Probably not the whole time though. We also discussed some rehab for her. And when we get back, I'll decide our next steps."

Raina stood. "Donna, I would like to help cover the cost of rehab and the trip. And don't worry about your business. It will be there when you get back, including your home. And if you decide to sell both we can make other arrangements then, but I don't want you to worry about that while you take time to heal."

"I can't accept charity, especially from the Nilssons. You'll understand after you read the letter."

"I think I already know what the letter is going to say. Which is why you're here. If you want, we can work out a plan for you to pay me back with an arrangement that works best for you upon your return, but for now, please let me help," Raina said.

"Why would you do this?"

"Because you're a part of Willow Bay, and we Nilssons help our own."

Donna crossed to Raina, hugged her, and shoved the letter into Raina's hand. "Please wait to read this until after I'm gone."

"I will. Celia, can you walk Donna to the door and get the specifics on where I can send the money?"

"Of course. I'll show you out, Donna," Celia said.

When Celia and Donna left the room, Aunt Kat said, "I'm so incredibly proud of you, Raina. I couldn't have handled it better myself."

"Thank you, Aunt Kat."

"Are you going to read the letter?" Conie asked.

"I will in a little bit, but for now I just want to be held by you, stare at the warm fire, and revel in my gratitude that I have all of you in my life."

Chapter
Thirty-Seven

Dear Wife,

If you're reading this letter, then I went through with taking my life. I've been planning it for months but just hadn't found the right time. You have to promise not to tell Donna any of this, but I feel like I owe you the truth. I lied to you. I lied to you so many times. I know I was mean. Poor Donna bore the brunt of it, and well, I suppose you did too.

This letter to you also represents my confession for something I can no longer live with.

I fell in love with a most beautiful woman. She was out of my reach in so many ways and yet she fell in love with me too. We didn't plan it. It just happened. The very idea that Catherine Nilsson could ever love me was beyond reason. She was lonely and hurt by a husband who ignored her. He didn't deserve her, but somewhere along the way she became an obsession for me. The idea that anyone else could have her made me crazy.

Our love affair lasted for about a year until the day she died. Until the day I killed her. I was losing her to her husband, and I couldn't stand it. She kept trying to slip away from me for months, but I wouldn't let her go. I was out of my mind trying to figure out how to keep her always. She told me she was pregnant with our baby, and she was going to tell her husband about us, so I packed my bags and waited for him to cast her aside, but he didn't, and I couldn't let her go. If I couldn't have her no one could.

When I arrived at their house to get her, no one answered the door, so I let myself in. I found my way into the living room where they were sitting on the couch, and he was kissing her. My Catherine. Everything just turned red. I tried to fight him, to hurt him, but he ran from me. Somehow, we ended up in the kitchen where I grabbed a knife, and I chased him into the library. I don't know how many times I stabbed him.

As he lay dying, I ran to find my Catherine. I couldn't find her until somehow, I found my way back to where Stefan Nilsson lay dying. She was taking the knife out of his body. When she saw me, she screamed at me and told me she hated me. She flung her body onto her husband's and sobbed. I tried to comfort her, but she pushed me aside. She told me she was going to call the police and I would pay for what I had done. I tried to hold her, but she said I would never touch her body again.

Something snapped inside me and then I noticed the gun. I don't know where it came from. I can only assume she had brought it with her to use on me. I picked it up and I shot her in the head. I didn't even think about it. She didn't even have time to plead her case. I just shot her, and she fell backwards onto the floor. I put the gun close to her hand and fled. I went to our place, mine and Catherine's, and wept until I fell asleep. When darkness came, I fled town.

The Nilssons didn't fire me. I just couldn't go back. I couldn't be in the place that took my love from me. I was hoping with time I would forget about everything, but I couldn't even sleep without seeing her face. For a time, I drowned my pain in the bottle, and the memories faded into the drink, but after a while the booze couldn't keep her out of my mind either.

I know I was cruel to you. I know I treated you unfairly. You asked me once what you did wrong. The answer to that is simple...you did nothing. You just weren't my Catherine, and Donna just wasn't me and my Catherine's baby.

I wish I could profess some sentiments of love for you before I end my suffering, but I can't, so just know that I wish I could.

Donny Strand

Tears slid down Raina's cheeks as she stuffed the letter back into the envelope and handed it to Jenks. She had read it to him after Aunt Kat asked him to come. Jenks took the letter and said he would be amending the file on the murder-suicide and would put out a statement. Raina thanked him for making it right and went to comfort her aunt.

"I'm okay, Raina," Aunt Kat said.

"Are you sure?" Raina asked.

"I'm happy the truth has come out. I just wish Del was here."

"I wish she was too."

Jenks took his leave and Annie said she and Murie would be heading out too. Conie offered to stay, but Raina said she wanted some time with her aunt. They were going to visit her great-grandmother's grave. Tomorrow was the last day of the festival, and she was looking forward to family dinner at his house. Conie kissed Raina and left.

Raina helped her aunt walk to the family graveyard. It was cold and late, and Raina suggested they wait until morning to do this, but Aunt Kat insisted they had to do it now. As they approached the gravestone, Aunt Kat burst into tears.

The two stood like statues until Aunt Kat collapsed to the ground with sobs shaking her body. Raina put her arms around her aunt and held her until she calmed. Aunt Kat eventually beckoned Raina to kneel on the ground next to her.

"Mother, I was so angry at you for so long," Aunt Kat said. "At times, I hated you. But the hate and anger has dissipated with my tears. I loved you. Del loved you. Father loved you. Gramma Melia loved you. And you loved us. Yes, you made a terrible mistake, but you did love us. And I know you didn't take anyone's life away from us. I had to come share this with you. My hope is that you're resting in peace now that the truth has come to light."

Raina helped her aunt back to her feet. They each kissed the top of the gravestone and started back toward the house. The weight of it all was left at the foot of the grave, and Raina knew the pain of it was finally healing in a way it never could before.

Chapter Thirty-Eight

Warmth from the sun radiated on Raina's skin as she made her way across the parking lot. Several people called a greeting to her as she wound through the cars toward the front of the new boatwerks and museum. They were offering a one-time chance to tour the boatwerks along with the museum and most of the town had shown up. The crowd made Raina giddy and she giggled. Aunt Kat spent most of her time in bed now, and Raina knew her days with her were numbered, but her aunt insisted she still have an opening celebration.

Conie kissed her cheek when she made it to the sidewalk where he was waiting for her. "Kat doing okay today?"

"For now, yes," Raina said, attempting to shove aside the realization she was about to lose yet another beloved family member.

"Did you see Annie?" Conie asked.

"I didn't. They made it back from their honeymoon?" Raina asked.

"Yes, late last night. Annie and Stu can't wait to tell you all about it."

"I can't wait to hear," Raina said, smiling up at Conie before asking, "Are Murie and Oliver going to make it? I know they were trying to move the last of his things into your house this week."

"They plan to, and speaking of them, my house is getting really crowded," Conie said.

"When is Stu and Annie's house going to be done?" Raina asked.

"Not for another month," Conie said. "Until then we will make it work."

"If you say so," Raina said with a laugh.

Henry waved at Raina, and she told Conie she would see him after. He hugged her and she went to give her speech as part of the opening. Henry said a few words first and Raina thanked everyone for coming. Her speech was short, and Henry cut the ribbon marking the grand opening. The crowd cheered as Raina went into the museum. She walked over to the main desk and smiled at Violet.

"Ready for this?" Raina asked.

"Ready as I'll ever be," Violet said with a sheepish grin.

Raina moved to walk away, but Violet called to her. "I never thanked you for offering me a job after I got home from rehab."

Violet and Donna had spent several months away from Willow Bay, but it wasn't until they had returned, and Violet had a relapse, that she finally got the help she needed. When she came back to Willow Bay a second time, Raina went to visit her and offered a way for them to mend things between them. Before she left, she told Violet she wanted her to work at the museum if she wanted the job. Two weeks later, Violet started helping the rest of the employees prepare for the opening.

"I'm glad it's worked out as well as it has," Raina said.

"Me too."

A line of people formed outside the front door, and Raina motioned for Henry to let them in. The throng moved toward the front desk and people started paying for their tickets. Raina left and went about her busy day. Conie caught up with her and they made plans for him to stop by the manor after he got off work. The rest of the day flew by, and she kicked off her shoes in the living room, thankful it was over. She had barely sat down when the doorbell rang. Surprised, Raina went to answer it.

As she opened the door, she burst out laughing at the sight of her love standing in the doorway with a bouquet of flowers and a bottle of champagne.

"Why didn't you just come in?" Raina asked.

"Because I wanted to surprise you with the flowers," Conie said.

"Fine, come in. I'll get some glasses and meet you in the living room," Raina said.

"Nah, I'll just come with you. I know the rest of your staff is off for the evening. I'll put these into some water while you get the goblets."

"Works for me," Raina said, leading the way to the kitchen.

As Conie rummaged through cupboards looking for a vase, Raina plucked the champagne flutes from their designated spot. She watched Conie move around and loved how at ease he seemed.

"I've been thinking about something for a while now," Raina said while Conie filled a vase with water.

Conie put the flowers on the island, grabbed the bottle of champagne and opened it. "Is the pause for dramatics, or are you afraid to tell me what you're thinking?"

"I'm just nervous," Raina said, grabbing the glass Conie offered to her.

Concern flashed across Conie's face before Raina left the kitchen to head back to the living room. She knew Conie was following her and she took the time to figure out the best way to explain herself. When they were seated next to each other on the couch, Raina took a sip of her champagne for courage and set it down on the table next to her. She grabbed Conie's hand in both of hers and took a deep breath.

"Okay, now you're making me nervous," Conie said, placing his glass on the table next to him. "What's going on?"

Taking a deep breath, Raina said, "I've decided, and Aunt Kat approves of my plan, when she passes away, I'm going to turn the manor and guest house into a museum and a bed and breakfast."

"How are you going to do that? Where are you going to live? I love you, but I'm not sure there is room at my house," Conie said with a laugh.

Raina chuckled. "I'm not asking to live at your house. The main house will be the museum and the guest house will be the bed and breakfast. I also plan to build a couple of cabins along the cliff to add space to accommodate more people."

"Okay this all sounds like a wonderful plan. But again, where are you going to live?" Conie asked.

"I'm getting to that," Raina said. "Come with me, I want to show you something."

"Um...okay. You forgot your champagne," Conie said as Raina left the room.

Raina went to the office and rummaged around on her desk until she found what she was looking for. Conie followed and she giggled, realizing he brought their glasses and the bottle.

"Couldn't leave it behind?" Raina asked.

"You may be trying to talk to me about something different, but I'm still trying to celebrate you and your success," Conie said.

"Come look at this," Raina said, reaching for her champagne from him.

"Okay," Conie said, walking around to stand next to her. "What is it?"

"It's a house."

"It's a big house. A beautiful house," Conie said, studying the plans.

"You like it?"

"I do."

"Would you make any changes to it?"

"If it were me, I would design the kitchen a little bigger and make something similar to my house off the back. But that's just me."

"What if I said I want you to design it as if you owned it?"

"What are you saying, Raina?" Conie asked, meeting Raina's eyes.

Raina took a sip of her champagne and set it down on her desk. She grabbed Conie's hand again. "Look I'm not saying we should get married tomorrow. But I know that is where I want us to head. I love you, Conie. And I know you love me. We make an amazing team when we work on Nilsson Family Enterprises. I see my future and it's with you, sharing all of this. I would like your help in designing my house because I want it to be our house."

Conie set his glass down and Raina thought her heart was going to pound out of her chest as she waited for him to respond.

Did she read the situation wrong? Does he not love her as she loves him?

Moving closer to her, Conie gathered Raina into his arms and stared into her eyes. "Raina, I would love to build this house with you."

Relief flooded through Raina, and she smiled. "Excellent. They broke ground yesterday."

"How did I not know?" Conie asked.

"It was hard, but I wanted it to be a surprise."

Conie kissed Raina. "I love you."

"I love you, too. Oh, and in the meantime, I thought since you have a full house, you might as well move in here."

"I love that idea, but you're sure Aunt Kat won't care," Conie said.

Raina smiled at his reference to Aunt Kat as though she were his aunt already and said, "She can't wait for it all to happen. It's comforting for her to know I'll not be alone when she dies, like she was for so long."

"How much time do we have with her?"

"Her care team says only a couple of weeks."

"I'm sorry," Conie said.

"I'm just happy she came for me when she did, and I got the time with her that I did."

"Where is our house going to be?" Conie asked, moving the subject back to their new house.

Raina knew he steered the conversation away from her aunt because he wanted to spare her sadness as long as possible. "It's going to be through the woods on the back side of the point just down from the guest house. We will have about five acres to ourselves, and we'll be overlooking the water. It's a beautiful spot. I know you'll love it."

"I can't wait to see it."

"Let's walk out there in the morning."

Conie yawned and Raina suggested they finish their champagne and celebrating in bed. Conie grinned at her idea and suggested they take the champagne to her bedroom. Laughing, Raina grabbed his hand and led him upstairs.

The bottle and glasses were secured before clothes went flying and Raina giggled as they dove into bed together. They celebrated long into the evening with love making, laughter, and drinks of bubbly liquid until Conie fell asleep. Raina played with his hair until she caught the moon on the water. She climbed out of bed and stood at the window enjoying the view until she saw the journal out of the corner of her eye.

Reaching over to pick it up, she turned to the page where she had left off the night before. She grabbed a pen, crawled back into bed, and leaned back against the headboard, tucking her legs under her.

She stared at the man she loved sleeping next to her, smiled, and began to write on the journal's empty page. As she wrote, she hoped someone in her family tree long into the future would find her journals, read her words, and get a better understanding of their deep roots too.

A Note to Readers

Thank you for reading *Roots of the Bay*.

If you enjoyed it, I would appreciate a review on your favorite retailer website.

And I'd love to hear from you. Drop me a line at: esther@theestherschultz.com

My website is theestherschultz.com

Acknowledgements

I can't close this next story without sharing my deep appreciation for all those who have helped me along the way. To my husband—your continued faith in me is unwavering and I couldn't do my work without you. To all four of my children—you are my personal cheerleaders and marketers, and I am so grateful for you.

Thank you to my close friends who continue to push me to keep moving forward. Andrea, Sarah, and Rhonda—your love and support on this journey is never ending and I can't tell you how much I appreciate you.

I couldn't do this work without my amazing proofreaders, especially Robin Dial and Megan Jeans. I can't thank you enough for your support, feedback, and encouragement. Last but not least, my amazing editor, Jeanne Felfe, I continue to learn from you every time we work together. Without your feedback and wisdom, I wouldn't have been able to publish yet another book. Words can't express how grateful I am for you.

About the Author

Esther Schultz is a freelance writer and author who believes everyone can live a peaceful, joy-filled life despite hardships, and attempts to spread that message in her work. Her favorite things include spending time in nature, especially along Lake Superior, and advocating for mental health. Esther lives in central Minnesota with her husband, four children, her dog, and horse. She invites you to visit her website at www.theestherschultz.com to check out her other work and to follow her on social media.

Facebook: Esther Schultz – Author

Instagram: esther_schultz_author

www.ingramcontent.com/pod-product-compliance
Lightning Source LLC
Chambersburg PA
CBHW050856210726
48290CB00004B/1255